MARTIN SUTER, born in Zürich in 1948, is a writer, columnist and screenwriter. He worked as a creative director in advertising before deciding to focus exclusively on writing. His novels have enjoyed huge international success. Martin Suter lives with his family in Zürich.

Praise for *Elefant*:

'A slick, very gripping story which tugs at your heart-strings ... Martin Suter has mastered a new genre: a mix of science fiction, thriller and fairytale' *NDR*, Hannover

'I loved *Elefant*! It was a complete tonic'

SENI GLAISTER, author of
The Museum of Things Left Behind

'A mind-blowing contemporary fable ... endearing, bizarre, irresistible and exhilarating' *Page des Libraires*, France

'The novel is artfully structured, and the unexpected shifts in narrative perspective guarantee a gripping read. I found it absorbing from the very start. Not a single page is superfluous' *MDR*, Leipzig

'A multi-layered, often moving novel, which, despite dispensing with brutal depictions of violence, reads in many parts like a gripping thriller' *DPA*, Hamburg

'The top   e swift,
the plot   Zürich

700043940386

'It's easy to fall in love with this novel because it's easy to fall in love with its main character: a tiny, glowing, pink elephant. But this is no children's novel. Instead, the story it tells is a timely reminder of the possible tragic results of unscrupulous genetic manipulation and the sanctity of life no matter how it is created. Ultimately, I was enchanted by the little elephant and cheered everyone in the story who protected her and wished ill on all those who quested after her for the purposes of greed and exploitation. I never thought I'd fall in love with a miniature pink elephant that glowed in the dark, but I did. I shall often think of her'

HOMER HICKAM, author of *Carrying Albert Home*

'Written in short chapters, like a thriller, and rich in flashbacks and jumps forward, *Elefant* is a gripping read'

Les Echos Weekend, France

'A quirky tale, composed with tangible joy, which affirms Suter's standing as one of Europe's most versatile authors'

Landshuter Zeitung/Straubinger Tagblatt

ALSO BY MARTIN SUTER

Small World
A Deal with the Devil
The Last Weynfeldt
The Chef
Allmen and the Dragonflies
Montecristo

Elefant

Martin Suter

translated from the German
by Jamie Bulloch

4th ESTATE • London

4th Estate
An imprint of HarperCollins*Publishers*
1 London Bridge Street
London SE1 9GF

www.4thEstate.co.uk

First published in Great Britain in 2018 by 4th Estate

1

Copyright © Martin Suter 2017
English translation copyright © Jamie Bulloch 2018

A catalogue record for this book is
available from the British Library

ISBN 978-0-00-826431-4

Printed and bound in Great Britain by
CPI Group (UK) Ltd, Croydon CR0 4YY

MIX
Paper from
responsible sources
FSC® C007454

This book is produced from independently certified FSC paper
to ensure responsible forest management.

For more information visit: www.harpercollins.co.uk/green

For Ana and Margrith

Part One

1

Zürich

12 June 2016

It couldn't be withdrawal syndrome as he'd had plenty to drink.

Schoch tried to focus on the object. A child's toy, a tiny elephant as pink as a marzipan piglet, but more intense in colour. And glowing like a pink firefly, right at the back of the hollow, where the ceiling of the cave met the sandy ground.

People sometimes stumbled across Schoch's cave, a hollow eroded from beneath the riverside path, and he might find the occasional junkie's gear, condoms or fast-food packaging. But he'd never seen evidence of a child's visit before.

He closed his eyes and tried to get something like sleep.

But then he had a 'merry-go-round', which was what he called those states of inebriation when everything started spinning the moment he crawled into his sleeping bag. In all these years he'd never managed to put his finger on what caused drunkenness to become a merry-go-round. Sometimes he was certain it was the volume consumed, while on other occasions he suspected it was down to the mixture of drinks. And then there were days like today when – so far as he could recall – he hadn't drunk more than yesterday, or anything different, and yet everything was still spinning.

Maybe it was something to do with the weather. On the way home the Föhn wind had chased the thick clouds over the river, intermittently tearing them apart to reveal a full moon. Full moon and the Föhn: maybe that was the reason for his merry-go-rounds, at least a few of them.

He'd never found out whether it was better to keep his eyes open or closed either.

Schoch opened them. The toy elephant was still there, but it appeared to be a little further to the right.

He closed his eyes again. For a moment the little elephant spun beneath his eyelids, leaving a streak of pink.

He immediately wrenched his eyes open.

There it was, flapping its ears and lifting its trunk into an S-shape.

Schoch turned over onto the other side and tried to stop the spinning.

He fell asleep.

2

13 June 2016

Schoch had been drinking for too long for this to be a hangover worth mentioning. But also too long to recollect every detail from the previous evening. He woke later than usual, with a dry mouth, gluey eyes and his pulse racing, but no headache.

The heavy raindrops were making the twigs of the bushes at the entrance to his cave bounce up and down. Beyond these, in the dawn light, Schoch could make out the grey curtain of rain and hear its even drone. The Föhn had abated and it felt unusually cold for June.

Schoch wriggled out of his sleeping bag, stood up as far as his low-ceilinged billet would allow and rolled up his bed tightly. He tucked his shirt into his trousers and reached for his shoes.

He always took them off by the opening to the cave – far enough inside so they wouldn't get drenched by a sudden downpour – but now he could only find one. After a while he located the other shoe outside the cave, lying in a puddle beside one of the dripping bushes. Schoch couldn't recall this ever happening before, no matter how hammered he'd been. Perhaps he ought to slow down a bit.

Cursing, he fished out the blue and white striped trainer, took the tatty Nivea towel from his holdall and tried to pat the shoe dry.

It was hopeless. Schoch slipped his foot into the cold, damp trainer.

A vague thought flitted through his brain, something from last night. Something strange. But what? An object? An experience? Like a forgotten word or name that's on the tip of your tongue.

He couldn't hold on to it, and meanwhile he was starting to freeze as the cold from the shoe crept up his leg. He needed to move and get some warm coffee in his belly.

Schoch put on a yellow raincoat that he'd pinched one day from a construction site. It had once borne the logo of the construction firm, but now it was flecked with tar and only the word 'Building' was still visible. He stuffed his sleeping bag into the stained holdall that contained a few more of his belongings. Pants, socks, T-shirt, shirt, wash bag and a wallet with his papers. The rest of his things were stored in the Salvation Army hostel; Schoch was on good terms with the man who ran it.

He pulled a baseball cap over his matted hair and stepped outside. He left nothing behind in the cave.

The rain was so heavy that he could only just make out the far bank of the river. Schoch struggled up the slippery embankment, losing his footing twice. By the time he'd reached the riverside path his trouser legs were smeared with mud up to the knees.

Schoch had inherited his sleeping place from Sumi, the man who'd introduced him to life on the streets

6

back at a time when there were still rules among the homeless. Such as the one that said you respected other people's sleeping places. Now it wasn't like that any more. These days you could come home to find someone else already camped there. In most cases it was a labour migrant, someone who'd come to the country in search of work.

Sumi had discovered the billet shortly after the flood of 2005, when the river level had risen so high that in several places it had hollowed out the ground beneath the path and washed away a large proportion of the vegetation.

By chance, Sumi had noticed the gaping hole from the other bank. The only downside was that the cave was easily visible. But luckily, one of his jobs before ending up on the streets had been as an assistant gardener. From further downstream, where the river basin was broader and the water hadn't reached the embankment, he'd dug out some shrubs and replanted them in front of the cave.

He baptised his sleeping place River Bed and spent almost eight years dossing there. Schoch was the only other person who knew of it. 'When I croak,' Sumi used to say, 'you can have my River Bed.'

'You'll drink us all under the ground,' Schoch would reply.

But then Sumi died suddenly. Drying out. Delirium tremens.

This had strengthened Schoch's resolve never to stop drinking.

Not a soul was about on the riverside path. The early joggers he usually met at this time of the morning had been kept at home by the rain. It wasn't long before Schoch's dry shoe was just as soaked as the wet one. The rain ran down his beard and into the neck of his coat. Jutting out his chin, Schoch wiped his beard with the back of his hand. He urgently needed his second coffee now; he'd slept through the first one.

Further along the path he passed a weir, where there was a small platform. Two concrete posts were sunk into the embankment, to which a rescue pole was attached. It was a notorious spot because a whirlpool formed on the downstream side of the weir, especially when the water level was high. Schoch could hear shouting coming from the platform.

He walked on until the vegetation on the bank no longer blocked his view. Two men, one tall, one shorter, were standing on the concrete platform, prodding the brown water with the rescue pole below the eddy.

'Need any help?' Schoch tried to shout, but his voice was so hoarse that he failed to utter anything audible.

He cleared his throat. 'Hey! Hello!'

The tall man looked up. He was Japanese or Chinese.

'Has someone fallen in?'

Now the man with the rescue pole looked up too. A redhead with shaven hair.

'My dog!' he cried.

Schoch raised his shoulders and shook his head. 'Whirlpool of death,' he shouted. 'Nothing gets out of there alive. It's swallowed plenty already. Forget the dog and concentrate on not falling in yourselves!'

8

The man with the rescue pole kept prodding the water. The other man waved to Schoch, said 'Thanks!' in English, and turned back.

Schoch continued on his way. 'I warned them,' he muttered. 'I warned them.'

3

Galle, Sri Lanka

25 April 2013

The ravens were skulking on the railings of the restaurant terrace, watching for the slightest inattention from the waiter guarding the warm buffet. From the terrace you could hear the waves of the Indian Ocean.

Jack Harris was sitting at the second table from the back. This gave him the best view of the assortment of backpackers, businesspeople and the last expats sticking to their *jour fixe* at the Galle Face Hotel.

He'd been waiting around here for three weeks now, glugging too much Lion lager. Occasionally he'd get into conversation with a tourist, and once an American woman travelling on her own was so impressed by his career that she followed him up to his room. Harris was a vet, specialising in elephants.

Mostly, however, he spent the nights alone in his room. It was nicely situated; it might not directly face the sea, but it did look out on the large grassed area where the colonial masters once played golf and where countless souvenir stands and food stalls now plied their wares. Sometimes during these lonely nights he'd open one of the two windows, light a cigarette and gaze down at the lights of the lively Galle Face Green and the fluorescent surf of the ocean.

Voices and laughter mingled with scraps of music, and clouds of smoke rose from the food stalls into the light of the outside bulbs, while now and then the wind blew over the aroma of charcoal and hot coconut oil.

Harris got up and helped himself from the buffet. For the second time. He shovelled a not particularly gastronomic hodgepodge of curry, stew and gratin onto his plate and returned to his table, where the staff, unprompted, had placed a 'Reserved' sign in his brief absence.

He was eating too much.

Jack Harris was forty years old, from New Zealand, and looked like Crocodile Dundee gone large. Or so he thought. His wife, who'd left him eight years before – how time flew! – thought he looked more like a sheep shearer.

The divorce threw him off the rails. He'd been living with his wife, Terry, and the twins, Katie and Jerome, in a large bungalow in Fendalton, the smartest suburb of Christchurch, running a veterinary clinic with his partner and earning good money.

Sure, he'd had the odd affair, but just when he was improving on this front he caught Terry with his friend and partner. A terrible shock. He was prepared to forgive the two of them and attempt a fresh start, but although Terry wanted a fresh start too, she didn't want a fresh start with him. After their divorce she married his partner.

Harris got himself hired as a vet on various game reserves in Asia. He'd only been back to New Zealand three times since, to see his children. They'd grown into

11

teenagers and on their last meeting had made it plain that they didn't think much of his rare visits. Contact with them was now restricted to modest bank transfers on their birthdays or at Christmas and the occasional awkward Skype call. Harris didn't need to pay any maintenance and his own infidelities hadn't been disclosed during the divorce.

A few tables further on two female tourists were feeding the ravens. He'd already noticed them on his first visit to the buffet. About thirty years of age, German-speaking, no beauties, but determined to experience more than just foreign culture and nature on their trip – this was something Harris had an eye for.

They were having great fun watching the birds land on the table and nibble their food. Harris could have impressed the women by pointing out that this was a good way of contracting cryptococcosis and psittacosis – not completely false, nor completely true either. He was just about to go up to the dessert buffet and make a remark to this effect when his mobile rang.

The display said 'Roux'.

Harris answered, listened, said, 'Hold on,' took a pen from his jacket and jotted down some numbers on the back of the list of daily specials. 'I thought it would never happen,' he said, before finishing the conversation and dialling another number.

'Kasun?' he said into his phone so loudly that a number of guests turned and stared. 'Get yourself to Ratmalana. Now!' He made the international gesture for 'The bill, please' to the waiter, and when it wasn't brought immediately Harris went up and signed the slip. On the way to his room he called his contact at the heliport.

Harris ordered a taxi and quickly put on his work clothes – khaki trousers and faded short-sleeve denim shirt. From the wardrobe he took his instrument case, which he'd already packed and checked over and over again for this long-awaited opportunity.

Barely five minutes after the phone call he was in a taxi on his way to Ratmalana Airport, fifteen kilometres to the south of Colombo.

A quarter of an hour later he was there. Kasun, the young man assigned to him by the Department of Wildlife Conservation, was waiting for him beside a Robinson R44, a light, four-seater helicopter. Its rotors had started spinning as soon as Harris's taxi came into sight.

When Harris got to the chopper, Kasun was already strapped into the back seat, his headphones on.

The pilot increased the rotor speed, the small aircraft rose slowly and hovered over the runway for a moment. Then the pilot lowered its nose and they set off towards the south-east.

4

The same day

They'd flown the last few kilometres at low altitude above the railway line and could see the stationary train from far away. A few metres behind the engine a group of people were gathered around the injured elephant.

The pilot flew higher to give them an overview of the situation. Not far from the site of the accident was a clearing, at the edge of which stood a few huts. Enough room to land.

Apart from a handful of old women and small children the village was deserted. Those not working in the fields had gone to the scene of the accident.

Laden with instrument case, a hard-shell cool box and various containers, the stocky Harris and his tall, loose-limbed assistant hurried along the narrow path that led from the clearing to the railway line in the forest.

As usual in Sri Lanka, it was over 30 degrees with more than 90 per cent humidity. When they reached the railway embankment Harris's shirt was sticking to his large torso. They laboured their way up the gravel and began heading northwards along the tracks. The site of the accident had to be just beyond the bend.

Not a scrap of shade fell onto the railway line; they were at the mercy of the roasting sun. It stank of the hot creosote that the wooden sleepers were impregnated with. And of the passenger lavatories.

Now they could see the train as well as the people grouped beside the embankment.

Just before they reached them, Harris instructed his Sri Lankan helper to go first to clear the way. Kasun barked some instructions in Sinhalese, and all Harris understood were the English words 'National Wildlife Department'. The curious villagers and passengers from the train immediately moved aside.

Before them lay the little elephant and beside it knelt a young woman, stroking its head.

'It's okay, it's okay,' she said, choking back the tears.

The animal's eyes were wide open, it was biting its trunk and its hind legs stuck out at an unnatural angle. Harris put down his case and opened it.

'Are you a vet?' the tourist asked him in her American accent.

Harris nodded. He took out a syringe and filled it from an ampoule.

'Will she be okay?' the American woman asked, worried.

Harris nodded. He lifted the injured animal's right ear. The network of veins on the back stood out prominently. Harris chose a swollen one as thick as a finger, positioned the needle, and injected the contents of the syringe.

'Painkiller?' she asked.

Harris nodded once more. 'Painkiller,' he muttered, checking his watch.

The elephant seemed to relax. The tongue slid from her mouth and lay on the trampled grass like a weary snake. The American tourist kept stroking the baby elephant's head, which was dotted sparsely with long hairs. 'Shhh, shhh,' she said, as if to a child going to sleep.

Harris checked his watch again and made a sign to Kasun. He understood and touched the woman's shoulder, who flinched and looked up at him.

Now Harris could see how young the tear-stained face was.

'Let's go, miss,' Kasun said.

The American looked at Harris for help.

He nodded. 'Everybody leaves now. We have to do some surgery.'

Slowly she got to her feet, looked back down at the baby elephant, wiped the tears away with the heels of her hands and looked at Harris. 'You put her to sleep, didn't you?'

He didn't reply.

She turned around and was led away by the train guard to the group of passengers waiting a few carriages further on in the shade of the trees at the edge of the forest.

Harris took off his sweat-drenched shirt and replaced it with a green surgeon's gown. Kasun clapped him on the back and handed him the disinfectant. Its glycerine content made it easier to put on the surgical gloves.

The vet listened to the little elephant through his stethoscope. After three minutes he nodded to Kasun, who was also now wearing sterile, disposable gloves. Kasun took the large scalpel from the instrument case and passed it to Harris.

Harris set the blade beside the eighteenth rib below the spinal column and opened up the lumbar region of the dead elephant.

5

The same day

Seat 11A had two advantages: there was no seat beside it and it was the furthest back in business class aboard this Boeing 787-9. Behind was room enough for the cool box carrying the baby elephant's ovaries.

Harris had just managed to catch the Etihad 265, which would take him from Colombo to Zürich via Abu Dhabi in a little over fourteen hours. He'd drunk his way through the champagne, claret and liqueurs on the menu and was now on his goodnight beer. Perhaps he'd get a little more sleep in the remaining four hours of the flight.

Business class was only about half full. Most passengers were asleep, but here and there he could make out the pale flicker of a screen.

All of a sudden a light went on above one of the seats. A few moments later the curtain of the galley moved and an air hostess emerged, went over to the light, bent down, exchanged a few words with the passenger and left. Shortly afterwards she returned with a tray carrying a glass and a can of beer.

Someone else who couldn't sleep.

Harris was pleased that this mission was coming to an end. He'd had enough of the tropics and was looking forward to Europe, cool nights and talking shop with colleagues. And to the recognition he'd receive – in the short term at least – for the project's success.

He put on the headphones and selected the Country channel. 'Lucille' by Kenny Rogers was playing, the song that had acted as a soundtrack to the most difficult period of his separation.

He was awoken by the captain's composed voice. They were entering an area of turbulence, he explained, and all passengers were requested to fasten their seatbelts.

In the past Harris used to suffer from a fear of flying. A pathological fear. Until the age of thirty-two he'd only got on a plane once. He was sixteen at the time and had won a round trip in a competition held by a cigarette firm. From Queenstown to Milford Sound in a Gippsland GA-8, a single-engine Australian aeroplane that seated seven passengers.

The aircraft got caught in a storm high above the rugged fjord and Harris swore he'd never get on a plane again if he survived this horror.

He made good on his promise right after the terrifying landing on the tiny Milford Strand airstrip. Harris refused to get back on board and made the five-hour trip back to Queenstown on the cargo bed of a timber transporter.

Harris took his next flight at the age of thirty-two, soon after separating from Terry. Air New Zealand from Christchurch to Perth via Auckland, and from there to Johannesburg and Cape Town, with South African Airways. His journey took almost thirty hours and not for a second did he fear for his life. He wasn't so attached to it any more.

Ever since that second occasion he'd actually enjoyed flying. He put his unconditional trust in the aircraft and its pilot like a baby kangaroo would in its mother's pouch.

And now, because of a spot of turbulence, this pilot was costing him the little sleep remaining to him before landing.

6

Zürich

26 April 2013

The rain had eased up and the sky had turned clearer. Roux could see the Etihad plane approaching. But the traffic hadn't got any better. He'd be stop–start for another two kilometres till reaching the airport exit.

Roux was angry. Angry at the weather forecast, which was only ever right when you weren't dependent on it. Angry at Zürich Airport, which was a permanent building site. And angry at himself, who couldn't even be punctual for this long-awaited appointment.

Of course Harris would call and wait at customs until he arrived with the necessary papers. But Roux was impatient. He was desperate to take possession of the delivery. He'd waited long enough to get it.

The airport exit came into view; just a few hundred metres more until he could peel off from the traffic jam and put his foot down. Adele sang 'Skyfall'. Roux's hairy fingers drummed out the rhythm on the steering wheel.

The song was interrupted by a traffic report, warning of the congestion he was stuck in on the A51. 'Oh really?' he muttered. 'Congestion?'

Roux was in his mid-forties. Although wiry and not particularly short, there was something squat about him, for which he had his large head and short neck to thank. He kept his sparse red hair shaved and his bushy eyebrows carefully trimmed, which emphasised the bulges above his eyes and lent a slight bull-like quality to his squatness too.

Finally he reached the place where the hard shoulder on the left opened up into the exit, but the gap between the road marker and the boot of the Volvo in front of him was too narrow for his BMW. If only the arseholes in front of him would move up a bit, he'd be at the airport by now.

Roux honked the horn.

Nothing happened.

He honked again, for longer this time.

The furthest car he could see up ahead moved forward a touch. The one behind closed the gap, and the next one and the next one. Only the Volvo stayed where it was.

Roux angrily pressed his horn, keeping his hand on it. The man behind the wheel of the Volvo responded by shaking his head slowly and deliberately. Then he started his engine and infuriatingly inched his way forward.

As soon as the gap was large enough Roux put his foot down and screeched off the motorway, still honking.

7

The same day

The customs area was a large room with stainless-steel counters. Passengers who'd chosen the green channel – nothing to declare – were streaming past the open exits. Only the odd person followed the red sign and entered clearance.

This is where Jack Harris had been waiting for twenty minutes now beside his wheelie case. He'd put the cool box onto one of the metal tables.

He wasn't sure if he'd recognise Roux; he didn't have a good memory for faces and had only met him once, on the fringes of an embryologists' conference in London on combating infertility. The two of them had attended a lecture on allowing elephant egg cells to mature inside rats. Harris was hanging around the conference because he hoped to make contact with researchers looking for experts in fieldwork. Roux needed someone who could procure some elephant ovaries for him.

They had met after the lecture at Ye Olde Rose and Crown, a pub next to the conference hotel. Harris sensed later that the meeting wasn't coincidental. Harris was sitting alone at the bar and Roux joined him with two pints of bitter filled to the brim. 'No sadder sight than a man on his own in a pub,' he said, in English tinged with a Swiss-German accent. By the second round – it was already Harris's third – Roux knew that he was a vet specialising in elephants, and when they were on their next drink he asked Harris outright if he knew the best way of getting hold of ovaries from an Asian elephant.

Harris knew.

'Sorry, Jack, traffic jam!' said the man approaching him now with an outstretched hand.

Harris had in fact failed to recognise him. He recalled Roux being shorter and fatter.

He took Roux's hand and shook it. It was clammy. That's right, he'd noticed this last time: sweaty hands.

Roux was already glancing past Harris at the cool box. Now he took his hand away and placed it on the lid of the container. 'At last,' he said. 'Finally.'

A customs official sauntered up to them. Harris had already informed him that this was an organ transplant and he was waiting for the recipient who had the necessary documents for the import formalities.

Roux showed the official his identification and handed him a slim dossier. The cover bore the red and yellow logo, Gentecsa, and the slogan: *Research for the Future*.

The customs official slid his finger across the rubric and found the information he needed to complete his form. When he was finished he pointed his chin at the cool box.

'Is that really necessary?' Roux asked. 'It's vital that the organ stays between 0 and 4 degrees.'

'I can't let you through without an inspection.'

Roux sighed and gave Harris a sign to open the box. 'No more than a second,' he said.

'As long as it takes,' the official corrected, also in English.

Harris snapped open the clasps and flipped open the lid. A sterile box made of milky plastic sat between blue freezer elements. Harris made no move to open it until the official asked him to.

'You're endangering a scientific project,' Roux grumbled.

'You're the one dragging this thing out,' the official responded.

Roux nodded to Harris, who reluctantly took the lid off the container.

What they glimpsed was as small as a child's fist, with a brain-like structure. It was grey and glistened damply.

'Don't touch!' Roux ordered.

The official slipped a mobile phone from a pouch on his belt and took a photo.

And that was how Sabu arrived in Switzerland.

8

Zürich

28 April 2013

Reflected on the wet asphalt of the car park were a few vehicles and some lit-up windows in an office block that had formerly been a wire factory. The lights still on were coming from the Gentecsa offices on the second floor.

Roux and two assistants were standing around a stainless-steel table, bent over Miss Playmate, as one of the assistants had christened the laboratory rat.

The rat was called Miss Playmate because she was naked. She was a neutered nude rat adapted to the requirements of the elephant tissue, a laboratory rat missing her thyroid gland to prevent her from creating T lymphocytes, the cells responsible for rejecting implants. This meant that Roux could implant the tiny section from the outer layer of the ovary without the foreign tissue being rejected.

Miss Playmate was anaesthetised and lay beneath the blazing surgical light, all four legs splayed apart and fastened with rubber bands. An incision had been made in her abdominal wall and Roux was working internally with a scalpel and pincers. One of the assistants held the wound open with tiny retractors, while the other passed him the instruments he barked for and dabbed, at ever decreasing intervals, the sweat dripping from his trimmed eyebrows between the surgical cap and mask.

The aim of the operation was to implant into Miss Playmate a piece of the Sri Lankan baby elephant's ovary with thousands of egg cells not yet capable of fertilisation. The cells would mature inside the rat's womb and after six months Roux would be able to genetically modify them.

He'd done this operation often enough, as testified by the tree shrews, rhesus monkeys and rabbits glowing green, blue and red in the darkened rooms along the corridor. But this was his first elephant egg cell. And – if everything went according to plan – the elephant he was going to create with it wouldn't just glow in the dark: the creature's skin would be an intense pink even in daylight.

This was Roux's great discovery, known only to his colleagues and, more recently, a silent partner – unfortunately. He'd managed to introduce into the egg cells a combination of luciferins and mandrill pigment!

Luciferins are the compounds that make fireflies glow, for example. And mandrill pigment is the compound that produces the colours in the face and backside of the mandrill. Roux had used the red of the nose.

The most beautiful result of these experiments was Rosie, a 'skinny pig', a hairless guinea pig. Roux had injected both genes into the egg cell, which he then fertilised and implanted into the womb of a normal guinea pig.

After two months the surrogate mother gave birth to two pink guinea pigs. One was dead, but the second,

Rosie, looked as if she were made from marzipan and glowed in the dark like a moving neon sign.

And without needing any light of a particular wavelength to be shone at it, dear Nobel Prize committee! Rosie didn't merely reflect, like the laboratory animals of Professor Dr Richard Gebstein.

Gebstein had been Roux's employer. He was the manager and owner of a genetic engineering laboratory that, among other things, undertook research into gene marking, which often involved the use of fluorescent proteins or enzymes. Roux came to Gebstein straight after he'd finished his PhD and worked for him for almost ten years as an underpaid researcher.

During this time he managed – partly by chance, partly intentionally – to generate a faintly fluorescent green rat, but made the big mistake of showing it to his boss. Delighted by this result, Gebstein gave Roux a not particularly generous pay rise and freed him up to undertake further research into his discovery, on condition that he didn't disclose it to anybody.

Roux worked day and night on his secret project, and in less than a year succeeded in repeating his experiment. His boss duly feted him, but only a few weeks after this triumph there was a spanner in the works. It began with a trifling argument, when Roux was caught by Gebstein eating his lunch – a sandwich, as always – in the laboratory. Eating in a genetic engineering laboratory with this level of security was an infringement of the regulations, but Gebstein had never commented on it before, except for the odd '*Bon appétit!*' On this occasion, however, he snapped at Roux, and Roux snapped back.

It was the beginning of a rift that soon led to his sacking. And when Roux read Gebstein's publication on the interim findings of his experiments, which didn't mention Roux once by name, it confirmed his suspicion that his dismissal had been carefully orchestrated.

The publication caused a sensation in the scientific and journalistic world and was even cited in research by Roger Tsien, Martin Chalfie and Osamu Shimomura, who'd been awarded the Nobel Prize in Chemistry for their discovery of fluorescent green proteins and their application. Roux felt great *Schadenfreude* at the fact that Gebstein's name was absent from the statement issued by the Royal Swedish Academy of Sciences explaining their decision.

Roux had been out for revenge ever since. He'd set up his own genetic engineering laboratory with a single objective: to compete with and outdo Gebstein's. For years now this thought had given him the strength and energy to work through the night, genuflect before bank employees and keep inventing new ways to see off the competition.

The scientific success of his firm had become increasingly incidental and the commercial success ever more vital.

His project had the potential to make a double breakthrough, bringing financial reward and scientific acclaim. If he succeeded in creating patentable animals that didn't just glow in the dark but also were spectacularly colourful in daylight, he would be made in every sense.

When Roux couldn't get to sleep in his short nights, he'd imagine Gebstein's face – his neat white beard, blow-dried white hair, feathery white eyebrows, gold rimless glasses, the entire face designed to look erudite – making him the takeover bid that would be so huge he wouldn't be able to refuse.

9

Zürich

13 June 2016

Schoch's hand wasn't the only one trembling. Around this time almost all of them had difficulty holding their cups in the Morning Sun. It smelled of filter coffee, boozy breath and damp clothes impregnated with smoke. The air was terrible, but if a newcomer stood in the open doorway for a moment, scanning the packed lounge for a free seat, those lucky to already have one would shout, 'Oi!' and 'Close it!'

Most had spent the night outside or in an unheated shelter and were here to warm themselves both externally and internally.

Schoch normally came here to drink his second coffee every morning. He'd have his first at Presto, a shop in a petrol station that opened at six.

But this morning he'd overslept and had come straight to the Morning Sun. He preferred the second cup anyway. You could sit down here and the coffee was better. Although he'd taken a while to get used to the pious sayings that hung on every wall in this small, plain lounge, when facing the choice between pious sayings and expensive coffee, a homeless person didn't have to think too long about it. Anybody who wanted to could get

31

something to eat here too. But Schoch didn't want to, not at this time of day. His stomach was still too unreliable. You could never be sure how you were going to react to solid nourishment. He needed to give it time. And a little coffee.

By noon his stomach had sufficiently settled down that he could give it something to eat. Depending on his financial situation he'd have his lunch either at Meeting Point, where people like Schoch came to shower and wash their clothes and could eat for four francs, or at the soup kitchen, where the food was free. If he needed something harder than apple juice to wash down his food, Schoch would dine at AlcOven, a meeting place for drunks, where you could also have a shower and wash your clothes, but were allowed to bring your own beer to accompany a cheap meal.

He usually took dinner at Sixty-Eight, where you could get a decent meal for free, but only in the evenings.

At this early hour – it was just after eight o'clock – most guests at the Morning Sun weren't particularly chatty. But there were always a few noisy ones, those who'd already taken their first drink of the day. Schoch was one of the silent ones. He never drank before ten. And even when he'd had something to drink he didn't say much. If he did speak, it was quietly, which lent him an aura of mystery. That and the fact that nobody knew anything about him. Everybody knew the stories of most of the others on the streets, knew what they used to be and what had made them end up here. But they knew nothing about Schoch. One day he just arrived on the scene with old Sumi. The two were inseparable, moved around together and supported each other when they were no longer able to stand up straight.

Supposedly, Schoch was also the one who found Sumi when he snuffed it. He didn't die from drinking, people said, but from having given up.

Schoch didn't get close to anyone else afterwards. He kept a friendly distance and remained a mystery.

A young man he'd never seen here before, probably a rejected asylum-seeker needing to go underground, freed up the seat opposite. Within seconds Bolle had sat down. Rapping his knuckles on the table by way of a greeting, he said, 'Shitty weather.'

Bolle was one of the loud ones. He always had something to say, but it wasn't always new. Schoch normally avoided him, but in this situation all he could do was acknowledge Bolle's presence. He shrugged and focused on his cup.

Bolle was blind in one eye, which looked like the white of an undercooked egg. Hence his nickname, Bolle, from the old Berlin folk song: '*His right eye was missing,/His left one looked like slime./But Bolle being Bolle,/Still had a cracking time.*'

Bolle tried to get the attention of the elderly lady, one of the many pious volunteers who helped out here. When she looked over at him, he called out, 'Coffee schnapps, please!' He was the only one who laughed; everyone else had heard the joke plenty of times before.

Or they didn't understand him, like the African man sitting next to him, who said, 'No German,' when Bolle, still laughing, repeated, 'Coffee schnapps,' and grinned at him.

'No alcohol,' Bolle explained in English.

His neighbour replied, 'No, thank you.'

Bolle now had a laughing fit. 'No, thank you!' he repeated. 'No, thank you!'

When he'd composed himself he turned to Schoch and said, 'They've got a new girl working at Sternen.'

Schoch's cup was by his lips. Before he took a sip he said, 'Aren't you banned from there?'

'I was,' Bolle corrected him.

Schoch put his cup back on the table and said in the same dispassionate tone, 'Because you've stopped begging the customers for beer?'

'Because the new girl doesn't care. It's all revenue, she says. Earned, stolen or begged, money is money.' Once again Bolle had a fit of coughing and laughter combined. 'Earned, stolen or begged,' he wheezed.

Schoch failed to react and Bolle tried to change the subject. 'Ever seen white mice? Not real ones, but in your head.'

Schoch shook his head. Pink elephants, on the other hand, he thought...

'I have,' Bolle continued. 'Last night.' His bloated red face suddenly assumed a troubled expression. 'Do you think that's a bad sign?'

Schoch wasn't listening. The memory of the tiny pink elephant had suddenly emerged from nowhere. Had he dreamed it? Or hallucinated?

'Oi, are you listening?'

'How do you know they don't exist?' Schoch said. He placed a franc on the table for his coffee, got up, rummaged on the rack for his yellow raincoat and left.

'He's right,' Bolle mumbled. 'How do I know they don't exist?'

10

The same day

All the washing machines at Meeting Point were being used and all the showers were occupied. At most tables in the cafeteria people were waiting for seats to become free. Their clothes were damp and dirty, and their frozen bodies were longing for a hot shower. It might be hours before it was Schoch's turn.

He knew most of the people waiting and nodded to some of them. Then he left.

The rain had eased up somewhat, but a spiteful little wind had picked up. Schoch pulled the coat around him more tightly and took longer strides.

After ten minutes he'd reached the shiny chrome WC container. It was occupied, but at least nobody was waiting outside. He put his heavy holdall down beside the door and sat on top of it.

Bolle was seeing white mice, and he was seeing pink elephants. Sumi had seen animals too: cockroaches. 'The size of your fist!' he'd claimed, clenching his tiny hand.

But that had been when Sumi was in withdrawal. Schoch wasn't. And Bolle? Unlikely, judging by the state he'd been in at the Morning Sun. But he hadn't said when he'd seen the white mice. Maybe it was yesterday. Maybe he'd tried to stay off the sauce and it had happened then. Schoch should have asked.

But was it important? If these visions only occurred when you were in withdrawal – which Schoch certainly wasn't – didn't that mean the little pink elephant had been no hallucination?

Pink elephants? Come off it!

11

The same day

The electric door to the WC slid open and a young woman stepped out. Her blonde hair hung down in thick strands, some of which were coloured green. She'd reapplied her lipstick and the dark red stood out sharply from her pale face. Eyeing Schoch with tiny pupils, the woman pressed the large shoulder bag more tightly to her slender body and walked away with faltering steps.

Schoch stood up quickly and darted into the WC before the door slid shut again, to save himself the franc he would have had to put in the slot otherwise.

The WC was constructed out of plastic and stainless steel, without gaps and cracks so it could easily be hosed down. The floor around the loo was wet from the water that sluiced the toilet bowl and flooded it each time the door was opened.

Beside the toilet was the loo paper that the woman had used to cover the rim. The smell of patchouli oil hung in the air.

In the metal basin he found a syringe like the ones you could get from the vending machine twenty metres away. Schoch threw it in the bin. Then he undressed, went to the

38

loo, took a flannel and soap from his holdall and washed himself.

In the mirror he saw a haggard-looking man with long hair and an unkempt beard, both blackish-brown and streaked with grey, just like his sparse chest hair.

He looked away and continued washing himself.

Had he drunk more yesterday than on other evenings? Or harder stuff than the litre cans of cheap beer from the supermarket? Where had he been anyway? With the dog lovers at the station as always? Followed by dinner at the soup kitchen? And a nightcap at Hauptplatz tram stop?

He couldn't recall anything unusual. But was this really his recollection of yesterday? How did it differ from the day before, the day before that, and the day before the day before that? If yesterday *had* been different from the evenings before and he had no memory of it, wouldn't the memory of the evening before that leap in to take its place?

Schoch had admitted to himself long ago that he was an alcoholic. But he was a disciplined alcoholic, he kept telling himself. He had his alcoholism under control. He could stop whenever he wanted, as he'd proved several times already. Stopped and, because he'd managed it, started again. He'd stop for good when there was a compelling reason to do so.

Was a pink elephant a compelling reason?

'Are you sick?' Giorgio asked.

Schoch had declined the beer he'd been offered. 'Just not thirsty.'

'Since when did you drink because you were thirsty?'

Schoch shrugged.

Giorgio was the down-and-out Schoch liked most. His sleeping place lay around one hundred metres upstream from Schoch's. It was also a hollow eroded by the river, only a little roomier. Giorgio needed more space because he had three dogs. Obedient mongrels with colourful scarves around their necks. He would starve for these dogs and sometimes he did if there wasn't enough for all four. His real name was Georg, but everyone called him Giorgio. It suited him for he had a moustache he spent a fair time looking after and he always wore a neckerchief like his dogs.

Giorgio was once an insurance salesman and he'd retained his verbosity from that time. Conversations between him and Schoch were very one-sided. But as Schoch liked listening to him – Giorgio was neither pushy, nor nosy, nor stupid – and Giorgio liked talking, this wasn't a problem for either of them. That's why Schoch enjoyed spending the hours before lunch with the dog lovers, even though he didn't really like dogs. There was always beer to be had, even when he'd spent the 986 francs basic subsistence that each homeless person received from the state per month. And they had a cosy regular plot near the station and the wholesaler CONSU. By the river when the weather was good and in the tram shelter if it was raining.

The few seats were occupied so Schoch sat on the ground, leaning against the back of the shelter, listening to Giorgio and watching the passers-by. He knew a few of them by sight because he'd sat here so often as they walked past without paying attention to him or anyone else in his group. Very occasionally he would recognise someone from his former life too. Men in suits, mostly, but also a few women in suits. All older and all passing by without so much as a glance in his direction. Even if they had taken notice of Schoch they wouldn't have recognised him, twelve kilos lighter, nine years older and with a beard.

'Got a fag?' Lilly's high-pitched whine tore him from his thoughts. Schoch took a packet from his pocket, tapped out a cigarette, but rather than offer it to Lilly, slid it out himself and passed it to her. He didn't want her jittery, filthy fingers touching the filters of the other cigarettes.

Lilly had appeared out of the blue five years ago as the girlfriend of Marco, a young junkie. She couldn't have been older than twenty at the time, pretty but prone to abrupt mood swings, and determined to get Marco off the needle. Soon she was addicted herself and when he died of an overdose she was four months pregnant.

The underweight boy she gave birth to was given up for adoption as soon as he'd completed his withdrawal treatment. Lilly stayed with the dog lovers, started selling her body to buy drugs, increased her doses and fell into increasing self-neglect. Now she looked about forty and with her thin, punctured arms and poor teeth couldn't find punters any more.

Schoch offered Lilly a light.

'I'll give her one thing.' Giorgio grinned. 'She's loyal to her brand. Only ever smokes Other People's.'

'Very funny,' Lilly grumbled, going over to the dogs.

Just after twelve Schoch headed for the soup kitchen. His stomach could cope with something to eat now.

12

The same day

Perhaps the macaroni cheese was too stiff a challenge for his stomach; the noodles were swimming in the fat of sweated onions, cream and melted cheese. Nor did the odours of the people sitting next to him help, or the smells drifting over from the kitchen. Schoch let some liquid drip from the baked pasta on his fork, then forced himself to eat a couple of mouthfuls.

The soup kitchen wasn't renowned for its cuisine, but the food was free. In Meeting Point the food cost four francs – for that you could get four litre-cans of 5.4 per cent beer at CONSU.

But seeing as he was dry at the moment, he could have shelled out the four francs, it occurred to him.

He speared three macaroni on his fork and watched the fat drip off, the process slightly accelerated by his trembling hand. 'Do you know why I drink?' Bolle used to yell. 'To stop my hands shaking!' Around this time of day Schoch's trembling had usually stopped. But apart from this, going without alcohol was – as expected – all right. It was just boring.

The rain looked as if it had set in for the day. Schoch walked close to the houses to avoid being splashed by the cars zooming past. Apart from him there was just an old woman and her dog on Blechwalzenstrasse. She was having a tussle with her umbrella, her large handbag and her overweight pet, who was mobilising all four of his skinny legs to resist this sodden outing.

Schoch went into the Salvation Army hostel, took off his wet coat and hung it on the rack. Behind the glass of the reception booth an elderly man looked up from his free newspaper. 'Is Furrer here?' Schoch asked.

The man nodded. 'In the office.'

Schoch went up to the door marked 'Management', knocked and went in.

Furrer was a shaven-headed man with a five-day beard. He was probably about fifty, wore jeans, a checked shirt and a corduroy jacket. 'Take a seat,' he said, pointing to one of the visitors' chairs from the junk shop.

Schoch sat down.

'I'll get us a coffee.' Furrer went out and returned with two large cups.

Schoch took a sip. Black with lots of sugar, just how he liked it.

He didn't know why Furrer was so friendly to him. He had been ever since his first day as manager of the hostel. For a short while Schoch thought it was because Furrer was gay. But a single glance in one of the few mirrors he came across was sufficient to eliminate this possibility. So he'd asked him, 'How come I get such preferential treatment?'

'You remind me of someone.'

'Who?'

'Don't know, but it'll come to me.'

After that he'd avoided Furrer, just to be on the safe side. But one evening Furrer intercepted Schoch outside Sixty-Eight and surprised him with the question, 'I've got a room free, do you want it?'

Schoch shook his head.

'Why ever not? Winter's on its way. Opportunities like this don't crop up every day.'

Schoch spent a moment searching for an answer, then shook his head obdurately. 'Homeless people don't have bedrooms.'

Sumi was still alive at the time and Schoch didn't have a fixed sleeping place. So he was happy to accept Furrer's offer to store his belongings at the hostel. And later, when he inherited the River Bed, he kept them there. They wouldn't have been safe in his cave.

Schoch wasn't the only one for whom Furrer put in safekeeping a few 'personal effects', as he called them. Schoch suspected that this allowed him to stay in contact with those homeless people who, like himself, wouldn't be domesticated. The lockers were in Furrer's office and it was difficult to access them without bumping into him.

Furrer asked the inevitable question, 'How are you?'

And Schoch gave the routine answer, 'Good.'

'You don't look it.'

'I haven't looked good since I was nineteen.'

'What about the shakes?'

'Didn't have them then either.'

Furrer laughed and shook his head. Then he turned serious. 'Dr Senn is coming at eight tomorrow morning. Shall I put your name down?'

Dr Senn was the GP who held a surgery once a week in the hostel for those who couldn't bring themselves to seek out a doctor in their practice.

Schoch shook his head. 'He's not going to make me any prettier.'

'Why don't you join the group?'

'The alky group?' Schoch said with a grimace.

'Hasn't hurt anyone yet.'

'If I want to stop, I'll stop.'

Furrer nodded thoughtfully. 'Well, that's good.'

Schoch stood up and went over to his locker. 'But if I do stop,' he said, more to himself than to Furrer, 'what will I do instead of drinking?'

The question was not meant as ironically as it sounded. When Schoch stepped out of the Salvation Army hostel, he didn't know where to go. Normally he would have headed straight for CONSU, the wholesaler with the cheapest beer, and bought himself a six-pack. If the weather was good, he would have then gone to Freiland Park and sat on a bench or joined the other homeless people, depending on who was there. In poor weather he might have taken the six-pack to the tram stop at the station and shared it with the dog lovers. And with today's weather as bad as it was he'd have taken himself off to the AlcOven, where it was warm and dry at least.

But without any beer? Without that spark of happiness that only ever lasted for two or three cans, then was replaced by something that might not have been satisfaction, but was at least its little sister, indifference? How was he going to kill the afternoons and evenings now?

Should he, as Furrer kept suggesting, register as a street vendor for *Gassenblatt*, the homeless newspaper? 'It gives you a structured day, your own income and you meet normal people,' he said. And you can't drink, Schoch thought. For him, those were precisely the 'advantages' that militated against it.

He'd tried it once. Furrer had lent him sixty francs, which had allowed him to buy twenty copies of the paper and keep 100 per cent of the income from these.

But after a short spell beside the escalator of the pedestrian underpass he'd had enough. He felt silly in the light-blue coat and matching baseball cap, and found it so embarrassing trying to talk to people. He recalled how he'd given the vendors a wide berth when he was one of those passers-by.

In almost two hours Schoch had sold a single paper, to an old lady who looked as if she needed the money just as much as him, and he sold the remaining nineteen copies to another vendor at half price. He invested his thirty-four francs in beer and cigarettes and still owed Furrer the sixty francs to this day.

Schoch stood indecisively beneath the porch of the hostel, staring at the pouring rain. He plumped for the closest option.

13

The same day

To begin with he thought the old man next to him was talking to the guy opposite, but then Schoch realised that both of them were talking to themselves. One he knew by sight, the other even by name: Ormalinger. He used to be with the dog lovers. He'd owned a large, shaggy mongrel, a 'Giant Schnauzer-Alsatian', as he used to call it. One evening during Carnival the animal had bitten a five-year-old dressed as Darth Vader, who'd threatened it with a light sabre. The injury was only slight, but the 'Giant Schnauzer-Alsatian' had been impounded and put down, which turned the alcoholic into a severe alcoholic. Schoch hadn't realised, however, that Ormalinger had now reached the stage of chatting away to himself unintelligibly.

He nodded, but Ormalinger didn't react. He probably couldn't remember Schoch.

The AlcOven was an institution for cases so hopeless that it had given up stopping them from drinking. Although no alcohol was offered for sale, visitors were permitted to bring their own wine and beer. And the management couldn't prevent people sharing the drinks they'd brought with others, nor stop money being exchanged under the table for such generosity.

There were a few who earned a bit of cash selling beer and wine at a slight profit to those who were stranded and couldn't summon the energy to make it to the nearby CONSU. When the weather was as bad as today, business was good. A lot of passing trade had joined the regulars: homeless people simply escaping from the rain. The dining room was jam-packed and everyone was drinking.

Everyone except Schoch, who wasn't consuming anything liquid apart from a bowl of free soup.

This he managed without a problem.

Which meant he wasn't dependent.

The next time one of the sellers offered him a beer he took it.

To combat the boredom.

14

The same day

After the AlcOven Schoch had passed by the dog lovers in the hope that Giorgio might be there, as they had the same route home. And by now Schoch was no longer feeling so steady on his legs.

But Giorgio had already left and at this time of day those who were still there didn't make much sense. He accepted the beer he was offered out of politeness and set off on his way.

It wasn't until he hit the riverside path that Schoch noticed it had stopped raining. The river was brown and churned up, taking twigs and branches in its wake. In the west a slim strip of clear sky brightened up the twilight gloom. Slowly and with the utmost concentration, Schoch put one foot in front of the other.

There was a man standing a little further along the path. He wasn't moving and seemed to be waiting for Schoch.

As Schoch came closer he could see that the man was from the Far East. Short and weedy-looking, but perhaps he had fighting skills.

Schoch made to go past him, but the man walked beside him and asked something Schoch didn't understand. He kept going.

'Where is cave?'

I see, Schoch thought, someone after our caves. 'There aren't any caves here,' he replied.

But the man wouldn't give up. 'You sure?'

'Piss off,' Schoch snarled. Now the man kept his distance.

At the whirlpool stood an elderly man that Schoch knew by sight. He had one of the nearby allotments. 'They pulled one out of here today,' he said.

'A dog?' Schoch said.

'A man. With a bag around his neck. Empty.'

The river tugged at some plastic tape that was tied to the trunk of a willow. It had red and white stripes like the tape the police used to seal off a crime scene.

'I wonder what was in it?' the elderly man muttered.

Schoch didn't reply.

'It'll turn up at some point. The whirlpool doesn't keep anything for ever.'

Schoch was about to mention the two men he'd seen early that morning, prodding around in the eddy with the rescue pole. But he had second thoughts. He didn't want to have anything to do with the police and, besides, there was nothing anybody could do for the drowned man now. So he continued on his way.

The gap in the clouds to the west had closed again, and the twilight blurred the contours of the landscape. Schoch had to pay close attention to the cracks and holes in the asphalt.

After about five hundred metres he'd reached the spot directly above his cave. As ever, he walked on past, in case anybody was watching. And, as ever, he peed up against a nearby poplar and looked around cautiously. When he

50

was sure there were no witnesses he clambered down the steep embankment.

The ground was slippery. Even for a younger, more sober man it wouldn't have been easy to come to a stop with the bulky holdall at the right place, then climb back up the two metres to the cave entrance. He slipped and caught a projecting root that had saved him more than once before. The entrance was now three metres above him.

Cursing, and on all fours, he waited until he'd got his breath back.

From here the entrance to his cave seemed to have changed. The bushes that partially concealed it in summer looked ragged. A result of the storm, perhaps.

His pause now over, he started scrambling up the slope on muddy hands and knees. When he got to the bushes he saw that they'd been mangled: leaves and twigs ripped off. That couldn't have been the wind.

Schoch pushed the bag past the bushes into his cave and then crept into the dim light.

There it was again, fluorescent pink and its ears cocked – the phantom from last night!

Schoch held his breath and didn't move.

The mini elephant stood there motionless too. So still that Schoch breathed out. It had to be a toy after all.

He crept completely into the cave and made a grasp for the elephant. But before he could touch it, it moved. It lowered its head and thrust its trunk into the air with a swing of its head.

Turning around, the creature moved right to the very back and narrowest part of the hollow. Where Schoch's hand couldn't reach it.

'I'm going mad!' he exclaimed.

And again: 'I'm going mad!'

Then, more softly: 'Or I am already.'

In the middle of the cave lay some leaves and stripped branches from the bushes by the entrance. Schoch picked some up and crawled as far back as he possibly could. He held out some leaves to the tiny creature, but it wouldn't be enticed. It just stood there, occasionally fanning its ears or raising its trunk menacingly.

Schoch clicked his tongue and spoke softly, 'Come on … come on … come on … tchick-tchick-tchick.'

The little animal put its ears back and started feeling the sandy ground with its trunk. Sometimes it curled the end of its trunk and sometimes it gracefully lifted a leg and let the foot hang there loosely. But it wouldn't come a single step closer.

15

Zürich

14 June 2016

At some point Schoch woke up, freezing. It took him quite a while to remember why he was lying like this. The elephant was nowhere to be seen and he was just about to put the whole thing down to a hallucination when he discovered the dung. The same crumbly mounds he remembered from the zoo visits of his past life, only much, much smaller, lay in the part of the cave where the ceiling was at its lowest.

He crawled backwards until he could just about sit up, and looked around. Apart from a few leftover leaves and twigs he didn't see anything unusual.

He took the sleeping mat from his bag, rolled it out, laid the sleeping bag on top, removed his shoes and got in. Now he heard a rustling by the entrance to the cave, saw movement in the bushes and finally the pink glow of his hallucination.

Schoch kept still and waited. And fell asleep.

He dreamed of a tiny pink elephant glowing in the dark. Someone he didn't know said, 'This is no dream, this is real.' When he looked again the elephant had turned into a little dog. Schoch wanted to stroke it, but the dog ran away. He wanted to follow it, but he couldn't run.

Suddenly he was beside the whirlpool of death, where Giorgio and Bolle were fishing with long poles. 'Has someone drowned?' he called out.

'You!' they replied.

Something warm, damp and soft enveloped his thumb.

He felt the dream departing, distancing itself rapidly and inexorably, and leaving him alone.

But the thing enveloping his thumb was still there. It moved, sucking and slurping.

Schoch opened his eyes. The dawn gave his cave a touch of light. The little elephant was beside his hand. It was standing on its hind legs, kneeling on its front ones and suckling his thumb.

Carefully Schoch lifted his other hand and brought it down gently. The pink skin felt warm and as soft as pigskin.

The creature flinched and scurried back to its hiding place. But not as far back as before. Stopping where Schoch could still have reached it, the elephant wiggled its trunk and looked at him expectantly.

Schoch crept out of his sleeping bag, squatted then knelt, and tried to breathe deeply and in a controlled manner to calm the pounding of his heart. What he could see wasn't a hallucination. You couldn't touch hallucinations.

But what was it?

A miracle? A sign? Something mystical?

Schoch had never been a religious man, but before his downfall he'd certainly believed in the existence of something that transcended his powers of perception and

54

imagination. A higher reality, and maybe a higher power too.

But like everything else, this belief had crumbled with his downfall. And hadn't made its presence felt in all the years since.

Until today. For the fact that this fabulous creature from another world, maybe even another dimension, had chosen to reveal itself to him – him! – must have a significance.

Schoch now did something he hadn't done since childhood: he crossed himself. But this form of homage seemed inappropriate given the significance of the revelation and the fact that it might be an Asian elephant before him, so he put the palms of his hands together in front of his beard and gave a deep Thai-style bow.

The animal felt around on the ground with its trunk.

'Hungry?' Schoch asked. He picked up a few leaves and held them out to the elephant.

Hesitantly, and with its trunk outstretched, the creature inched closer. It grabbed hold of the leaves, lowered its wedge-shaped jaw and stuffed them in its mouth. Schoch's hand brushed the tip of the trunk, which felt soft and silky.

The elephant raised its trunk, indicating that it wanted more.

Schoch put on his shoes. 'Stay here,' he ordered. 'I'll fetch you some more.' He pushed past the bushes and got to his feet.

The clouds hung low and the river was still brown and flowing rapidly. But at least it wasn't raining. Schoch went over to the old willow growing a little way downstream and broke off a few branches. Then he pulled up some clumps of grass and a bunch of buttercups that were growing just above the high water level.

With this harvest he struggled back up the embankment and crept into his cave.

His visitor, still standing in the same place, shot out its trunk when it saw the food.

Schoch fed the little animal with fascination and patience. It was so hungry that he had to go out twice for more. With his penknife he also cut off the lower third of a plastic bottle, filled it with water from the river and watched the elephant sink its trunk in, suck up the water and empty it into its mouth.

Thus the morning passed without Schoch having eaten or drunk anything.

His cheap plastic watch showed 2 p.m. when his little guest went for a lie-down. Schoch thought this was a good idea and lay down beside it.

When he awoke the mini elephant was on its side in a different spot. Its stomach was rising and falling rapidly and its trunk was being thrust out and curled up at irregular intervals. On the ground everywhere were puddles of runny excrement.

Schoch gently laid a hand on the little body as if it were the forehead of a feverish child. It didn't react. He carefully took hold of the elephant and placed it upright. It stood there, legs splayed, ears and trunk drooping, and beneath its tail the contents of its bowels gushed out, as thin as water. The little creature lay back down even before it had finished. In fact it was more like falling down than lying down.

Drink lots of fluids when you've got diarrhoea, Schoch thought. He took an empty bottle and went back down the embankment. It was much easier now; after twenty hours without any alcohol he was quite steady on his feet again.

But he was still panting heavily when he entered his cave with the full bottle. The tiny, pink, magical creature now lay there peacefully, its chest no longer rising and falling and the trunk not twisting any more, but resting limply beside its front legs.

Schoch panicked. 'You're not going to die on me,' he muttered. 'You're not going to die on me.'

He shook out the contents of his holdall, wrapped the droopy animal in the towel with the Nivea logo and placed it inside the holdall. Then he hung this over his shoulder and left.

16

Eastern Switzerland

6 June 2013

A director is only ever as important as the business they preside over. And unfortunately Circus Pellegrini wasn't as important as it once had been.

That's why most of the employees and all the artists who worked for Carlo P. Pellegrini just called him Carlo. Only those veterans of the circus who'd been taken on by his father called him 'Herr Direktor'.

Back then Pellegrini was still one of the three most important circuses in the country. It played the same venues as the national circus and although its gala premieres may have been rather middle-class events, they were still part of the social calendar.

Its decline began right after the sudden death of Pellegrini's father, Paolo, at fifty-two. He was the victim of a lion attack, or rather, the victim of the abrupt end of an affair between the animal trainer de Groot and a Chinese trapeze artist, who on the orders of her father, the head of the troupe, had to submit to family discipline and terminate the relationship.

De Groot, an alcoholic who'd stayed dry for fifteen years, suffered a relapse and was confronted by Carlo's father at a training session where he was clearly drunk. The circus director marched into the cage as he'd often done before – he'd worked with lions himself in the past – and gave de Groot a piece of his mind. Pellegrini ordered him to take the lions back to their cages and sleep off his inebriation.

Tarzan, the star of the lion routine, came to his boss's aid and attacked Paolo Pellegrini.

He died on the spot.

Carlo had just turned thirty and was unprepared for the role of circus director. His dream was to become a musician, but his plans had been thwarted by his sister Melanie. She had been an enthusiastic circus child and they were agreed that when the time came for the hand-over she'd become the first female circus director in the country. While he, Carlo, would continue the circus life-style, but on tour with a rock band.

Then, however, his sister fell in love with the magician and son of an American circus family, and followed him to the States. Which meant Carlo had no choice but to take over his father's role.

He might have enjoyed more success if it hadn't been for his father's widow. Following the death of Carlo's mother, Paolo had got married again to Alena, a Russian circus princess who was as old as his son. Although he'd bequeathed the circus to whichever child was going to continue it, he'd set aside a generous pension for his widow, which placed a major burden on the circus budget. Moreover, because she no longer did her horse routine, for which she'd once won a prize, Carlo had to hire an external artiste as a replacement.

He'd never got on with her even while his father was alive, but afterwards open hostility broke out between them. She constantly interfered in the management of the circus, undermined the little authority he had and kept causing upheaval in the team by embarking on affairs with the artistes. Carlo was delighted when she stayed on after a holiday to Ibiza and only returned sporadically. Sporadically, but always unexpectedly.

In his will, Carlo's father had guaranteed her the right of abode for the rest of her life, which meant that the circus always had to shunt around her luxury caravan.

Another problem was that Carlo Pellegrini had no affinity with animals. He was a poor rider, he'd never been able to overcome his fear of horses and he had zero understanding of them. Losing Alena's equestrian skills left him in a fix, and he ended up hiring rather mediocre acts twice in succession.

After the tragedy with his father he struck large carnivores from the programme, replacing them with pigs, dogs, goats and other pets in acts that were amusing rather than striking and which could have been entertaining if he'd had a better feel for the routines. The same was true of his choice of artistes. He lacked sufficient professional knowledge or interest to spot the really exceptional artistes. And he couldn't afford those with the best reputations in the circus world, a problem that worsened each year.

Soon this was even the case at the top venues in the country. He had to make do with the second- or sometimes third-best choice.

The last remaining showpieces of Circus Pellegrini were its Indian elephants. Four cows and an adolescent bull. They'd been the pride of Carlo's father, who was known as an eminent elephant trainer. After his death

Carlo took over the elephant act, even though he didn't have a clue about these animals either.

That this was at all possible was down to Kaung, his Burmese oozie. Oozie, or neck rider, was the name given over there to elephant keepers.

It was Kaung who'd been training and looking after the elephants for years and who led them around the edge of the ring at every performance. Even Paolo Pellegrini's act with the elephants had been a bit of a sham. He pretended that the grey giants were obeying him, when in fact they only listened to Kaung.

Keeping the elephants was a costly affair. A fully grown animal ate 200 kilograms of fresh twigs, hay, leaves, fruit and vegetables per day. A year after he'd taken over the circus, Pellegrini was determined to sell them. And he would have done if it hadn't been for Kaung, who one day came up with the idea of submitting the cows to an international breeding programme. He knew that during the pregnancy a client would pay for feed, veterinary services and care, and then hand over a wad of money after the birth.

Pellegrini was convinced. He applied to a programme that worked with artificial insemination. Three of his cows had already produced babies using this method and prospects were good that this part of his business, at least, would continue to prosper. The clients were most satisfied. The elephants were healthy and so well trained that they patiently allowed the procedure to be carried out.

'Carlo!' called the woman who looked after the ticket sales, book-keeping, correspondence, telephone and all the other administrative tasks. 'That Roux guy is here!'

She'd opened the door to his caravan without knocking, pointing behind to a squat man with shaven hair, carrying an open umbrella and a briefcase.

'Show him in, he's got an appointment,' he said gruffly, watching as she – also holding an umbrella – went back over to Roux and indicated the caravan.

17

The same day

The red, white and yellow striped tent with the Pellegrini logo was pitched on the recreation ground beside the recreation hall in a town in eastern Switzerland near Lake Constance, a good hour's drive from Gentecsa. A dozen circus wagons in the same colours and a motley collection of just as many caravans and mobile homes were clustered behind the big top.

The picture might not have looked so sad if this hadn't been the penultimate stop before the end of the season and if it hadn't been chucking it down so persistently from a murky grey sky.

The bad-tempered woman from the office pointed to the caravan that said 'Director'. 'He's expecting you,' she said, before hurrying back to the box office.

He walked the few metres up to the caravan and knocked. Pellegrini opened the door and invited him in.

Roux knew the man from the media, particularly from the time when his father was 'Torn to shreds by lions!' as one tabloid put it. For a while the same rag ran stories on the circus takeover and the rather indelicate question of when Pellegrini would get married. After that, however, media interest in the director and his circus died down.

Roux recalled Pellegrini as slimmer, but otherwise he hadn't changed much in the intervening seven years. Pellegrini was a head taller than him, his shoulder-length hair a touch too black and he stood slightly stooped, as many tall men do.

The director's caravan was dominated by a huge desk with three visitors' chairs. The rest of the space was taken up by three armchairs and a sofa. The walls were covered with old circus posters and photographs from eighty-five years of Circus Pellegrini. The director seemed to be pondering whether to offer his guest a seat by the desk or take him to the more comfortable armchairs; he opted for the latter.

'I'm intrigued,' Pellegrini said.

Roux placed his briefcase on the floor beside the armchair. 'I'm looking for a surrogate elephant mother.'

Pellegrini smiled. 'You mean an elephant cow for artificial insemination. You could have told me that over the phone. It's no secret that we do this.'

'But in this instance it needs to remain one. You see, we're not talking about artificial insemination.'

Pellegrini looked at him expectantly.

'It's a blastocyst transfer. We place a 0.2 millimetre embryo directly into the womb.'

'And?'

'It's a genetically modified blastocyst.'

'Oh, I see. Would you like a coffee?'

'I'd love one.'

Pellegrini went over to the espresso machine on the chest of drawers. 'Lungo or espresso?'

'Espresso please, black, no sugar. Don't you want to know how?'

Pellegrini took a capsule, placed it in the machine and waited for the espresso to pour out. 'You mean how it's been genetically modified?'

Roux nodded.

Pellegrini made himself an espresso too, put both cups on the coffee table and sat down. 'No,' he said, 'I don't want to know how. I don't even want to know that it has been.'

'I understand.' Roux was fine with that. He wasn't going to tell Pellegrini the truth anyway. He would have said he was working on a project to make elephants resistant to herpes. Elephant herpes was one of the most common causes of death among Asian elephants in captivity.

'There's another issue,' Pellegrini now explained. 'Rupashi is pregnant, so is Sadaf, Trisha is breastfeeding and Fahdi is a bull.'

Roux realised that this was all about the price. He'd done his homework beforehand: the fourth cow, Asha, was available. She was also the most experienced. 'What about Asha?' he asked innocently.

'Asha is reserved,' Pellegrini came back quickly.

'Is that a binding commitment?'

'Sort of.'

'What does that mean?'

'Nothing's been signed yet. But we made a verbal agreement.'

'Given the special nature of our project, we'd be prepared to go above the usual rate.'

'Who is we?'

'Me and the international group that's behind me.'

'May I know which group?'

'No, but I can assure you that they are a most solvent partner.'

Pellegrini nodded. Then sighed. 'Turning down our other clients would have a very negative impact on any future projects with them.'

'Well, of course we'd take this into account,' Roux assured him.

'As well as the fact that the project is secret, I assume. An additional complication.'

'Naturally.'

Pellegrini took Roux to the animal tent to show him Asha, the elephant cow who was a possible surrogate mother.

It was quiet in the stalls; the only sounds were the occasional snort from a horse and the rustling of hay that the elephants were eating. Asha was the furthest away in the elephant pen. An Asian keeper was standing beside her, feeding her carrots and talking softly to her in a foreign tongue.

'May I introduce Kaung, our elephant-whisperer? Kaung, this is Dr Roux. He wants to borrow Asha as a mother for his baby.'

Kaung put his palms together in front of his face and bowed. Roux nodded, gave him a 'Hello' and turned back to Pellegrini.

* * *

It was already getting dark when Pellegrini went to get changed for the performance. The bad-tempered woman was garishly made up, and sitting at the evening box office, waiting for the first spur-of-the-moment customers.

18

The same day

Kaung's father had been an oozie too, as had his father. They lived near Putao, in the very north of his country, and worked in logging camps. At the age of five Kaung was already riding a bull elephant that dragged teak trunks weighing tonnes.

When he was eleven Kaung ran away, and after months of roaming the country he ended up as a boy monk in a Buddhist monastery to the north of Mandalay. He was a good pupil and was sent to university.

On 8 August 1988 he took part in the demonstrations against government oppression, which later became known as the 8888 Uprising. The military killed thousands of people and tortured tens of thousands more.

Kaung managed to flee, making his way across Laos to Thailand, where in Bangkok he signed up on a freighter under the Liberian flag.

It wasn't until summer 1990 that he dared go ashore. Kaung jumped ship in Rotterdam and applied for asylum, which he was granted on account of the situation in Myanmar.

More difficult was finding work. He had to draw a veil over his dream of continuing his studies and becoming a teacher. Eventually he managed to get a job as an assistant in a circus, where they found out how good he was with elephants and from then on employed him as an elephant keeper.

After two years the Dutch circus sold two of its elephants to Paolo Pellegrini. Kaung accompanied the animals on the journey and was scheduled to spend the first two weeks with them, but Paolo Pellegrini immediately recognised the skill the oozie had with elephants and made him an offer. Although it was scarcely more generous than his Dutch wages, the food was better, the accommodation more decent and he was treated with respect. Kaung accepted.

He'd been looking after the Circus Pellegrini elephants ever since. And since the sudden death of Paolo Pellegrini, he'd also been responsible for training them behind the scenes.

19

Romania

29 October 2013

Ashok stood serenely in the area in front of the elephant pens. His right hind leg and left front leg were tied with rope.

Ashok's mahout held the bull's trunk and comforted him with some words. Beside the animal an assistant was waiting with a fishing net on a pole. The net was covered with a plastic bag.

The young man behind the elephant was standing on a solid platform. He wore a plastic apron, arm-length surgical gloves and was removing dung from the animal's rectum. When it was empty an attendant handed him a hose with which he flushed out the rectum. Then he inserted his arm up to the elbow and started kneading and massaging the prostate.

Ashok patiently allowed all this to happen. It wasn't his first time; he was a trained sperm donor – the pride of a small zoo in provincial Romania.

The grey penis slowly grew from the wrinkly foreskin. The young man on the platform doubled his efforts and the S-shaped penis became erect to its full length of two metres. 'Get ready to receive!' the man gasped.

The assistant held the collection bag on the long pole at the end of the penis and caught the sperm that came flowing out soon afterwards.

A lab technician poured it into a glass specimen jar, added the nutrient solution and a little glycerine, to protect the cells against the sharp ice crystals. He labelled the jar 'Roux/Gentecsa' and placed it in a freezer that gently chilled the contents down to minus 196 degrees. Twenty minutes later he put it in the steam of a liquid nitrogen container.

20

Zürich

4 November 2013

Twenty days before, Roux had finally received the good news that Asha's LH test was positive. This meant that the egg cells would be ready in twenty-five days; with elephants it was possible to predict this accurately.

To ensure that the cells developed into blastocysts at the right stage at exactly the right time, they had to be fertilised precisely five days before transfer. Which meant now.

Roux's hand was never steady enough for this job. He'd wired a monitor up to the microscope where his assistant, Vera, was doing the work, and he was following the process volubly.

'That one, yes, that one! No! Not that one, the other one. Yes, that one!'

Vera was staring concentratedly into the eyepiece, her right forearm resting on a small cushion to allow her to manoeuvre the wafer-thin glass needle with greater accuracy.

On the monitor you could see the sperm in the petri dish, swimming in a viscous liquid that was meant to reduce their speed slightly. Vera's glass needle was following them. She aimed for the sperm Roux was talking about.

'Yes, yes!' he cried. 'That's the chap! Get 'im.'

Vera tried to place the needle on the sperm's tiny tail, but it got away.

'My God, is it really that difficult?' Roux groaned.

Vera had worked long enough for Roux not to feel nervous in his presence. Another three failed attempts followed, but on the fifth try she got it. The sperm was kept in place for a moment by the glass needle before it went on swimming with a kink in its tail. But slowly enough that Vera had little trouble sucking it up in her pipette.

'Finally,' Roux grumbled.

Vera took the petri dish containing the sperm from the stage of the microscope and Roux fetched the first dish with the now fertile egg cell from the incubator.

He carried it over to the table with the microscope with great solemnity, for in his hands was the result of many years' work, the reason why he was up to his eyeballs in debt and why he'd had to sell half of Gentecsa to a silent partner whose name was a secret only he knew.

Roux had genetically modified the egg cells he hoped would liberate him from this hopeless situation. As with Rosie, the glowing pink skinny pig, he'd inserted the pigment from the noses of mandrills and the luciferin from the *Lampyris noctiluca* species of firefly.

He – or more accurately Vera, under his instruction – had prepared six egg cells in this way in case the highly complicated implant of the ovum in the elephant cow went wrong. Those that weren't used would be frozen for future opportunities.

Vera placed the petri dish into the specimen jar and Roux sat back down in front of the monitor.

'Now concentrate!' he ordered.

She looked up from the eyepiece and shot him a weary look. Then, taking a deep breath, Vera got on with her work.

The glass needle appeared on the screen, gently pushed the egg cell to the end of the holding needle then vanished from the picture.

Vera's respiring penetrated the silence of the room before she held her breath.

Now the razor-thin tip of the micropipette appeared in the picture. It moved closer to the egg cell, touching it in the very middle. There was a slight indentation as the cell wall offered some resistance before giving way and the pipette entered.

The two of them were still holding their breath.

Vera carefully began the injection.

Roux could clearly see the sperm being pushed down the thin channel and leaving the tip.

As gently as she could, Vera removed the pipette from the cell.

Only then did they exhale and take another deep breath.

'Yes!' Roux cried, clapping Vera on the shoulder. Then he stood up and fetched the next egg cell.

21

St Gallen, Switzerland
8 November 2013

Dr Horàk was one of the foremost experts in the artificial insemination of elephants. And one of the few who, together with his team, had succeeded in implanting a fertilised egg cell.

Although he didn't know Roux, the latter's lengthy collaboration with Professor Gebstein, a leading researcher in gene marking, was an excellent reference. And the project of immunising elephants against herpes sounded interesting. Horàk didn't think it would work, but he didn't want to let slip the opportunity of practising his team's blastocyst transfer techniques – flights, hotel, expenses and fee included.

He also knew Pellegrini and his experienced elephants, but especially his oozie, a true elephant-whisperer and a great help.

Kaung led Asha in without rope or stick. She walked beside him as quietly as the barefoot Burmese trainer.

They were in an empty barn in a village near St Gallen. A low platform stood beside a pillar supporting the gable roof, and behind it were a few tables full of electronics. Dr Horàk was accompanied by four assistants, all in green gowns, aprons and gloves.

Roux was there too. He stood in his green surgical outfit at a safe distance next to Pellegrini, who looked slightly disguised in his freshly ironed overalls bearing the circus logo.

In response to some words from Kaung, Asha stopped, turned around 180 degrees and stepped onto the platform from the side. The oozie placed a piece of carrot on the pink tip of her trunk, which she curled inwards and put in her mouth, unbothered by the assistant who was emptying and washing her rectum. She didn't even react when Dr Horàk inserted the rectal probe to check on which side her ovulation had taken place.

Now came the fiddly part. Horàk had to position the four-metre-long endoscope in the right part of the uterus. The route went through the metre-and-a-half-long vaginal vestibule, ninety centimetres horizontally, then sixty vertically. Then it passed the hymen, which in elephants only tears at birth before growing back, and further on through the vagina, its many folds repeatedly obstructing the path of the endoscope. Finally it had to negotiate the uterine wall until it got to within a metre of the place of ovulation.

The man on the endoscope opened the vent for the carbon dioxide channel.

Asha had stopped eating during this procedure, her only reaction to Dr Horàk's interventions.

The endoscope had three working channels: one for guiding the catheter; one for the saline solution that could be used to clean the lens if it got smeared; and one for the carbon dioxide to puff up the cervical canal and give a better overview.

It took half an hour for Horàk to navigate the end of the four-metre-long endoscope to where he wanted it. He had an assistant take over, then directed the five-metre-long guide tube through the work channel of the endoscope. And a metre further to the tip of the uterus.

By now the two other assistants on the loupe microscope had loaded the tip of the transfer catheter with the blastocyst, as the embryo was called in this stage of development. They passed the catheter to Horàk.

With the greatest of care he fed it into the guide tube and pushed it slowly to the end of the endoscope.

Asha was slightly unsettled for the first time. Kaung stroked the root of her trunk and whispered words of comfort to her in Burmese.

Horàk pushed the transfer catheter further.

This was the most critical phase of the implant. If the tip of the catheter came too close to the wall of the cervical canal, or the assistant, out of nervousness, triggered the mechanism a split second too soon, the embryo would be lost.

But the assistant kept his nerve. Horàk was able to guide the end of the catheter to the uterus.

'Now,' he said calmly.

The assistant released the blastocyst. Horàk started pulling out the catheter and another assistant sucked the CO_2 back out through the relevant work channel.

'So?' Roux said impatiently.

'Everything's fine,' Horàk replied.

Roux applauded enthusiastically. Pellegrini joined in.

Horàk waved a hand dismissively at them. 'I'm the sort of pilot who doesn't like it when passengers applaud after landing. Landing's my job.'

22

Late 2013 to June 2014

Seven weeks later Dr Horàk came again with an assistant and performed the first transrectal ultrasound.

Horàk established that the embryo had embedded itself in the mucous membrane of the uterus.

Roux celebrated this finding with a visit to Red Moon, which cost his silent partner 4,000 francs, including champagne, a hotel room and a 'present' for Semira from Bucharest.

After four more weeks the embryo was 'developing well' and the hormone values of the urine test were satisfactory.

A further four weeks down the line and it already looked like a little elephant. Dr Horàk's verdict: 'Nice development, maybe a bit on the small side.'

In the sixth month he said, 'Stagnation. At this stage the embryo ought to be twice the size.'

One month later he paid his last visit to Asha. 'Not viable,' was his diagnosis. 'Make sure she expels the foetus if it dies in the uterus. You don't want to lose the cow too,' he said as he left.

23

Graufeld

21 June 2014

Dr Reber got caught up in the affair the very next day.

Dr Hansjörg Reber was Circus Pellegrini's vet. He had a one-man practice in Graufeld, a backwater in the Berner Oberland. Three mornings a week he saw patients in his surgery: dogs, cats, even pigeons and guinea pigs. The rest of the time was spent conducting house visits to farmers and horse-owners.

His passion was for elephants, however. He had undertaken further training in this area, as a volunteer at the zoo and on a six-month internship at the Pinnawala Elephant Orphanage in Sri Lanka.

Unfortunately there weren't too many opportunities to apply this knowledge, which was why he offered his services to Circus Pellegrini for nothing, billing only for the horses and two lamas. Pellegrini, on the other hand, permitted himself to pass on costs for Reber's treatment of Asha to Dr Roux.

The day after Dr Horàk's diagnosis Dr Reber arrived for routine ultrasound scans of the two pregnant elephants, Rupashi and Sadaf.

Pellegrini, who'd so far kept knowledge of the embryo

implant from Reber, now let him in on the secret and asked him to perform an ultrasound scan on Asha too.

Dr Reber confirmed what Dr Horàk had said: far too small, not viable.

'But is it still alive?' Pellegrini asked.

'The heart is beating.'

'If it dies how will you get it out?'

'I assume Asha will miscarry.'

'If she doesn't, will you remove it?'

'I can't – too dangerous. I couldn't get to it. And surgery's out of the question.'

'So I'd lose her?'

'I assume that she'll get rid of the foetus herself. I've even heard of cases where elephant cows carry a dead foetus around in the womb for years without any problems.'

Pellegrini wasn't convinced. 'I hope you're right.'

'Don't worry. I'll be coming every month anyway to check on Rupashi and Sadaf, so I'll examine Asha too. If things aren't right with her in the meantime Kaung will notice and call me, won't you Kaung?'

The oozie, who'd been following the conversation silently and blankly, his arm wrapped around Asha's trunk, nodded.

24

Austria

June to November 2014

Roux didn't waste any time. Once it was absolutely certain that the experiment had failed, he started looking around for another surrogate mother and found one at a small Austrian circus, which was less convenient logistically, but far more economical. This was important, because he was contractually obliged to pay for Asha's care, food and veterinary treatment until she was ready for breeding again. He hoped that Asha would miscarry soon to rid him of the double burden.

He couldn't wait to examine the foetus either, to see if it was pink and contained luciferins that would have made it glow.

Roux had left it that Pellegrini would contact him as soon as the surrogate mother miscarried.

In Austria the implanting of the blastocysts didn't go as smoothly as with Asha. The elephant cow was not as stoical and on Dr Horàk's instructions Roux had to have a metal cage made specially. It almost wasn't ready on time and they only just caught the ovulation.

The transfer still failed. On both attempts the cow moved suddenly and Horàk lost both the intended blastocysts as well as those he had in reserve.

They had to wait four months until Roux had prepared new blastocysts and the elephant's cycle allowed for another transfer. Seven more weeks would pass until there was absolute certainty that the embryo had embedded.

From time to time he rang Pellegrini and on each occasion the circus owner assured him that the heart of Asha's foetus was still beating.

'Are you sure?' he asked him, when he heard the same news five months after the vets had declared it to be not viable.

'That's what Dr Reber says,' Pellegrini told him.

Roux suspected that the circus director was drawing the whole thing out so as not to lose the contributions. 'When's he next coming?'

'In around four weeks. We haven't fixed a specific date yet.'

'I'd like to be there. Let me know.'

25

Circus Pellegrini

19 December 2014

When it wasn't on tour, Circus Pellegrini was housed in the industrial and agricultural zone of a village in the canton of Thurgau. Pellegrini's father had built stables and storage sheds there, put up two container offices and negotiated a twenty-year contract for a farmhouse, where the family lived between tours.

This is where Dr Hansjörg Reber paid his next veterinary visit to the circus. The elephants were billeted in a dividable concrete stall with metal posts and heavy gates that led into a small outdoor area, also secured with heavy posts.

Pellegrini was waiting for him in Asha's stall with the oozie and a man he didn't know. Pellegrini introduced him as Paul Roux, the researcher and owner of the embryo.

Reber took an instant dislike to the man. And his first impression was soon confirmed by Roux's overblown confidence, his authoritarian way of expressing his wishes and the condescension with which he treated the oozie.

'Let's take a look,' he ordered.

The foetus was now almost fifty-eight weeks and could be seen with an ultrasound device. Reber put it on the folding table that stood beside Asha. It looked like a laptop from the time when they were still heavy and chunky.

Kaung rubbed plenty of gel on the surrogate mother's flank and Reber started moving the sonic head around.

'I don't see anything,' Roux said disdainfully after a few seconds.

'You're looking at the mother's intestines. It can take a long time for the foetus to appear,' Reber said, before adding spitefully, 'That's if we do actually see it.'

Roux shot Pellegrini a look of reproach and turned back to the screen. 'Are you sure it's still there?'

'Where else would it be?' Reber asked.

'Miscarried.'

'Kaung would have noticed.'

The oozie shook his head. 'Not gone, still there,' he said.

And all of a sudden it emerged among the fluid grey outlines. A tiny toy elephant, its trunk clearly visible. Just for a moment, before disappearing again.

'Is it still alive?' Roux asked.

'I think so.' Reber played the film several times over in slow motion.

'Well?' Roux asked.

Reber didn't reply. He played back the sequence another three times, then he was certain. 'Its heart is beating,' he declared.

'Does this mean it might survive the pregnancy?'

'I can't rule it out altogether. But whether it's viable or not with this growth deficiency ...'

'But the foetus is growing?'

'If so, then incredibly slowly.'

'So how big would it be at the normal point of birth in – how many months?'

'Between seven and eight, maybe nine.' Pellegrini didn't have to count; the dates of this deal, which might now slip through his fingers, were fixed in his head.

'It's impossible to say how big it would be. First we'd have to know whether the embryo was growing at all,' Reber pointed out.

'How can you find that out?' Roux asked, sounding reproachful again.

'By comparing it with the last recording.'

'So compare them!'

Reber nodded. 'I shall. And I'll pass on the results to Herr Pellegrini.'

'You'll pass them on to *me*!' Roux ordered. 'The foetus is *mine*.'

Reber looked at him calmly with his eyes enlarged by spectacles. 'Herr Pellegrini is my client.'

'But I'm his,' Roux barked.

Hansjörg Reber hadn't been deceived by his first impression.

26

The same day

The road was lined with apple trees on both sides. The BMW was going a little too quickly; Roux was lost in his thoughts. About the small elephant and the future.

The vet couldn't rule out the possibility that the animal might be born alive. It was conceivable, therefore, that in nine months he could be the owner of a tiny pink elephant that glowed in the dark!

A slight bend forced him to cut his speed; only now did he realise how fast he'd been driving.

This wouldn't just be a great scientific breakthrough, but a commercial one too! His silent partner knew how to manage something like that. International patents, PR work, market positioning. Was there a Saudi prince who wouldn't wish to buy a little glowing pink elephant for his children? Were there genetic researchers who wouldn't be delighted by the possibility of marking cells in any colour they liked?

His silent partner was a Chinese genetic engineering firm. One of the biggest. One that decoded masses of genetic material on a daily basis. One that experimented with the CRISPR/Cas system, a method of cutting and modifying DNA.

For someone like Roux this was a hard secret to keep. He, the small researcher with his three-man firm, had a foothold in China's gigantic genetic engineering industry! In the country with the fewest qualms about genetic manipulation. Where a factory already existed that could clone 100,000 cattle per year, with the aim of increasing this to a million. A country that had undertaken the task of decoding the genome of all its 1.4 billion inhabitants and was in the process of developing the largest genetic database in the world!

His Gentecsa was working together with this great power in bioengineering. And nobody was allowed to know. Not yet!

In the distance a barrier came down and once again Roux noticed while braking how his speed had crept up inadvertently.

A locomotive painted white, red, yellow and black went past with a single coach. The few passengers were all absorbed in something he couldn't see.

The barrier opened again and the warning light stopped flashing. Roux put his foot on the accelerator and his car started moving again.

Towering in front of him was a black bank of cloud, as if the little train had pulled it here.

27

Zürich

9 January 2015

Having measured the stills from the two last sonographs, Reber had come to the conclusion that the foetus had grown. Not much, a centimetre and a half perhaps, but it had grown.

He told Pellegrini this over the phone. He couldn't tell whether the circus director was pleased or disappointed by the news.

An hour later his mobile rang. To his surprise it was Kaung, the oozie.

To begin with Reber found it hard to understand what Kaung wanted. But soon it became clear that he had to talk to him. 'Are there problems with the elephant?' he asked.

'Yes, problems.'

'Shall I come over?'

'No, I come.'

'When?'

'Tomorrow.'

'Is it so urgent?'

'Very urgent.'

They arranged to meet in a pub near the old barracks, which Kaung knew because Circus Pellegrini had performed there.

It was three o'clock and Sternen was almost empty. It smelled of the lunch that had just gone and of the dinner that was to come. Reber was punctual, but Kaung was already sitting there, alone at a table next to a window with a tulle curtain from the time before the smoking ban. He looked small and thin as he waited there with a bottle of mineral water, wearing a shirt and tie. When he saw Reber approaching the table he got up and offered him his hand.

Scarcely had they sat down than Kaung blurted out, 'Little elephant not belong Herr Roux. Belong Asha.'

Reber didn't know what to reply to this. Eventually he said, 'It won't survive anyway.'

'Will,' the oozie said defiantly.

'What makes you so sure?'

'Asha good mother. Baby not sick, just small. Kaung small too.'

The waitress cleared the glasses from a vacated table and came to take Reber's order.

'What can I get you?' She could have been around fifty but had tried in vain to wipe a few years off that with make-up.

Reber ordered a coffee and turned back to Kaung. 'We can't do anything except wait. Every time I come I'll check how she's getting on and whether the foetus is still alive. And you call me if there's a problem.'

The waitress brought the coffee in a large cup with brown glaze on a saucer that also carried a biscuit.

'Do you mind paying straight away?' She didn't trust guests she'd never seen before.

Reber wanted to pay for them both, but Kaung had already been made to settle the bill for his water.

When they were alone again Reber asked, 'What were you hoping to get out of this meeting, Kaung?'

The oozie hesitated. He drank a sip of water, put the glass down, sat up straight and looked Reber in the eye. 'You protect little elephant. Maybe sacred.'

Reber knew that in Myanmar white elephants were considered sacred. He'd learned too that it was a white elephant who had announced to Maya in a dream that she would give birth to the Buddha. He also knew that in Hinduism they revered the god Ganesha, the elephant-headed son of Shiva and Parvati. The imminent birth of a sacred elephant in the middle of the canton of Thurgau, however, was something he hadn't reckoned with.

But Kaung was looking at him so seriously and with such expectation that all he could do was nod without irony and say, 'Maybe.'

Now the oozie smiled for the first time and said, 'So you help.' Then his smile faded as he looked past Reber and up. When Reber turned around he saw a bearded, unkempt man standing behind him and looking with one red-ringed eye – the other seemed to be blind.

'Could you pay for our beers? I'm afraid my wallet was stolen.' He pointed to a table at the other end of the room, where two men were sitting who also looked as if they were homeless. They waved over at him.

Reber took his wallet from his pocket and looked for a tenner, but could only find a twenty-franc note, so gave this to the bearded man.

'Wow! You're a real gent!' he bellowed, shaking Reber's hand keenly and returned to his table.

'Have you done it again, Bolle?' Reber heard the waitress say.

Kaung had followed the scene with interest and now smiled again. 'You good man,' he said. And after a pause, looking serious once more, added, 'Roux not good man.'

Reber didn't object.

'If little elephant live, Roux must not have it,' he declared. An irreversible decision.

'How are you going to prevent that?'

'You help.'

28

Austria

28 January 2015

Every time he had to crawl along the Austrian motorways at 130 kilometres per hour, Roux wished the surrogate mother was in Germany, where he'd be able to push his BMW 218 to its full 200 kph.

The surrogate mother in the Austrian circus was causing problems. The foetus had developed normally until now, but the cow's hormone values were suddenly 'a touch borderline', as Horàk said. Horàk, who got on his nerves more and more each time Roux met him. But what was he to do? Horàk was the only one who could implant an elephant blastocyst with any degree of reliability.

The driver behind was tailgating him and flashing his headlights, even though he was driving at 130, just like the Mercedes in front. He didn't want to cross over into the right-hand lane and get caught among the lorries doing 100.

And now fat drops of rain were splattering on his windscreen too.

Roux maintained his speed, refusing to give in to the jerk hassling him from behind.

Bryan Adams stopped singing and the phone rang. The dashboard computer said, 'Pellegrini'.

'I hope you have some good news for me,' Roux said.

This greeting kept Pellegrini quiet for a moment, then he said, 'I don't know if you'll regard this as good news – the mini foetus didn't survive.'

Now it was Roux who was lost for words. He indicated right, took his foot off the accelerator and slotted in between two lorries. The tailgater sped past, hooting his horn, and showed him the finger.

'Miscarriage?'

'Yes.'

'Just now?'

Pellegrini cleared his throat. 'Last Thursday.'

'What? And I'm only finding out about this now?'

'I've been away for a week.'

'Away? Why away?'

Now Pellegrini started shouting too. 'Looking at circus acts, for God's sake! I need to sort out next season's programme!'

Roux took a deep breath, then asked more calmly, 'What does it look like? Anything unusual about it?'

Pellegrini had to clear his throat again before answering. 'Nothing unusual, apart from the fact that it was very, very small.'

'If you've got it in a normal freezer, please turn it down to its lowest temperature. Minus 18 degrees is too risky as far as I'm concerned. Minus 23 would be safer.'

Pellegrini didn't reply.

The downpour became heavier and the lorry in front of Roux slower. 'Hello? Did you hear what I said? Minus 23 degrees!'

'The foetus isn't frozen,' Pellegrini confessed in a soft voice.

'What then?'

'It's not here any more.'

'Where the hell is it then?' Roux was shouting again.

'Kaung took it to the animal corpse disposal centre.'

'But you knew that—'

'Yes, I did. But Kaung didn't.'

'I hope you booted him out.'

'I'd have to boot out the elephants too.'

'I'm going to sue you,' Roux screamed. He darted out of the convoy of lorries and put his foot down.

Just before the Feldkirch/Frastanz exit he was stopped by the motorway police. He'd been driving at 178 kph. Roux's BMW was confiscated.

29

Zürich

14 June 2016

Sixty per cent of her time was spent working in the animal hospital and the rest was taken up by free consultations in the back room of a second-hand clothes shop. Having set up the street clinic, she now ran it and was its sole employee.

Valerie was in her early forties and an attractive woman, but not immediately. She had short black hair and occasionally disguised her shyness by being excessively tomboyish.

The last patient had left and she opened the window of her surgery to let out the pong of the dog and its master.

Then someone else arrived.

She'd seen him before but she didn't know he had a dog. Or was it a cat he had in the holdall? He placed it on the examination table.

'I'm closed, actually,' she pointed out.

'It's an emergency.'

Now she recalled where she'd seen him: with the dog lovers at the station. She'd occasionally pass by to check whether there were any new dogs that hadn't been seen by her and were lacking a chip or their inoculations, and whether there were owners who hadn't completed the obligatory dog courses. In fact all this was rather rare. The homeless adored their dogs and wouldn't risk them being taken away. She knew owners who'd come running to her with their four-legged friends at the first sign of any pain, whereas they'd never go to the doctor themselves, however urgent the need.

Valerie kept an eye on the dog scene all the same. She felt responsible for the pets of those without a home. She wouldn't have had to start up the street clinic otherwise.

The man now in her surgery after closing time sometimes hung around with the dog lovers. He was one of the silent ones. And she'd noticed something else: his teeth. Most of the alcoholics and junkies on the streets had terrible teeth, whereas he seemed to care for his. Valerie had seen him laugh once and it looked as if they were still all there and white. Perhaps he visited the outpatient clinic of the institute of dental medicine, which offered free treatment to the homeless and marginalised.

'What have you brought me?' Valerie asked. She didn't know his name.

He hesitated. 'This comes under doctor–patient confidentiality.'

She smiled. 'Vet–patient confidentiality. Even stricter.'

He opened the zip. 'You won't have seen anything like this before.'

'I'd be very surprised.'

The man put his hands into the bag, carefully took out a pink toy elephant and laid it on the examination table.

Valerie grinned. Either the guy was pulling her leg or he wasn't quite right in the head. It was quite common among addicts.

But then the toy moved. The trunk coiled, the small body convulsed and something flowed out of its mouth. The creature threw up.

Valerie put a hand over her mouth as if suppressing a scream. The man was right: she never *had* seen anything like it before. It was a tiny elephant, forty centimetres long at most and thirty tall. It had the proportions of a young animal and the skin of a ... a marzipan pig! Just a bit wrinkly, and with pink hair on its back.

'Where did you get that from?' she blurted out.

'I'll tell you later. Do something – it's dying.'

The tiny elephant doubled up again. Now something flowed out from behind. Watery, mixed with undigested green matter.

Valerie went to a cupboard and tied a rubber apron around herself. She put on some surgical gloves and came back to the little patient. 'What did it eat?'

'Grass, leaves, that sort of thing.'

'Can you be more specific?'

'Well, the stuff that grows where I sleep.'

'Where's that?'

'By the river.'

'What did the grass look like?'

'Like ... like grass. Long, thin, green. With flowers.'

Valerie's ears pricked up. 'Yellow ones?'

'Yes. Buttercups.'

She went back to the cupboard, took out a rubber pump and filled it with water. She pushed the hose end into the creature's mouth. It struggled a bit, but Valerie was able to carefully push the hose deeper into the gullet until it felt slight resistance.

'What are you doing?' the man asked.

'Flushing out the stomach. The poor thing's poisoned.'

'By what?'

'Buttercups.'

'Buttercups are poisonous?'

'Yes. Some slightly, others seriously.'

'But they've got such a wholesome name,' he said, surprised.

She pressed gently on the water-filled rubber pipe. Soon water mixed with plant residue was flowing out of the trunk.

Valerie repeated the procedure until the water running out was almost clean. Then she gave the elephant an enema until the water that end was no longer cloudy.

She went to the medicine cabinet and mixed a black liquid, which she drew up into a transparent tube, the end of which she inserted into the patient's gullet again. Then she pumped the contents of the tube into its stomach. 'Physiological saline solution to combat the loss of liquid. And charcoal powder, which binds the toxins,' she explained.

During the treatment, which took almost an hour, the owner of the strange creature stood there anxiously and helplessly. She kept listening to the elephant with her stethoscope and taking its temperature, and each time he asked, 'Is everything all right?'

Each time she replied, 'I don't know,' which was the truth. She had no idea what the pulse of a thirty-centimetre-high pink elephant should be; she doubted that anybody on earth did.

She fetched some towels, gently patted the patient dry, laid it down on a second towel and covered it with a third.

After a while the elephant stopped curling and stretching its trunk, and it closed its eyes.

'It's dying,' the alcoholic said.

She took her stethoscope and listened. The pulse was considerably lower than before.

'I don't think so. I think it's better. I think it's asleep.'

It sounded as if the man wanted to say something in reply, but couldn't because his voice was refusing to play along. Valerie looked at him and saw that his eyes were moist. He turned away and coughed.

She went to the sink, filled two glasses of water and passed one to him.

He thanked her and gulped it down.

'What's your name?'

'Schoch.'

'First name?'

'Everyone calls me Schoch.'

'Okay, Schoch, where did you get this?'

'It was suddenly there in my sleeping place.'

'Where do you sleep?'

'I don't like to say.'

'Vet–patient confidentiality.'

'In a cave by the Limmat.'

'Hmm.'

'It glows in the dark.'

Valerie looked at him in amusement. 'It wouldn't surprise me.'

They both gazed down at the tiny creature, which now was breathing deeply and calmly.

'Let's sit down,' she said, pushing over one of the bar stools that the patients' owners sat on, and taking one for herself.

'Who knows about this?'

'I haven't told anyone.'

'Good. Keep it like that, Schoch, do you understand? Tell no one. Whoever it belongs to will want it back at any price.'

He nodded.

'What you've got here is an impossibility. It's a global sensation. Do you understand me, Schoch?'

'Yes, for Christ's sake.'

It went quiet until Schoch said, 'If it's an impossibility, then how is it possible? How come it exists?'

'Genetic manipulation.'

'Oh, you mean …'

'What else? It's the great industry of the future. The Chinese are the ones doing it most brazenly. For example they've bred and patented tiny pigs. They did it for research purposes to begin with, because pigs make the ideal laboratory animals. And mini pigs are much simpler and more economical to deal with. But now you can buy them as pets and toys. I bet you can make mini elephants with the same technology too.'

'Crazy,' Schoch murmured.

'Have you ever heard of glowing animals?'

Schoch shook his head.

'Come, I'll show you.' She went over to her computer and turned the screen in his direction. Then she typed the words into the search engine. Monkeys glowing green, hares glowing blue and sheep glowing red appeared on the screen.

Schoch stood up and came to the screen. 'Are those for real?'

'As real as that over there,' she said, pointing to the mysterious animal. 'Someone even won a Nobel Prize for it.'

Shaking his head, Schoch moved over to the examination table and looked at the creature like a father gazing at his sleeping baby.

Valerie stood beside him.

'Is it going to survive?'

She shrugged. 'Poisoning can cause permanent damage. Kidneys, liver, circulation, etc. I don't know, we'll have to nurse the poor thing back to health and keep it under observation.'

Schoch sighed. 'Great. My cave's going to be ideal for that.'

30

The same day

It was dark when Valerie Sommer's clapped-out Peugeot estate stopped outside a villa high up on the Zürichberg. A hedge that hadn't been clipped in ages blocked the view of the building.

Valerie rummaged in her bag and finally found the remote control. She turned around to Schoch, who was sitting in the back beside the bag with the pink dwarf elephant, and said, 'This comes under vet–patient confidentiality too.' She pressed the remote control and a metal gate rattled and creaked to the side, revealing a double garage behind. She drove the car forward and waited till the gate behind them had closed.

Now one of the two garage doors opened and she drove in.

A green vintage Mercedes was jacked up in the other half of the garage. The number plates had been removed and the cream-coloured roof carried a thick layer of dust.

Once the garage door had closed again Valerie motioned to Schoch to get out and she went ahead. She took him through several utility rooms into a kitchen and then into a large, dark room.

103

'Look!' Schoch said. Valerie came closer. He'd opened the zip of the holdall completely and let her look in.

The elephant was lying on its side; the eye facing them was open. And the tiny pink body was glowing.

They stared at it in silence for a while, then looked at each other. Valerie smiled and shook her head in disbelief.

'I told you,' Schoch whispered.

She pressed a switch and a few of the candle-shaped bulbs on a brass candelabra lit up, bathing the entrance hall in gentle light. The room was panelled up to the ceiling and a drab oriental carpet covered the parquet floor. In the middle stood a round table bearing a brass sculpture. A stag being brought down by half a dozen hounds.

The decoration on the heavy front door was repeated on the five other doors that led off the hallway into other rooms. Above each of them was a light patch in the wood panelling in the shape of a shield, like the ones for mounting hunting trophies. It smelled of dust and stale air.

'Who lives here?' Schoch asked.

'Nobody.'

She went and opened one of the doors. Behind it was a lift, also entirely clad in wood. A mirror with black spots was set into the central panel.

They went up to the first floor, where the air was even mustier. The light from the lift fell into a landing from which three corridors led. This was laid with a thick carpet and it had a round table precisely in the middle, bearing the bronze of a naked female archer.

Valerie led the way down one of the corridors. At the end she opened a door into a spacious room with a double bed, sitting area and a door that led to a bathroom.

It smelled of drains. Valerie turned on the sink and bath taps and flushed the loo. 'The traps dry out if they go too long without any water flowing through them. That's why it stinks in here.'

In a cupboard she found a towel that she handed to Schoch. 'Wait an hour if you don't want a cold shower. I'll go and switch the boiler on now.'

When Schoch hesitated, she added, 'It wouldn't do any harm.'

They went back into the sitting room. 'Take a seat, I'll be right back.'

She left the room and returned with a small dog bed, woven from wicker and painted light blue. The rim was lower in the middle to make it easier for a small dog to climb in. In many other places it had been gnawed away. Inside was a small mattress with holes revealing the yellow foam inside.

They lifted the small elephant from the bag and laid it in the basket.

'I don't know much about elephants, but if I'm not mistaken they're nursed for the first two or three years of their lives.'

'What with?'

'Elephant milk.'

'How do you get hold of that?'

'I don't know if they can cope with cow's milk, it might be too fatty. I'll find out tomorrow.' She took a mobile phone from her pocket. 'Do you know how to use one of these?'

'I'm told they're getting simpler. If that's true, then yes. I used to be able to.'

'I'll dial my number, see?' She showed him. 'All you've got to do is press the green 'Dial' button and it will call my phone. Do it the moment you think that something's not right with the elephant and I'll come straight away.'

'You're not sleeping here?'

She shook her head. 'I can't.'

'Whose house is this?'

'My parents'.'

'Where are they?'

'Dead.'

'I see.'

'Stay inside, don't show yourself, don't open the door to anyone and keep quiet. Tomorrow I'll bring you both something to eat.' She pointed to a huge antique cupboard. 'The bedclothes are in there.'

'I don't use bedclothes.'

'Will you manage without food till tomorrow morning?'

He nodded. 'I'm not much of an eater.'

'And without drink? Will you cope without that, Schoch?' She stared at him sceptically.

'I'm not much of a drinker, either.'

31

The same day

The Persian carpet was softer than Schoch's cave. He'd taken the flowery throw from the bed as a blanket and as a pillow he used a seat cushion from one of the armchairs. This allowed him to look into the light-blue dog basket where the miniature elephant lay.

It hadn't vomited for three hours, nor had any diarrhoea. Once it tried to scrabble to its feet, but failed.

But the elephant wasn't asleep; its round eyes were wide open, it kept moving its head restlessly and most of the time its trunk was flailing around.

Schoch had tried several times to lay his hand on the warm, soft body, but on each occasion the fantastical creature became more unsettled, as if wanting to shake him off.

Now he was just lying beside the elephant, watching it.

In the distance a bell chimed three times and he could hear the wind rustling the old trees.

The shutters and curtains were closed, but Schoch had opened a window to let in some fresh air.

Who has a house like this, but doesn't live in it? he wondered. Can't sleep in it, but holds on to it?

The elephant drew in its front legs, pushing them beneath its body, and tried to get up.

'Shhh,' Schoch said. 'Shhh, shhh.'

It seemed to respond to him. At any rate it turned its head slightly in his direction and laid it back down on the tatty mattress.

'Shhh, shhh, shhh,' Schoch said again, placing his hand gently on the small, faintly quivering body.

'Shhh, shhh, shhh.'

This time it let him keep his hand there. It even seemed to relax.

'Shhh, shhh, shhh.'

The round eyes closed. Opened again. Closed. Opened. Stayed open.

Schoch didn't dare withdraw his hand. He tried to make it as light as possible and gazed at the slumbering creature as it lay peacefully in its own pink glow. A creature from another planet.

Schoch's gaze fell on his hand: coarse, dirty and shaky. He got up gently, went into the bathroom and found a nailbrush. There was also a new bar of soap in one of the many drawers. When he unwrapped it from the crinkly lime-green paper, something flaked away from the now crumbly outer layer.

He held the soap under the running water and rubbed it between his hands until it lathered. Then he washed his hands thoroughly, brushed away the black beneath his long, brittle nails and trimmed them with some nail scissors that he found in an incomplete manicure set.

Schoch tiptoed back into the bedroom.

The tiny creature was lying a metre from the basket, trying to stand. Schoch hurried over, squatted down, picked it up, stood it gently on its feet and let go carefully.

Now the elephant, legs apart and its trunk hanging down, stood there shakily, as if it might topple over again at any moment.

Schoch lifted it up and laid it back down in the basket. 'Don't worry, I'm not going to leave you, erm …' What were elephants called?

He only knew one elephant name: Sabu, the beast who a few years ago had escaped from the circus in Zürich, taken a long bath in the lake and then gone for a stroll along Bahnhofstrasse. He'd remembered the name because the elephant's story had struck a chord. Like Schoch, he'd bailed out of a comfortable life.

'Don't worry, I'm not going to leave you – Sabu.'

32

15 June 2016

He was woken up by somebody sucking his little finger. Sabu had left the basket and was glowing beside his left hand.

He took it away circumspectly and checked the time. Seven o'clock already. Some light was seeping in through a chink in the curtains. He pushed the curtain a little to one side. In one of the shutters a louvre was missing, allowing Schoch to see some fir trees in an unmown meadow and a pavilion with garden chairs tilted against the edge of a table.

Schoch was startled by a handful of chords from a rock guitar. Sabu, too, spread its ears and raised its trunk.

It took him a while to realise that the music was coming from Valerie's mobile. He pressed 'Accept call'.

'Everything okay?' her concerned voice said.

'The elephant's hungry.'

'How do you know?'

'It's sucking my finger.'

'That's a good sign. I'll bring something over as soon as the shops have opened.'

'Those I know are already open.'

'But they don't sell coconut oil.'

In the two hours he spent waiting for Valerie, Schoch got to grips with the mobile phone. In his past life of course he'd had mobile phones, but back then you couldn't take films with them. He had a few attempts at videoing Sabu, who kept trying to suck his little finger.

Eventually they heard the squeaking of the electric gate. Soon afterwards a heavily laden Valerie came into the room.

She unpacked her shopping bags. Thermos flask, Tupperware, twigs with green leaves, bottles of mineral water. 'Coconut oil is the base. Baby elephants can't digest the fat in cow's milk. Coconut oil is enriched with all manner of minerals and vitamins. I'll teach you the recipe.'

She shook one of the baby bottles, removed the protective lid, and gave it to Schoch.

'Me?'

'If it's suckling your finger …'

He crouched down to Sabu and offered it the teat.

The elephant took it in its mouth without hesitation and started sucking.

'There you go!' Valerie beamed.

Schoch smiled. 'Do you think it'll pull through?'

'That depends on you.'

'Me?'

'Whether you manage to do this every three hours. And spend twenty-four hours a day with it.'

Schoch looked at Valerie aghast.

'Those are the rules of the game for hand-rearing elephants.'

'I can't do that without help.'

She shook her head. 'Don't look at me. I've got a job.'

'Me too.'

'What's that then?'

'Homeless person.'

They watched the baby elephant sucking eagerly at the bottle. 'Sabu,' Schoch said. 'I've named her Sabu.'

'What makes you so sure it's a girl?'

'Well, there's nothing underneath.'

'Male elephants keep their testicles in the abdominal cavity. And their penis in the skin of their stomach.'

'So she could be a boy?'

'You call a male elephant a bull.'

'A bull,' Schoch said with a grin as they continued to gaze at Sabu.

'There was an Indian Hollywood actor called Sabu,' Valerie said.

'And that female elephant who escaped from the circus.'

Sabu had drained the bottle. Valerie held out a twig. The elephant fished it with her trunk and stripped the leaves off with her mouth.

'You must be hungry too.' Valerie took a couple of ham rolls from one of the shopping bags.

'Thanks.'

'And something to drink.'

She put a bottle of mineral water beside the rolls.

'Or would you rather have this?' She took out a litre can of beer.

Schoch shook his head. 'You can take that back.'

She packed the beer away again.

Sabu tossed the bare twig in a high arc and clearly wanted more. Valerie put the greenery she'd brought on the floor and Sabu launched into it.

'To think she almost died yesterday,' Schoch said.

'Maybe it was more of a bad stomach upset than poisoning,' Valerie said.

As if by way of confirmation Sabu dropped a few balls of dung onto the carpet. Valerie laughed. 'You'll never get her house-trained, that's for sure.'

She put two mugs on the chest of drawers, unscrewed a Thermos flask and poured steaming coffee. 'Milk? Sugar?' she asked.

'Sugar. Lots.'

She handed him the mug and took one of the ham rolls from the wrapping. To his surprise he was able to eat it, even though it was before ten o'clock.

'What now? Where do we go from here?' he asked, his mouth full.

Valerie raised her shoulders to her ears and let them drop again.

'Maybe there's a place where they look after laboratory animals. Some sort of organisation,' Schoch suggested. 'Or the WWF, maybe the animal protection association.'

Valerie was doubtful. 'Associations that protect animals are usually rather naïve. What we need are people who are as tough as nails. They have to set up a kind of witness protection scheme like you see in films.'

'When I used to watch films those sorts of schemes tended to go belly up in the end.' He sipped his coffee.

Valerie had an idea. 'Greenpeace! This is perfect for them. They're well organised and they've got money.'

'Greenpeace? They're good at getting their message out. But can they do the opposite?'

Valerie got ready to go; she was expected in the animal hospital. 'I'll ask around and do a bit of research. I'll come back after work. Maybe by then I'll have found a solution. Don't forget – a bottle every three hours, not too much greenery and, as for you …' she said.

'I've got it under control, for Christ's sake,' he snapped.

33

The same day

Sabu was sleeping and Schoch could feel the creeping anxiety at having missed his ten o'clock beer. He decided to take a shower. But when he saw the large tub with its lion's claw feet, he ran a bath instead. His first for ... he couldn't say how many years.

The water flowed a rusty red from the tap and took a long time to turn clear.

In a china pot he found some bluey-green bath salts, which were so stuck together that he put the whole chunk in the tub, hoping that they would dissolve.

Sabu slept on, disturbed neither by the rushing of the water nor the whistling of the pipes. Schoch got undressed, wrapped the bath towel around his waist and took his clothes down to the ground floor, where he'd seen a laundry room on their way in.

The washing machine was an old model, but not much older than the ones he was familiar with from the charitable washing facilities. He even found an open packet of a brand of washing powder that no longer existed. It had amalgamated into a single clump, but he managed to break off a chunk. He switched the machine on and went back upstairs.

Sabu was still asleep.

The bath was full, the salts had almost completely dissolved, and the water had taken on their bluey-green colour and smelled good in an old-fashioned way.

Leaving the towel on a bathroom stool, Schoch climbed in. The water was too hot – it was a good while before his body got used to the temperature and he was able to sit, then lie down.

His head back, his eyes closed, Schoch allowed his restless hands to swim in the water, like when he was a boy.

What would he have given as a child for a small, living pink elephant that glowed in the dark? He'd only had a guinea pig. Johnny. After a year Johnny turned out to be a girl and died soon afterwards. Of a fatty heart, as his father claimed. If he was being honest, Schoch hadn't been upset at Johnny's premature death. It meant he no longer had to muck out the cage and his mother didn't nag him any more about the stink.

Schoch woke up because the bath had turned cold. He ran some more hot water and washed himself with the flaking soap, which he had to use for his hair and beard too, having found no shampoo.

When he climbed out of the bath and the water level sank, Schoch could see a dark ring around the tub. Even blacker than when he'd been a boy.

He scrubbed the bath with a brush, which lost a large proportion of its bristles in the process.

Schoch then heard a strange noise coming from behind him, something in between squealing, squeaking and chirping. He turned around and there stood Sabu, her trunk and ears raised, staring at his naked form. Schoch put the plug back in and filled the tub to ten centimetres. Then he picked up Sabu and lowered her into the water.

She hesitated for no more than a moment before plunging her trunk into the water and showering her back.

34

The same day

In his search for something to wear Schoch had stumbled across the parents' bedroom. It was twice the size of the one he'd slept in, had a bathroom with a jacuzzi and a walk-in wardrobe, two-thirds of which was filled with women's clothes, the rest with men's suits.

He took one of the suits from the rail and held it up. Three-piece, colour an indeterminate grey. He laid it on the vast double bed, took the jacket from the hanger and tried it on.

Valerie's father must have been roughly the same height as him. But much fatter. The jacket hung off Schoch like a clown's costume. In the past it would have fitted him.

Schoch found some braces and tried on the trousers. The same clown-like effect, but it would do until his own clothes were dry. The stripy shirt he chose was passable if he rolled up the sleeves.

The socks fitted him, but the hardly worn suede shoes were far too small. He had to make do with his worn-out trainers.

Thus dressed, Schoch made a tour of the entire house. On the ground floor was a living room and dining room, both with French windows that presumably led out onto a terrace. Here too the curtains and shutters were closed.

At right angles to the two large rooms were smaller ones – a library, a television room, a billiard room and something that looked like a trophy room: faded patches on the panelling indicated that hunting trophies had been unscrewed from the walls. Many pictures must have hung here as well, judging by the pale rectangles with nails on the upper edge.

Hunting weapons were displayed in two glass cabinets, both locked. But the cupboards beside them were open and full of hunting literature, mugs and cups from shooting matches, a collection of tankards and schnapps glasses with hunting motifs, and piles of framed black and white photographs showing hunting parties with their kill. Each of them featured the same man, sometimes fatter, sometimes thinner, mostly with a broad smile. Presumably Valerie's father.

The contents of these cupboards had been randomly stuffed in, and were probably from the empty cabinets and shelves in the room.

In one of the cupboards he found a cocktail cabinet full of glasses in all shapes and sizes. At the very bottom was a small built-in fridge, its door wedged open with a cloth. Above it was a humidor containing a few dozen cigars.

Bottles were lined up on the shelf above the glasses, some opened, some not – single malt whiskies, gin, vodka, liqueurs and schnapps.

Schoch closed the cupboard and continued his tour.

In the library was an entire shelf of hunting books: *The Magic of the Hunt, Before and After Your Hunting*

Licence, Hunting in the Landscape, Big Game Hunting in Africa. The jacket of the last of these featured an elephant cow with her calf. Schoch took it from the shelf; he might be able to learn something.

In the television room he came across a wrought-iron magazine rack. He skimmed some of the publications, all of which were from 1997 and most of them addressed to Frau Johanna Sommer, presumably Valerie's mother.

The kitchen looked like it belonged in a restaurant: large stainless-steel work surfaces, a cooker with gas and electric hobs, several fridges, all with cloths to keep them ajar and prevent mould from forming inside. There was also a pantry with two hatches and a small staff area with cloakroom and loo. A chef's outfit was hanging in one of the lockers; in another he saw a waitress's apron and a starched cap.

In the corridor that went back to the utility rooms and the garage were some steps that led downstairs. Below was the boiler room with a large oil heater and beside it another door. Schoch opened it and turned on the light.

He found himself in a large wine cellar. The shelves were two-thirds empty, but he reckoned there must still be 300 bottles stored here, all neatly arranged by area, domaine and vintage.

Schoch didn't stay long in there, but long enough to note that not a single bottle was younger than twenty years old.

When he came back Sabu was standing by the door, as if she'd been waiting for him. Schoch crouched down beside her. At once she wrapped her trunk around his index finger, pulled it towards her with astonishing force and put it in her mouth.

'I know, second breakfast,' Schoch said, freeing his finger and going over to the chest of drawers where Valerie had put her shopping. From one of the Thermos flasks he filled a bottle to the mark that Valerie had shown him and held the teat out to Sabu. She began drinking greedily.

'Know the feeling,' Schoch muttered.

35

The same day

Valerie used the first opportunity she had to put her animal hospital work to one side and embark on her research. She couldn't find anything on projects to miniaturise animals while also making them glow in different colours. Nor did she have any luck with which organisation to turn to with their Sabu problem. However, soon she came across a disease which in human medicine was called 'microcephalic osteodysplastic primordial dwarfism type 11', caused by a problem with the protein responsible for cell division. A similar protein substitutes for the defective one, but the person remains small.

There were adult people with this disease who were no taller than fifty-six centimetres. But Valerie found no indication that animals could be affected too.

She was called to an emergency: a highly elegant, highly distressed lady had run over her Scottish terrier in the entrance to her garage. The animal had broken both its hind legs and two vertebrae, and had to be put to sleep. She gave the woman a sedative and, because she was now unable to drive her Porsche home herself, Valerie had to keep her company until the driver of her husband's firm arrived to chauffeur her home.

When she was finally able to turn back to her monitor, she resolved to reduce her workload in the animal clinic to 40 per cent and increase her time in the street clinic to 60. She read more about primordial dwarfism.

Valerie learned that those affected by the disease had a lower life expectancy. Their blood vessels formed protrusions or constrictions, often leading to brain haemorrhages or strokes.

This information made her feel both sad and hopeful.

36

The same day

Schoch took the bottles from the cocktail cabinet down to the wine cellar, locked it and put the key in his trouser pocket. He intended to give it to Valerie. For safety's sake.

He was just filming himself feeding Sabu the bottle when Valerie came back. She didn't know whether to feel perturbed or amused when she saw him in her father's suit. She decided to ignore it.

'She's not a bull,' he told her.

'Have you looked?'

He nodded. 'There's nothing in the skin folds.'

'All the better.'

Schoch contradicted her. 'No, it's not better. Elephants are matrilinear. The females always stay with their mothers and are shaped by them. It's all in there,' he said, pointing with his chin at the big game hunting book he'd left on the bed.

'And it looks as if I'm the mother now.' He smiled down at Sabu, who was sucking powerfully on the bottle. 'I can't spend the rest of my life here playing hide-and-seek and elephant mum.'

'You won't have to. She probably won't live very long.'

Seeing his reaction she wished she'd said it a little less bluntly.

'Where did you come up with that nonsense?' he asked angrily.

'I've been doing some research into this form of dwarfism. Not those who are born normal size, then grow disproportionally. But those who suffer from microcephalic osteodysplastic primordial dwarfism type 11. They are born very small and grow slowly, but proportionately, and in the end look like miniature versions of the original. This is what Sabu has.'

'Why do you say she won't live very long?'

'Because people with this disease often die young.'

'Sabu isn't a person.'

'All I'm saying is that if you're fretting over the decision of whether to – how can I put this? – adopt Sabu or not, it wouldn't be for life.'

Both of them looked at Sabu drinking from the bottle, her head slightly to one side, her trunk raised and curled inwards.

'How old is she roughly?'

'She's still got the proportions of a baby. I'd say she can't be much older than a year.'

Schoch gave Sabu a probing look.

'You could live here,' Valerie said.

'What would I do all day long alone in this huge house?'

'You wouldn't be alone.'

Sabu had finished the bottle. Schoch put it away and started feeding her bits of carrot. He placed one in the palm of his hand and Sabu's trunk picked it up and put it in her mouth.

'How many muscles does a human being have?' Schoch asked.

'About six hundred and fifty if I remember rightly.'

'An elephant has around forty thousand. In its trunk alone. *Forty thousand!*'

'Just think about it.'

'What would I do all day long?'

'What do you do all day long at the moment?'

Schoch pondered this question.

Valerie encouraged him. 'It would be a job.'

'Exactly.'

Realising that Valerie was waiting for an explanation, he gave one: 'That's precisely what I don't want. Do you think I would be homeless if I wanted a job? People like me don't want a home or a job. All people like me want is some peace and quiet!'

Valerie, who liked to have the last word, said, 'You'd have that here.'

When she'd gone he remembered that he'd wanted to give her the key to the wine cellar.

37

16 June 2016

Schoch was woken shortly after two in the morning by Sabu's strange, high-pitched trumpeting sounds.

He'd watched the sleeping elephant from his improvised bed until late into the night and mulled over Valerie's suggestion. He must have fallen asleep thinking about it; he couldn't remember having reached a decision.

He was still lying on his side, his eyes pointing towards the basket. It was empty, and something was pressing against his stomach.

Sabu was lying on her side, her head lying on her bent right front leg, her trunk curled slightly inwards and her back nestled into his tummy.

She must have sensed that Schoch was awake, for she lifted her head slightly and opened her eyes. She met his gaze. Sabu put her head back down, closed her eyes and went back to sleep.

Schoch didn't bother turning off the light, but put his hand on the small body and was soon asleep himself.

He was woken a second time by the presence of somebody in the room. Valerie. She'd put down her shopping bags and was taking a photo of the idyllic scene.

Schoch carefully removed the bed throw that served as his blanket and stood up.

Valerie took a video of him standing by the tiny pink elephant, looking dishevelled in crumpled shirt and ill-fitting trousers. 'I can safely say that this is the first time those clothes have been slept in.'

'I'll change in a minute. My things must be dry.'

Valerie put away her mobile and started unpacking what she'd bought for Sabu and Schoch. 'Have you thought about it?' she asked, trying to sound as casual as possible.

Schoch nodded.

'And?'

'I'll do it,' he muttered, then added quickly, 'for the time being.'

38

17 June 2016

The following morning Sabu had disappeared.

When Schoch woke up – ever since he'd stopped drinking he'd been sleeping through the night – the dog basket was empty, and she wasn't lying in front of or beside it. He got up and started looking. She was nowhere to be seen in the bedroom. Nor in the bathroom. But she couldn't have left the room.

Or could she? Might he, half asleep in the middle of the night, have mixed up the bathroom door with the bedroom one and Sabu slipped out unnoticed after him?

Unnoticed? A glowing pink dwarf elephant?

All the same he opened the door, turned on the light and looked around the landing. Nothing.

Eventually he found her under the bed, standing motionless right at the back. Like during their first encounter in his cave. A toy out of reach.

'Come on, Sabu,' he called out.

But she didn't move. Her head was lowered and her trunk pointed straight down with a little hook at the bottom.

Schoch went into the bathroom, put on Valerie's father's dressing gown and looked under the bed again. The same picture: a tiny, glowing pink elephant.

Schoch went down into the kitchen and heated up the leftover coffee from the day before. Then he mixed up Sabu's formula milk for the day, cut up some apples and carrots, toasted two slices of bread, spread them with honey, placed everything on a tray and went back upstairs.

Now Sabu was in the middle of the room. She'd made her way over to his trousers, shirt and underwear and flung them about the room. Her ears were spread wide and she was swinging her trunk from side to side.

She may have been tiny, but she still managed to look menacing.

When he told Valerie about this later that evening she said, 'She's trying to earn respect. I've seen lapdogs who thought they were big bad beasts. And do you know what? Their owners thought so too, right up till the end.'

Schoch nodded. 'There are human beings like that too. I've known a few in my time.'

'You must tell me about your past life some time.'

'Some time.' He paused. 'Do you think she knows she's small?'

Valerie thought about it. 'No. She hasn't got anything to compare herself with. But she certainly feels like an elephant. As proud as an elephant. As dignified as an elephant.'

'And she thinks we're not paying her the respect an elephant is due.'

'We're not.'

From now on their relationship changed. Valerie and Schoch treated Sabu with the awe you show such an unreal creature and left it up to her to decide whether she wanted to be trusting, reserved, playful or strange.

Schoch found this reassessment of his relationship with the little elephant rather convenient, as it gave him the opportunity to read more. For after all these years he'd rediscovered books.

Valerie had brought him everything she could find or order about Indian elephants. She'd also bought him a pair of reading glasses. Or two pairs, in fact. The first hadn't been strong enough. He'd asked for a pair of 1.5 strength reading glasses. That's what he'd always had, 1.5. It turned out, however, that now he needed 3.0. He'd read virtually nothing for nine years.

Schoch didn't just read books about elephants. The villa's strange library contained a real mixture. Unopened luxury editions of great classics, German translations of international bestsellers from the 1980s and 1990s, as well as the complete works of Annette von Droste-Hülshoff.

He'd chosen the laundry room to read in. It had a barred window that he could open because it was hidden by a large cherry laurel. When you'd spent as much time outside as Schoch had, you sometimes needed daylight and fresh air. The laundry also had a brick floor and two drains, which meant he could hose it down after reading. Sabu, who kept him company as he devoured the books, wasn't making any effort to become house-trained.

Sabu had begun to determine her mealtimes herself. She kept refusing the bottle at the regular times, demanding it whenever she was hungry instead. Occasionally Schoch tried to ignore her, but she became fractious, made her strange noises, nudged him with her head and wouldn't let up until he'd put his book down and fed her.

He, on the other hand, kept to his mealtimes. At noon he cooked himself something small. His repertoire wasn't particularly wide, but it included spaghetti with tomato sauce, a variety of egg dishes, roast meatloaf, bratwurst and suchlike.

While he cooked, Sabu amused herself in the kitchen. She liked playing with a red rubber bone that Schoch had found in a storeroom with other dog equipment, or she'd ceremonially parade around the room, or adopt one of her meditative poses.

After four in the afternoon the clock tended to tick more slowly. This was the time when he most missed his drink. He didn't have any withdrawal symptoms, if you could describe the slight trembling of his hands for what it was: nervousness.

But once again he was tortured by the symptom that had turned him into an alcoholic in the first place: bloody boredom.

39

18 June 2016

For lunch Schoch made himself a cheese toastie with ham and a fried egg. The idea had come to him by chance. In one of the many kitchen cupboards he'd found a gratin dish of the sort he remembered from the past: orange on the outside and glazed white on the inside. These were the dishes they used for toasties in the restaurant cars of trains. The moment he found it Schoch had the smell in his nostrils and taste in his mouth. His decision was made: today he would have a cheese toastie.

He heated up the oven, cut a thick slice of bread, and placed a slice of ham and three slices of Emmental on top.

Schoch deliberated for a moment, then went down the corridor and the steps that led to the boiler room. He opened the door to the wine cellar and chose a bottle of white – coincidentally there happened to be an Aigle les Murailles, the wine he'd always ordered to accompany his toastie in the restaurant car.

In the kitchen he uncorked the bottle, poured some into a bowl, removed the ham and cheese then placed the slice of bread in the bowl and let it soak up all the wine, before everything was reassembled in the gratin dish and put into the oven.

Schoch heated some butter in a frying pan and cracked two eggs. When they were fried he took the toastie from the oven, placed the eggs on top and brought his lunch to the table.

The shining yellow cheese had oozed out beneath the fried eggs and was sizzling at the edges of the dish. Where the white of the eggs was thinnest it gave a bluish shimmer, while the butter had crisped the edges. He could barely see the ham.

And as for the aroma! Melted cheese, baked ham and hot butter and – white wine.

Forgoing alcohol wasn't a problem. As a drink. But as a condiment …

That day the boredom set in after lunch already. The prospect of spending from now till evening without human company made him feel edgy.

He tried to take a siesta, but soon gave up and left the room.

'Are you coming?' he asked Sabu.

She was standing in the middle of the carpet, swinging her trunk mechanically from left to right and from right to left.

He left her where she was and started prowling around the house.

Shortly after half past two he decided to take a dose of the only psychotropic drug that helped combat these symptoms.

Less than half an hour later he felt relaxed and went back up to see Sabu. She was in a better mood too. She'd stopped swinging her tail and came up to him when he entered the bedroom.

Schoch played with her for a while and made some videos. Then he returned to the wine cellar.

As he came back upstairs he had an idea. On one of his forays around the house he'd noticed in the storeroom a bag of the type used to carry lapdogs. He found the bag and took it to the bedroom.

It was made of slightly tatty, dark blue suede, with a long shoulder strap and decorated with golden rivets. The bag was perforated at both ends and along the sides were plastic windows, which had turned slightly yellow and opaque.

Schoch opened the zip, put Sabu inside and paced up and down.

He didn't know if she liked this or whether the movement was too much for her, but anyway she lay down.

Schoch put the bag on the chest of drawers. He could barely make anything out through the window, but when Sabu lay like that and her skin touched the plastic it didn't look like a dog in there.

The right volume of white wine is known to stimulate creativity, and indeed Schoch had another idea. He hung the bag over his shoulder and went to the walk-in wardrobe in Valerie's parents' bedroom, where he'd seen a number of furs. Schoch plumped for a simple black Persian stole and took it with him.

After another bottle for them both he was sitting in the tram heading for the city centre, the dog bag containing his dwarf poodle on his lap. He'd be back in plenty of time for the seven o'clock bottle.

40

The same day

Bolle's old sleeping place had been all right. Underground car park, barely frequented at night, warm, dry and near the places he liked to hang out. The one downside was that they didn't tolerate him being there during the day, which was a bit of a problem for someone who enjoyed the odd doze in the afternoon. The homeless shelters didn't allow people to kip there in the daytime, while you kept getting disturbed in entranceways, on park benches and at tram stops.

From that perspective Schoch's disappearance had been a stroke of luck, although the fact that Bolle had found out about it at the right time had nothing to do with luck. He had his network to thank for that. Bolle knew everyone living on the streets and he cultivated these relationships. He'd visit the relevant meeting points, exchange a few words, crack the odd joke and see to it that people liked him. Through his careful nurturing of these contacts Bolle had found out about Schoch's sleeping place. And that it had become free.

He was drinking a coffee in the Salvation Army hostel lounge. Beside him was Karlheinz, sipping a peppermint tea. Both were silent until Furrer, the manager, came in, walked across the room, nodded to the handful of guests and went into his office.

'He's got more junk to store now,' Karlheinz muttered.

'Why?' Bolle asked.

'Schoch's stuff.'

'Why?' Bolle asked again.

'He's disappeared.'

'Since when?'

'Dunno. Giorgio, the guy with the three dogs ...'

'Yeah, yeah, I know. He's got three dogs ...'

'He found the things in Schoch's sleeping place. Schoch always takes that stuff with him in the mornings.'

'Where is his sleeping place?' Bolle asked.

'No idea. But it must be wonderful, given how long he's crashed there.'

Later Bolle quizzed Lilly, the junkie who hung around with the dog lovers. He contrived it so that she begged him for a cigarette, which wasn't difficult as she was always begging everyone for cigarettes. He gave her half a packet and asked casually if she knew where Giorgio's sleeping place was.

In the end it cost him an entire packet plus five francs before she spilled the beans.

That same day he packed his rucksack and went to the place she'd described to him. He found Giorgio's cave even though it was well camouflaged by all sorts of bushes and grass. From there he went a little further along and found Schoch's hideaway. Slightly less well hidden – the bushes in front were rumpled, a bit smaller and lower – but the cave was dry and comfortable. Plus a toilet and running water right by the door, as he quipped to himself.

It smelled a little strange, like in a stable; there were patches on the sandy floor that looked as if someone had spilled soup, while dry twigs and hay were scattered everywhere.

But this wasn't a problem for someone who in his last regular job had been team leader in an office cleaning company. He bundled up the twigs to make a brush and swept the muck out of the cave. Then he unrolled his mat, put down his sleeping bag, took a can of beer from the rucksack and toasted his new lodgings. Then he made his way back into town.

The only disadvantage was the distance. From the station it took him between fifteen and twenty minutes, depending on his alcohol level. A bit too much effort for an afternoon sleep. But walking's healthy, he told himself. And he didn't need a siesta every day.

He certainly needed one later that afternoon, however. He'd been celebrating this serendipitous change for the better rather over-exuberantly and needed a nap if he was going to spend the evening in company again.

He was heading along the river path, staggering occasionally, and deep in a semi-audible conversation with himself, towards his new home. Some of the allotment-holders were using the rain-free afternoon for a little garden work, but the banks of black cloud were already gathering in the west.

He saw a bench roughly level with Giorgio's cave and took a brief rest there.

Bolle stared at the rapid, brown river making mischief with its flotsam, and nodded off.

He was awoken by a gust of wind. The bank of cloud had moved closer. Bolle trudged the last hundred metres to the point where he had to leave the path and negotiate the rest of the way along the steep embankment.

Maybe the access issue is another disadvantage with this new billet, Bolle thought. It wasn't completely without risk if you'd had one too many – which wasn't a particularly uncommon scenario, if Bolle was being honest.

Now right below the cave, he started scrambling up. Twice he slipped down again, but when he'd finally made it to where he could peer inside through the bushes, he saw that someone was there.

Schoch!

He had his back turned to Bolle and was crouching on the ground, talking to someone. Schoch's right hand appeared, which had been hidden by his body. It was holding a piece of fur, which he placed on the ground.

Bolle was about to announce his presence, but what he now saw made him lost for words.

Behind Schoch's silhouette emerged something that looked like a tiny elephant. It was pink, it was moving and it was glowing faintly in the gloom of the cave!

Bolle rubbed his eyes and brow with his hand, shook his head like a wet dog and turned away.

Half running, half slipping, he fled from his vision. When he got to the river path and started hurrying back to the city with a jiggling rucksack there was only one thought in his mind: stop drinking!

Part Two

Part Two

1

Circus Pellegrini

28 January 2015

Kaung stood in the director's caravan, his head bowed. Pellegrini and Reber were sitting down, while a scarlet-faced Roux was standing right beside Kaung, bellowing at him.

'Fool! You've ruined a scientific experiment that cost many times more than you'll earn in your entire life! What a bloody idiot!'

Reber made use of the pause to draw breath. 'For goodness' sake please stop! This isn't going to bring the foetus back.'

Roux ignored him. 'What the hell were you thinking of, you imbecile?'

Kaung said something so softly that Roux couldn't understand.

'What?' he yelled.

Slightly louder, Kaung said, 'Baby was dead.'

'Not for science it wasn't! For science it wasn't dead until it was burned like rubbish!'

'Sorry,' Kaung muttered for the umpteenth time.

'Your apology is of no bloody use to me! I can't put it under the microscope! I can't give it a chemical analysis. I can't even wipe my sodding arse with your apology!'

Reber stood up. 'Come on, Kaung. Let's go and see the elephants.'

The oozie looked at his boss uncertainly. Pellegrini nodded.

'I'm coming with you,' Roux snorted, following the two of them.

When they entered the stalls, the cows started moving and rattling their chains. Trisha's calf, untethered, was standing next to his mother. Now more than a year old, he no longer fitted underneath her. Fahdi, the bull, was in a separate pen.

'You can stay here if you promise to keep calm and not drive the animals crazy,' Reber said curtly to Roux. 'Otherwise I'll have to ask you to leave.'

'No worries,' Roux snapped. 'This isn't the first time I've been close up with elephants.'

First they went over to Rupashi, the elephant cow who was in her nineteenth month. She'd been artificially inseminated by Dr Horàk's team and so far had enjoyed a problem-free pregnancy.

Due dates for elephant cows are difficult to predict. They barely exhibit any pregnancy symptoms and are fully fit until just before the birth. Kaung thought she'd be giving birth in less than three months and Reber was inclined to believe him because he'd predicted the birth of Trisha's baby almost to the day.

Reber wanted to carry out an ultrasound scan none-theless, and Kaung helped him.

Everything about Rupashi looked normal. Kaung was probably correct with his prognosis.

All was fine with Sadaf too, an artificially inseminated breeding elephant in her seventeenth month.

Reber started packing up the ultrasound device.

'What about Asha?' said Roux, who'd kept quiet as ordered until now.

'What about her?'

'I want you to give her an ultrasound too.'

'Why?'

Roux gave no answer, he just raised his eyebrows scornfully.

Reber understood. 'I see, you don't trust me.' He exchanged glances with Kaung.

'Let's just say I don't trust that one over there,' Roux said, pointing at Kaung.

Reber thought about it briefly, then waved the oozie over and they carried the device to Asha. Roux followed them and bent over the monitor.

Reber smeared gel over the elephant's wrinkly grey skin and applied the sensor.

There was movement on the monitor. Shapes and contours, areas with changing tones of grey, outlines and structures appeared and disappeared.

For several minutes Reber scanned Asha's flank, while Roux peered over his shoulder at the screen. Kaung watched with bated breath.

'Tell me when you've seen enough,' Reber said coolly.

Roux let him scan for another couple of minutes then left the stalls without saying a word.

When he was sure that the man was out of earshot, Kaung asked, 'How you do that?'

Reber started packing the device away. 'Something so little,' he explained, 'is hard to find.' He smiled. 'And easy not to find.'

Only now did Kaung see that there was sweat on Reber's brow.

2

9 April 2015

This was the first time that Kaung felt conflicted in his loyalty to the Pellegrinis. He owed them a debt of gratitude, especially Paolo Pellegrini, the father.

Although the old director hadn't understood much about elephants, he knew a bit about people. And Kaung soon learned that to run a circus it was more important to understand people than animals. For this was how you identified those who did know a bit about animals.

He wasn't bound to Carlo by the same feelings. Kaung's loyalty was to the father, the circus and the elephants. Which is why he didn't feel particularly conscience-stricken about the fact that he'd gone behind Carlo Pellegrini's back and defrauded him of some of the money that Roux owed him.

Kaung worked every day with the animals as usual. He taught them new tricks, helped look after Trisha's baby, a bull calf by the name of Nilay, kept a close eye on the two pregnant cows, Sadaf and Rupashi, and an even closer one on the officially not-pregnant Asha.

But it wasn't long before the secret was in danger of being exposed. In spring, Pellegrini received a request for another surrogate pregnancy.

This request came right on cue, for Circus Pellegrini had just experienced a slow season and they were missing the contributions for Asha's sustenance and care that had stopped when the foetus was miscarried.

Of the four cows, one was nursing and two were pregnant. But in theory Asha was a possibility.

More than two months had now passed since she'd lost her foetus. For elephants in the wild it could take up to two years for the cycle to begin again. But for an elephant cow in captivity it was possible for this to happen only two months after a miscarriage.

Once again the request came through Dr Horàk. He wanted to measure Asha's progesterone levels every week to check for her receptivity.

When Kaung was instructed by Pellegrini to take a weekly urine sample from Asha he rang Dr Reber in horror.

Reber was horrified too. If Horàk got hold of a urine sample from Asha he'd know by the following day that she was pregnant.

'Kaung, can you spot when an elephant cow is ready for the bulls?'

'Yes.'

'Is Trisha ready?'

'No.'

They hung up.

Shortly afterwards Kaung was able to take some urine from Trisha.

3

17 April 2015

After the evening performance Pellegrini wanted to take another look at Rupashi. He never usually did this, but Kaung had hinted that he didn't think Rupashi would be able to perform the following day.

He entered the animal tent and put his wet umbrella in a bucket by the elephant stalls. An inspection lamp shaded by cardboard, which hung in the bars of the stalls, cast some light on the elephants. They were all lying down. Kaung had arranged a place to sleep in the corner with a horse blanket and he leaped to his feet to give the director an appropriate welcome.

'Have you started the night watch?' he asked.

'Baby come tomorrow or next day,' Kaung said.

'How can you tell?'

'The eyes.'

Pellegrini peered long and hard though the bars at the elephant's visible eye, but saw nothing. He turned to the neighbouring pen, where Asha was sleeping, and moved his head to the thick, widely spaced bars that were set in the upper third of the wooden construction until they touched the brim of his top hat.

He stood there, silently watching the sleeping elephants,

then said, 'It would be good for the circus if Asha were ready for the bulls again.'

'Yes, I know. But is not. Is not for long time.'

Pellegrini tore himself away from Asha. 'There's no reason why Dr Horàk needs to know that though, is there?'

'No.'

Pellegrini stood there in his tailcoat, tall and troubled. Then he nodded, turned around, grabbed his umbrella and left.

The following day Rupashi became unsettled and jumpy. She urinated at short intervals and kept dropping small balls of dung. The unease spread to the other elephants. Kaung decided to leave her in her pen during the performance. Too risky, he thought.

The next day the unease and jumpiness escalated. Rupashi stopped eating and tossed sawdust beneath her and on her back.

In the night Kaung noticed that she'd lost some mucus. When morning came he went to his boss and said, 'Doctor must come in evening.'

Before Dr Reber arrived Rupashi lost the mucus plug that surrounds the cervix during pregnancy. Two circus workers put up a partition wall to separate off an area where Rupashi wouldn't be disturbed by the other elephants. When Reber got there she was having her first contractions, which were pushing the baby into the birthing position.

She lay on the floor, rolled around, stood up again, hit herself between her legs with her tail, all the while appeased and comforted by Kaung.

At dawn Rupashi broke off the birth.

Dr Reber stayed for another two hours, but the elephant cow gave no more signs apart from losing a little more mucus and blood.

Reber had been amazed by this phenomenon at other elephant births. To avoid being disturbed mothers gave birth at night. But because a single night often wasn't sufficient to complete the process they would pause in the morning and not resume until the following evening.

He drove off to his clinic and came back later.

Rupashi was in the litter stall, picking up sawdust from the ground and throwing it onto her back. Kaung was crouching and talking to her softly in Burmese. Otherwise nobody was around. The show was about to begin.

The other elephants were already decorated for their performance. They wore leather headdresses covered with glittering studs and colourful coats that hung down to their knees on either side.

When Kaung saw Reber he got up. 'Must change,' he said and hurried out. Rupashi swung her head from side to side, as if in disapproval at Kaung's departure. Then she lay down. Trisha, who was right next to Rupashi's pen, came as close as the chain tied to her foot would allow and stretched her trunk through the bars.

Kaung returned. He was now wearing a red turban, a white collarless shirt and yellow Indian trousers. He crouched down to Rupashi and spoke to her again.

The circus orchestra struck up. It consisted of three men and a lot of electronics. What they played was anything but a suitable accompaniment to the thrilling spectacle the audience witnessed.

Rupashi moved her trunk as if she were looking for Kaung. He held out his hand and she grabbed hold of it tight. She lay peacefully like this for a while until Pellegrini came with two circus workers. He was wearing his tailcoat, top hat and red riding trousers.

'Where are you?' he called out into the stall.

Kaung got up and Rupashi copied him. He whispered something, stroked her trunk and called the elephants, who followed him reluctantly. Fahdi, the bull, went first, then Asha and Sadaf, while Trisha and her baby brought up the rear.

Now Reber was alone with Rupashi. He heard a plodding elephant tune coming from the orchestra.

The elephant cow started playing with hay and scattering sawdust around. From time to time she struck her belly with her trunk or bit its tip.

Reber grew nervous and hoped that Kaung would be back soon. Although he'd been present at many elephant births, he had never been alone before. If something went wrong he'd need help. And much could go wrong with an elephant birth.

Rupashi turned around 180 degrees as if in the circus ring. She thrashed about with her trunk and Reber saw a small bulge beneath the tail root.

The ponderous elephant march was still playing.

Rupashi sank to her knees, stayed there for a while, then stood up again.

Reber took a carrot from a bucket that Kaung had prepared and offered it to Rupashi. She took the carrot, toyed with it briefly, then tossed it across her back. She lay on her stomach and stretched out her hind legs.

By the time Rupashi was back on her feet the edge of the amniotic sac was sticking out of her like a ball. Reber tied the rubber apron around his waist and put on surgical gloves.

Finally the music stopped and he heard a thin applause. Soon afterwards Kaung was back beside him.

Rupashi made a noise that sounded like a scream. Kaung went up to her and laid his hand on the top of her trunk.

Now the circus workers led the elephants in and back to their pens. But Kaung instructed them to leave them outside Rupashi's stall. The animals crowded around the bars and watched.

The final contractions had started. In the cramped space Rupashi was going around in circles, from right to left and back again. Once more she made the noise that sounded like a scream and the other elephant cows answered her.

She hunched her back then stretched it out again.

All of a sudden the baby's hind legs slid out.

In the distance a drumroll from the orchestra announced another act.

Rupashi squeezed the baby out. It hung there briefly before falling to the ground in a gush of amniotic fluid and blood.

The elephants outside the stall trumpeted.

Rupashi turned around and, swiftly but carefully, freed the baby from its sac.

It lay there for a second without moving or breathing.

Rupashi knocked the baby with her feet and trunk, as if trying to shake it awake.

The baby raised its head and looked around.

At that very moment the circus orchestra played a fanfare.

Kaung said something in Burmese to the new arrival.

The elephants greeted the baby noisily.

Reber started crying, as he did at every elephant birth, whether it went well or not.

Less than twenty minutes later the little elephant was on its feet.

It was already getting dark when Kaung accompanied Dr Reber back to his car. This was the only opportunity they'd had that evening to speak in private.

'I'm worried about Asha's baby,' Reber began.

'No worry,' Kaung said. 'All good.'

'With elephants the babies trigger the birth. Asha's is too small for that.'

Kaung smiled. 'Asha do it herself. All good. No worry.'

4

8 June 2015

Some two months later Pellegrini received a short message from Dr Horàk saying that he didn't need any more urine samples from Asha. The progesterone curve wasn't showing any change and he'd decided he needed another surrogate mother.

Alena – Pellegrini's stepmother who was young enough to be his sister – had returned from Ibiza bloated by lovesickness, and she proceeded to tyrannise him and the entire circus from her luxury caravan.

The next setback was the birth of Sadaf's baby. Everything went fine until Sadaf tried to remove the amniotic membrane with her trunk and front legs. It was her first birth and, whether out of inexperience or aggression, she kicked the little one so hard that – as Dr Reber later diagnosed – it suffered multiple skull fractures and died.

Pellegrini was saved by the fact that Trisha, the mother with the two-year-old calf, finally showed symptoms of being on heat. He was able to offer her as a surrogate mother. This was also a stroke of luck for Kaung and Dr Reber. Monitoring Trisha's pregnancy gave the doctor an excuse to keep a discreet eye on Asha's too.

Which in truth was progressing most peculiarly. Now in its sixteenth month, the foetus was fully formed, but hardly growing. Reber estimated its shoulder height at less than twenty centimetres. He'd have loved to examine the baby with special transrectal ultrasound equipment like Dr Horàk had. But he had to make do with his conventional device and remain patient each time until the mini foetus manoeuvred into a position where it was visible.

The tiny heart kept beating and all Asha's blood values fell within the normal range.

H

5

Summer 2015

Dr Reber didn't feel comfortable with the situation. His decision to get involved had been a spontaneous one, even though spontaneity wasn't one of Hansjörg Reber's most obvious qualities. He was more of a systematic, organised and focused individual. 'A cold fish', as his ex had sometimes called him. But that wasn't true. He could be emotional too. 'Sentimental' was what his ex had said.

'If one of your bloody animals snuffs it,' she said once, 'you're inconsolable. But you don't give a shit about the fate of your fellow beings.'

'Which fellow beings?' he asked.

'Me, for example,' came her reply.

And he had to admit that she hadn't been entirely wrong in this. He'd already become indifferent to her in the first year of their marriage. It wasn't something that just happened; he consciously engineered it. The persistent dissatisfaction she expressed about him, herself, her life, their fellow human beings – in short, about everything – got so badly on his nerves that one day he resolved not to care less what she said, felt or thought. In line with his systematic and focused approach to life he consistently maintained this detachment, and soon felt liberated. He realised that the logical outcome of his stance must be a growing indifference to her as a person too, and accepted that their marriage was ultimately doomed.

The loss of his marital status was balanced by a gain in freedom. The freedom to abandon a career in the large animal clinic where he worked. The freedom to become a small country vet. The freedom to undertake voluntary work and traineeships so as to develop an expertise in elephants. The freedom to not become a rich man.

No doubt his ex would have added to this list: the freedom to let himself go. Another example of her not being entirely wrong either.

Since their separation he'd put on eight kilos, one for each year. And even before that he hadn't been a slim man. His gait had become somewhat ponderous. His wardrobe consisted of comfortable, practical clothes that he bought large enough and kept wearing until even the farmers noticed how shabby he looked.

Dr Reber lived in a secluded farmhouse that he'd bought cheaply in the second year of his practice. He'd been the first person to discover that it was for sale.

Brudermatte Farm was a small, half-timbered house with four rooms and a spacious kitchen from which you could heat the sitting room stove.

Attached to the house was a large barn which consisted of a stable for twelve cows and a few calves, a shed he used as a garage and a hayloft still containing some left-over hay from the previous owners.

One day he intended to renovate the barn, he just didn't know what for.

The house came with eight hectares of pasture, arable land and some woodland, all of which he'd leased to a neighbour.

Outside, beneath the windows of the sitting room, stood a bench where he could sit in the evenings and gaze at the rolling hills, the black stands of fir trees and the three farmhouses where his neighbours lived.

When he bought the property he'd pictured himself sitting on this bench watching dusk slowly envelop the surrounding countryside. But he can't have sat there more than about twice; Reber didn't have time to enjoy the sunset.

He didn't mind living alone at Brudermatte Farm. Three times a week Frau Huber came to tidy and clean – which was permanently necessary – and to replenish his supplies. He either ate in the pubs of nearby villages or he put frozen pizzas, *tartes flambées* and cheesecakes in the oven, or cooked tomato spaghetti, his signature dish.

Reber spent the evenings watching the television news and reading specialist literature on the internet. Recently he'd been looking at dwarfism in humans and animals, and he was especially fascinated by microcephalic osteo-dysplastic primordial dwarfism type 11, where the foetus barely grows in the womb, but otherwise develops normally. Like Asha's foetus.

Judging by Roux's surprise at the fact that his embryo had stopped growing, dwarfism couldn't have been the goal of his experiment. But Reber doubted his aim was to breed herpes-resistant elephants. He'd done some back-ground research on Roux and learned that he used to work for Gebstein, who experimented with glowing animals. He wouldn't be surprised if Roux was involved in a similar commercial project.

At any rate it was significant how suddenly his interest was aroused once he spotted the possibility that the foetus might survive to become a mini elephant.

Kaung was right when he said Roux wasn't a good man. Which was why Reber didn't feel any guilt. Although hiding from Roux the fact that the embryo was still alive wasn't strictly ethical, Reber was certain that Roux's intentions weren't either.

Any qualms that Reber may have felt were short-lived, for surely it would only be a few more days before Kaung rang to tell him that Asha had lost the baby. They were agreed that the most important thing to do when it happened was to get rid of the dead foetus and afterbirth as quickly as possible so that Roux didn't get his hands on a single cell.

Reber wasn't a particularly outspoken opponent of genetic engineering. He just didn't like it. He found he had nothing in common with the people who were interested in it. At university these had generally been the technocratic researchers and scientists.

Although it was principally the student number quotas rather than a pure love of animals that drove him into veterinary medicine, he did like animals. And people who liked animals.

But since he'd given up his work in the large animal clinic and been working as a country vet, his relationship to the job had changed. He had – how should he put it? – become more idealistic. The farmers he dealt with, most of them at any rate, had a natural affinity with their animals. Not sentimental, but it wasn't value-free either. The animals might be livestock, but they weren't mere commodities. And certainly not organisms or clusters of cells to be experimented on willy-nilly.

The more he read about the subject of genetic engineering the more dubious it seemed. But it was only when he learned of the discovery of a system that allowed simple, cheap and efficient interventions into the genome, that he became a convinced opponent.

The system was called CRISPR/Cas and it allowed targeted genes to be destroyed, repaired or modified. You could use it to modify specific gametes. And changes in the genome of a living being affected all its descendants too.

Reber had enough professional experience to know how quickly mistakes could occur and he was concerned by the idea that each of these would be passed down to future generations.

He gradually became anxious that the tiny embryo might be one such mistake.

The due date came ever closer and the mini foetus was still alive. Reber and Kaung had to brace themselves for the prospect that the elephant might be born alive. Kaung was sure of it, and Reber himself slowly started to accept this possibility.

If it did happen, he'd agreed with Kaung that they'd try to keep the birth secret and Reber would hide the creature on his farm. For the duration of what was likely to be a short life.

6

12 August 2015

Just for once Reber was sitting on his after-work bench outside the house. Throughout the entire rainy summer he'd been able to blame the weather for not doing it. But that evening the atmosphere before the next looming storm was so wonderful that he simply had to sit out there, enjoying a bottle of wine and the paper.

The grass was tall and dark green; no farmer had dared make hay. Like a wound, a red-rimmed gash on the horizon gaped in the ash-grey blanket of cloud.

The bottle was already half empty when he noticed that the light had changed into an unreal yellow. Shortly afterwards stormy gusts started tugging at his paper. He made for the shelter of the house.

Before he'd got to the front door his mobile rang. On the display it said 'Kaung'.

'Must come,' Kaung said. 'Taxi not find house. GPS not find house either.'

That was true. His house didn't have a GPS locatable address. 'Where are you?'

'Graufeld. Must come. Quick.'

'Has Asha lost her baby?'

'Not lost. Alive. Quick!'

As Reber was reversing his SUV out of the shed the first lightning flashed in the sky. Halfway to the village the deluge almost defeated the windscreen wipers. Streams flowed from farm tracks onto the narrow road.

Alive? If that was the case then the baby had arrived before the earliest date. And without any signs from the mother.

It stopped raining abruptly. The road led through a little wood. Reber accelerated.

A few seconds later the car hit another wall of rain. Reber braked, the SUV skidded, but he regained control. The wine, Reber thought. He hadn't expected he'd have to drive.

Shimmering through the downpour by the side of the road were the lights of Waldhof, the last farm before the edge of the village. Soon afterwards Reber saw the Graufeld sign and the speed limit.

They hadn't arranged where to meet, but it was a small village. Even from a distance Reber could see the taxi sign shining and reflecting on the wet roof of the vehicle.

He flashed his lights and saw a door open and Kaung get out. He turned around, picked up a bag and waited for Reber in the pouring rain.

Reber stopped, Kaung opened the back door, put the bag on the seat, pushed it to the middle and said, 'Must pay please. Kaung not enough money.'

The taxi driver made no move to get out, but just put the window down, said, 'One hundred and fifteen thirty,' and held out his hand.

Reber gave him 120 and hurried back to his own car.

The taxi drove off, but Reber didn't start his engine. Kneeling on the seat he peered behind at the bag.

The zip was open. Kaung was holding the two sides apart.

At that moment the courtesy light inside the car automatically went off.

Inside the bag he saw something that was pink and glowing.

7

Circus Pellegrini
The same day

Kaung had been certain that it was imminent; he could read the little signs. Asha had started making the same steps forward and backward for hours on end. Although it was common for elephants living in captivity to display such mechanical behaviour, for Asha this was new. Nor was it like her to throw food and objects around. She also had diarrhoea, another indication that she was nervous.

Then Kaung saw that she'd lost some mucus. By now at the latest he ought to have informed Dr Reber. But a visit outside his scheduled calls would have raised eyebrows in the circus. Kaung could still ring him if it were absolutely necessary and he could be here pretty quickly because their current venue in the Oberland was only about half an hour away from Dr Reber's village.

But Kaung didn't think it was necessary. He was almost sure that it would be an easy birth. Yes, the doctor was afraid that such a tiny baby might get stuck and suffocate in the long birthing canal, but he had never believed it would survive anyway. The doctor was a good man, but he didn't believe in miracles.

Kaung was now sleeping beside Asha, which didn't arouse any suspicion as it wasn't unusual for him to spend the night with a poorly animal, talking to it and feeding it little treats. And Asha was poorly. She had a gastrointestinal infection, or at least that's the excuse Kaung had given Pellegrini for her not being able to take part in the performance.

Kaung sat in Asha's stall in the lotus position, meditating. The rain made a dull thud as it drummed onto the roof of the animal tent. The smell of the elephant dung mingled with that of the wet grass that drifted in through the half-open entrance.

A noise from far beyond his consciousness alerted Kaung. Opening his eyes he saw that Asha was thrusting her trunk high in the air and hunching her back.

The noise was coming from Trisha, who had stood up and was blurting out the sounds. Kaung immediately knew what they meant: Asha's contractions had begun.

He stood up, went to the entrance to the tent and closed the tarpaulins. Then he hurried back to Asha, laid his hand on the root of her trunk and spoke some words of comfort.

As a young boy he'd learned how to read the eyes of elephants. He could spot their fears, their anger, their happiness and their pain.

Asha wasn't in pain. Although her body tightened once more she didn't seem to feel any resistance.

She pushed again. Kaung leaped behind her – just in time to catch a little bundle in a jet of amniotic fluid.

Asha turned around.

Normally she'd now free the baby from the sac, but Kaung didn't dare put this tiny creature at the feet of the mighty animal. He hurriedly ripped open the slippery membrane with his bare hands. And got a fright.

It was as if he were peeling an exotic fruit from its plain exterior.

The skin that appeared was a deep, schid, shining pink.

Kaung took the animal completely out of the sac and nudged it to get it moving.

Yes, it was breathing!

Asha gave the small creature a fleeting examination with her trunk and turned away. Kaung fancied he'd seen something in her eyes that told him it was advisable to leave.

He carried the newborn out of the stall. No sooner had he secured the heavy bolt than Asha gave the partition wall a thundering kick and trumpeted briefly but angrily.

Kaung went past the stalls with the sleeping horses to the tack room, where he dried the baby with a towel and bedded it down on a blanket.

In front of him lay a perfectly formed elephant. Not twenty centimetres tall.

It was pink.

And it radiated a holy aura.

Kaung knelt and prayed.

The creature moved its trunk and tried to lift its head.

Kaung covered the body with the loose end of the blanket and left the tack room.

A few planks formed a slippery path across the soaked meadow to the caravans. Only in one of them was there a light still on, while a television flickered in another.

He opened the door to his small caravan and went in. Without turning on the light he pulled out a bag from under the bed and returned to the tack room in the pouring rain.

The small elephant appeared to have moved; the blanket had slightly slid to the side. Kaung covered it up again, took a Thermos flask from the bag and went to the elephant stalls.

All the elephants were on their feet. Asha still looked as if she ought to be given a wide berth. He went into the others' shared pen and approached Rupashi, who gave him a brief hug with her trunk.

Kaung patted Rupashi, led her calf to the udder and waited until it started drinking. An elephant cow can only be milked when a calf is suckling on the other teat.

He stroked Rupashi's udder and she let him milk her.

Kaung filled the Thermos with a litre of her milk.

When he returned to the saddle room the small elephant was standing on wobbly legs. Kaung filled a baby bottle with some milk and offered it to the elephant.

It hesitated, examined the teat with its trunk then eventually lifted it, opened its mouth, put its head slightly to one side and started to suck.

Kaung watched the tiny fairytale creature, which wasn't even twice as big as the baby bottle, as it drank almost 100 millilitres of Rupashi's milk.

The rain kept thundering on the tent roof.

'*Barisha*,' Kaung muttered, the Hindi word for rain.

And from that moment on, this would be the little elephant's name.

8

Graufeld

Autumn 2015 to spring 2016

Barisha's entry into the life of Hansjörg Reber challenged almost everything that he'd hitherto thought incontrovertible, and cast a shadow of doubt over what he'd always imagined to be cast-iron certainties.

His scientific understanding was shattered, he doubted his powers of medical judgement and he was doing things for which he needed reserves of dishonesty he never knew he possessed.

He kept telling himself, of course, that his motives were nothing but ethical. In this case someone had intervened in nature not for the sake of scientific progress that would cure illnesses or save lives. He'd done it to produce a sensation and possibly earn a fortune too. Was his intention to produce a living toy? Was that what Roux was trying to do?

Reber didn't spend long pondering the question of how unethical one could be to prevent something unethical.

That he'd appropriated something that didn't belong to him wasn't in doubt. Something that was the result of years of expensive research activity. However contemptible Roux might be, Reber was guilty of cheating him out of the fruits of his labour and of withholding a scientific sensation.

But he didn't feel the slightest pangs of conscience. The only worry plaguing him was the fear of being caught.

Although Reber had taken precautions to ensure that this didn't happen, he'd been obliged to widen the circle of those (partially) in the know. Frau Huber knew that for research purposes he was keeping an animal in quarantine in the stables, which were now permanently locked.

And every day Hans, her unemployed son, drove in his tuned and lowered Opel Astra to wherever Circus Pellegrini happened to be performing. He brought with him an empty Thermos sterilised by his mother and came back with a full flask that Kaung would hand over in a place specified by text message.

Hans wasn't interested in the content of the Thermos flasks, only in the money per kilometre that Reber paid him, which was higher than usual: one franc. For greater distances, Hans also received an expenses allowance, which given his huge bulk was not inconsiderable.

In the end Reber knew exactly why none of these ethical questions bothered him: he was completely in love with Barisha.

Not as a vet, not as an elephant specialist, not as a scientist. Ever since his first encounter with the tiny creature he'd been entranced by its – charm.

Yes. He was overwhelmed by a feeling that he'd only experienced once before, and very briefly at that, in the first few weeks after meeting his ex. When he was in love with her freshness, her naïvety, her chubbiness.

Now he felt a similar affection for Barisha, a comparable urge to protect.

No doubt anyone else would have felt the same. Barisha was captivating. She – Reber had identified her sex – possessed the charm, curiosity, awkwardness and attachment common to all baby elephants. Only she was much, much smaller. And pink. And she glowed in the dark like an alien.

His feelings towards Barisha were different from Kaung's. Reber felt affection, whereas Kaung felt reverence. Kaung prayed to her and venerated her like a deity. On the visits he made on his days off he placed small flower garlands around her neck.

Barisha was doing well with Rupashi's milk. She'd weighed 2.45 kilograms at birth and now was putting on about twenty-five grams per day. And she was thriving in Reber's care. After her birth he'd disinfected her navel, as he would with any normal baby elephant. Later he'd immunised and vaccinated her with a fraction of the usual doses.

Barisha was an adventurous baby and Reber noticed that she was getting bored in the pen of the old cowshed – she kept running against its confines.

When the air was pure and the weather decent, Reber took Barisha outside. She loved vanishing into the unmown grass between the trellis and the vegetable garden, only to appear again by the edge of the gravel path that led to the house. Sometimes she'd roll around, leaving marks in the grass that must have looked like little corn circles to Frau Huber.

Reber's veterinary work suffered as a result of his new

housemate. He couldn't leave Barisha for longer than three hours, because that was how often she needed her milk. On several occasions he'd had to call on an astonished colleague and competitor when he'd been summoned to attend a calving cow at an awkward time of day.

But Reber didn't care; he had more important priorities than his reputation as a vet. He wanted to spend as much time with Barisha as possible, because he didn't think she'd live long. From what he'd found out, brain haemorrhages and vasoconstriction were common in humans with microcephalic osteodysplastic primordial dwarfism. Why should it be any different with elephants?

Barisha was kept in the stables only on those days when Frau Huber was in the house or when Reber was in his practice or out on a call. Otherwise she kept him company in the kitchen or sitting room. She also spent the nights on a blanket beside his bed. He'd rolled up the rugs, put them in the hayloft and was always armed with a roll of absorbent paper and dog waste bags. This was more out of consideration for Frau Huber than any need for cleanliness. He liked the smell of elephant stalls.

His evenings were spent reading in the sitting room beneath the standard lamp on the threadbare sofa, both items his predecessor had left behind. Or he'd watch Barisha, who slept either on the sofa or at his feet. And glowed silently.

He couldn't remember ever having felt so happy.

9

Circus Pellegrini
Autumn 2015 to spring 2016

Kaung's daily routine was less tranquil. He still spent every day training the elephants on his own, for Pellegrini claimed he was far too busy with the preparations for next season. And there was plenty of time to integrate him into the act in a way that made him look like the trainer.

Kaung was pleased as it meant every day he could milk Rupashi unobserved and hand over the Thermoses to Hans at the waste disposal point at the entrance to the village.

On every second Monday, when there was no performance, he'd get into the car and Hans, a silent, daredevil driver, would whisk him off to Barisha in record time.

Each time Kaung brought an offering: a few flowers in a basket or woven into a garland; a small, decorative offering of fruit – bananas, apples, oranges – and always plenty of incense sticks. He would offer these things to the sacred elephant in a little ceremony. Although the vet never let it show, Kaung knew that he was secretly amused by these rituals. For Reber, Barisha was the result of a scientific experiment gone wrong. Kaung forgave him for this; he didn't know any better.

Kaung spent a lot of time with Barisha, praying and meditating until Reber dragged him into the kitchen for the inevitable spaghetti with tomato sauce.

Afterwards he'd spend the night in Reber's guest room, which otherwise remained unused, and drove back with Hans to the circus on Tuesday morning. He'd milk Rupashi again and take the bag with the Thermos back to Hans, waiting for him in one of the village pubs.

But on this particular Monday Kaung was greeted by a peculiar situation when he arrived. Dr Reber opened the front door and took him without further ado into the kitchen. There, beside the wood-burning stove, stood Barisha. She was as still as a statue, and held in her trunk a small bundle of pine chips that Reber used as kindling. The other bundles of kindling that Reber kept in a nickel-plated bin were strewn across the kitchen floor.

When she noticed Kaung she lifted her head slightly, as if wanting to show him her trophies.

Kaung unpacked his basket of offerings, lit some candles and incense sticks, knelt, put his palms together in front of his face and muttered a prayer.

Reber left the kitchen.

It wasn't until dusk fell that Kaung came into the sitting room, followed at a slight distance by Barisha, still aloof.

Reber glanced at Kaung uncertainly and was about to go up to Barisha.

'Leave in peace, please,' Kaung said.

Reber paused. 'Why? What's wrong with her?'

'Sit, please.'

Reber sat in his padded armchair. 'What's up with her?'

'Barisha is elephant. Small, but elephant. Doctor think Barisha is toy.'

Reber looked shocked. 'No, no, I don't think that at all.'

'But Barisha think doctor think that.'

Reber frowned.

'Barisha sacred creature,' Kaung declared solemnly. And when he sensed Reber's scepticism he added, 'Doctor need not believe. But must believe that is elephant. Must take seriously. Must respect.'

Reber nodded.

'Barisha do with wood what elephants do. Wants to show that is elephant.'

From now on Reber tried to pay the glowing pink mini elephant some respect. Which he didn't always succeed in doing.

It was now February. Barisha was six months old, but had scarcely grown any bigger. She wasn't just living on Rupashi's milk any more; Reber gave her vegetables, fruit, leaves and twigs too. He was also able to leave her for longer than three hours at a time and without food. But this almost never happened. He didn't feel comfortable with the idea of her being unsupervised and unprotected. And he missed her, probably more than she did him.

10

10 May 2016

The winter break was at an end and the circus was appearing at Dondikon Common, a place that had become stuck in the transition from village to agglomeration and which, if one was being kind, could be counted as part of the Zürich commuter belt.

Audiences for the shows were poor, which wasn't just down to the programme, but also the cold, wet May and the persistent technical problems of the heating system.

To compound the misfortune, it had also snowed overnight. The big top, the caravans and the mobile stables all lay beneath a heavy, wet covering of snow that had begun to melt before it started getting light.

It smelled of the slurry that the farmer deposited in brown lines on the neighbouring field.

Kaung had spent the night with Barisha and driven back with Hans, who was now waiting in one of the village pubs for Rupashi's fresh milk.

On this Tuesday he had to leave him waiting for ages, because as Kaung approached the animal tent he could hear Pellegrini's voice coming from inside.

He was standing in Asha's stall, talking to someone that Kaung only recognised when he got closer: Roux.

And another man Kaung didn't know, partially obstructed by the elephant cow. He was holding a stick, attached to the end of which was a bucket, as if he were waiting for the opportunity to collect some of Asha's urine.

Asha was agitated, and Kaung could immediately see why: all four of her legs were chained up.

Only now did Kaung spot the fourth man: Ben, the unpleasant circus worker who sometimes helped out with the elephants. He was wielding an elephant hook, a tool that Kaung never used. It was a stick with a barbed metal hook for leading animals by pressing on their most sensitive spot behind the ears. Ben must have been the one who'd chained Asha up.

Roux noticed Kaung at once. He broke off mid-sentence, looked at Pellegrini and indicated Kaung with his chin.

Turning around, the director gave the oozie a nod. 'This is Dr Hess; Dr Roux you know already. The gentlemen would like to repeat the experiment with Asha.'

'Asha not ready,' Kaung replied.

'Dr Hess would like to verify this personally. He believes that sixteen months after the miscarriage should be sufficient.'

'Dr Reber says—'

'Don't give me Dr Reber!' Roux interrupted.

'Trisha better. Trisha soon ready,' Kaung said.

Pellegrini shook his head. 'But Dr Roux would like to work with Asha.'

'Why?'

The director was going to answer, but Roux got in there first. 'Because he does.'

At that moment Asha urinated, and Dr Hess caught some in the bucket. He filled the sample bottles.

Kaung watched him and noticed that in the case from which the doctor had taken the bottles were six full blood sample tubes. They'd taken blood from Asha.

Kaung knew it was possible that Asha was ready for a new implant. You might almost think she hadn't had a baby. The afterbirth had only weighed two kilos – compared to twenty-five for a normal baby elephant – and Asha hadn't produced any milk either.

The doctor packed away his things and the three men left the stall. Kaung started unfastening Asha's chains. She spread her ears and swung her head back and forth.

'Better get out before chains off,' Kaung said. 'Otherwise dead.'

Ben gave a scornful smile and left the stall.

Kaung spoke words of comfort to Asha as he undid the chains. As soon as she was free he fetched carrots and fed her. Only then did he milk Rupashi and bring the bag with the milk to the pub, where Hans had just polished off his second breakfast.

11

Graufeld

11 May 2016

Dr Reber was worried. Barisha was standing beside the kitchen door, playing with her bundle of kindling. Kaung had called him to say what was happening at the circus. Reber was not at all happy to hear that Roux was visiting Pellegrini again, but what was worse was that he'd brought along his own vet: Joachim Hess! Reber knew him too well for comfort. They'd called him Joa, or maybe that's what he'd called himself – Reber couldn't really remember. The two of them had studied together and he'd always been puzzled by how Hess had come to veterinary medicine. He had no connection with animals; he merely regarded them as objects of study, which he observed with interest but absolutely no compassion.

It was only later, when Hess specialised, that Reber understood why he'd become a vet. He acquired a qualification in equestrian medicine, became a vet for riding, showjumping and race horses, and now moved in those circles he'd always felt attracted to.

The last he'd heard of Hess was in connection with a doping scandal a few years back involving a legendary showjumping horse. But it was news to Reber that he was now working with elephants.

Reber understood why Roux had turned up with his own vet: he didn't trust him. Reber could hardly blame Roux.

But why was he insisting on Asha as the surrogate mother?

Reber could only come up with a single explanation, which did nothing to lessen his concerns: Roux didn't just want to repeat the experiment; he wanted it to fail again. And in exactly the same way as the last time. Roux probably thought that the foetus's growth deficiency was down to the surrogate mother.

Another proof that the dwarfism was coincidental rather than having been planned in advance as part of the experiment.

Roux had intended to create a normal, large, pink elephant. To begin with he'd probably thought that it was a fault in the CRISPR/Cas technology that was responsible for Barisha's size. But perhaps he hadn't succeeded in repeating this and was now attributing the result to Asha.

Barisha dropped the bundle, lay down and rolled on her back. Her mouth was visible beneath her trunk. It looked as if she were laughing.

During those many days and nights with Barisha, Reber had undertaken detailed research into the status and especially the dangers of genetic engineering. The more he found out, the more convinced he became that what he and Kaung had done and were doing was not only defensible, it was their duty and obligation, to use a favourite phrase of his former professor of biomedical ethics.

When Reber first came into contact with the topic, decoding the genome was still one of the biggest problems of genetic engineering. Nowadays it was routine.

The genetic databases were growing daily, allowing those with access to them to produce genetic maps from which they could establish someone's provenance. And obviously this would be a recipe for a new, more nuanced and more targeted form of discrimination than the one humanity was already familiar with. It would also allow, for example, the development of new weapons that were only effective against certain genetic make-ups. It would be possible, therefore, to attack a country with chemical weapons that were harmless for certain ethnic groups, but deadly for others.

As a medical man, of course Reber could see the benefits of decoding and modifying the genome too. You could, for example, switch off the genetic functions that triggered Alzheimer's, cancer or the ageing process, or other scourges of humanity.

But it also meant that you could reconfigure the genomes of plants, animals and humans. You could design them.

Barisha was the most spectacular proof of this technological feasibility. And not only that. She was also a delightful advertisement for its desirability and harmlessness.

Reber went to his computer and searched for Hess's telephone number. He couldn't locate one. But he did come across a website called Ask a Vet. In a long list of specialists he found Dr Joachim Hess, zoological veterinary medicine. A wording Reber had never come across before.

If you clicked on Dr Hess, it opened a window in which you could type your question.

'Hello, Joa,' Dr Reber wrote. 'Do you remember me? Hansjörg Reber. I hope you're well. There's something I'd like to ask you, but not so publicly. Can I reach you by phone? Till then – Hajö.'

Less than two hours later Reber heard the ping announcing the arrival of a new email. It was from Hess and consisted merely of a telephone number and the three letters JOA. He dialled the number and Hess picked up straight away.

'Hajö, old chap, how are you? Good, I imagine, seeing as you're a bachelor again.'

'I've been worse,' Reber replied.

'I've been expecting to hear from you. About the elephant thing, no? All I can say was that I didn't go looking for it, it was thrust on me.'

'Whatever – that's not what concerns me. I still look after the other elephants. If Roux had asked me I would have declined.'

'Oh really? Why?'

'Because Roux's an arsehole.'

Hess laughed. 'I can't be so picky.' And after a pause, 'So what does concern you?'

'Why's he insisting on Asha? After the bad experience last time? The miscarriage. Trisha is ready.'

'He says the foetus didn't grow. And that's what he's after.' Reber could picture him grinning. 'A cute mini elephant. That's what he's hoping for.'

'I thought he was involved with experiments in Austria.'

'He was. Two. Both failed.'

'Also dwarf foetuses?'

Hess didn't reply.

'Anything else particular about them?'

Silence.

'Colour? Glowing?'

'Sorry, Hajö, I've said too much already. Bye.' He hung up.

May snow lay on the ground outside and Reber was freezing. He'd heated up the stove and went into the kitchen to put more wood in. He cut up an apple and carrot into small pieces. When he returned to the warm sitting room Barisha was waiting for him by the door and raised her trunk in greeting.

Reber squatted and stroked the tiny creature. 'Don't worry,' he muttered. 'I'll look after you.'

12

Circus Pellegrini

5 June 2016

Ben's real name was Tarub. Tarub Ben Bassir. But everyone called him Ben. He came from Morocco and had joined the circus shortly after the death of Pellegrini's father.

His job at the circus consisted of helping put up and take down the big top, and setting up the props in the dark between acts and putting them away again. Apart from that he had to clean the stalls and perform all manner of other menial tasks.

But Ben had no intention of spending his whole life as one of the lowly circus workers. He was good with animals and one day hoped to have a career as an attendant, then to become a trainer and finally to perform with them in the ring.

Kaung was in his way.

Kaung, the 'elephant-whisperer'! 'Better get out ... otherwise dead'! They'd see who was 'otherwise dead' first, now that Ben had discovered Kaung was dealing in elephant milk.

It had struck him some time ago that Kaung was behaving strangely, as if he had something to hide. He always waited till he was alone, then he did something nobody was allowed to know about. Ben hadn't cared what it was until now. He wasn't one to interfere in other people's business. But now, after this insult, it was no longer just someone else's business.

Kaung was milking Rupashi! Every day! Ben had secretly watched him. Kaung would take the milk to a fat young man who waited for him in a car in various locations. He'd noted the registration number.

'Better get out ... otherwise dead!'

13

The same day

To begin with Carlo Pellegrini didn't know what to do with this information. Kaung was milking Rupashi? And taking the milk to a car with a Zürich number plate? For what purpose? What could anybody do with a litre of elephant milk?

Was Ben telling the truth, or did he just want to get one over on Kaung? The two of them couldn't stand each other, something Pellegrini had realised early on. Ben's treatment of the elephants was a thorn in Kaung's side. And vice versa.

Ben stood keenly facing Pellegrini, expecting praise.

Another mistake, this Ben, the circus director thought. Clearly not all Moroccans were born circus workers. And this one wasn't even popular with his fellow countrymen, the ones who had been hired by Carlo's father.

'Thanks, you can go now,' was all he said.

Ben looked as if he wanted to add something, but changed his mind and left the director's caravan.

Carlo sat there at a loss, holding the piece of paper on which Ben had noted the registration number in rather crude writing. Then he turned his chair to the monitor, opened the Swiss vehicle index website and typed in the number. The owner was 'Huber, Hans', resident in Graufeld.

Graufeld?

Pellegrini put 'Graufeld' into his contact database and, indeed, Dr Hansjörg Reber appeared on the screen. Veterinary practice in 8323 Graufeld.

That couldn't be a coincidence. Was Kaung sending a litre of elephant milk every day to Reber's practice?

Pellegrini typed 'Dr Hansjörg Reber, vet' into the online telephone directory and got two results. One was the practice in Graufeld. The other address was Brudermatte Farm, 8323 Graufeld.

Pellegrini checked the time. Just after six o'clock. He could be there within the hour.

14

Graufeld

The same day

He hadn't expected so much snow in June. The area where Reber lived was at a slightly higher altitude than Dondikon. The wet snow that had already melted there in the morning still covered the fields and pasture here by the road. And with the snow now falling again it settled immediately. He had to cut his speed and it took him an hour before he finally saw the Graufeld sign.

Putting 'Brudermatte Farm' into his GPS had brought no results, so he had to ask the way in the village pub.

A sign on the front of the half-timbered building announced the pub's name as Löwen. The chit-chat died down as he entered. This is where, it seemed, all the farmers in the village came to enjoy a beer after work. He went up to the bored young woman pulling beers at the bar.

'Could you tell me how to get to Brudermatte Farm, please?'

'Tell you? Yes, I could tell you.'

'But?'

'But would you understand?'

As a circus director he wasn't used to a huge amount of respect, but some, at least.

'It's all rather complicated, you see.'

'Try me,' he replied, somewhat resigned.

'Fancy one too?' she said, pointing with her chin at the glasses of beer she was pulling.

'No thanks, I've got to drive.'

'Oh, but it would help. It's even more difficult to find sober.'

Pellegrini took one, paid immediately and gave her a tip. She took a beermat and drew him a sort of map.

When he opened the door to the porch he heard one of the farmers call out, 'That was the guy from Circus Pellegrini, the director in person!'

He found the first two turnoffs without difficulty. But he had to spend a long time looking for the third. Now there were a few centimetres of snow on the ground and the road he was meant to take had no tracks on it.

He drove slowly and with dipped headlights over the virgin snow, which was falling ever more thickly. He didn't see the lit-up window until he was almost right in front of the building. Pellegrini turned off his engine, got out and went over to the light. All that now marked the path to the house was a gentle depression in the white. He passed through an open gate on which hung a weather-beaten sign. He was able to make out the name 'Brudermatte'.

On an impulse he left the path, walked up to the bench that stood beneath the lit-up window and climbed on it. By stretching he could peer into the room.

Reber was crouched on the floor, feeding a – tiny pink elephant!

Pellegrini had to get back down on his heels.

Had he seen correctly? A pink dwarf elephant?

He went on tiptoes again. There was no doubt about it: that *was* a tiny elephant! Reber was holding out a little piece of something to the creature, who grasped it with its trunk and put it in its mouth like a big elephant.

Asha's foetus that refused to grow! She hadn't lost it; she'd given birth to her baby and Reber had stolen it! And Kaung was in on the act – he was helping rear the baby elephant with Rupashi's milk.

Pellegrini pondered the situation as he stood on the bench. Should he ring the bell and confront Reber?

He had a better idea. He took his mobile from his breast pocket, held it up to the window and filmed for a good minute. Then he viewed the result. He couldn't use the footage; his hand had been too shaky. Pellegrini made a second attempt, this time pressing the mobile against the window to stabilise it.

Now the picture was sharp. You could see Reber feeding the animal. All of a sudden Reber glanced up and looked as if he were staring straight into the camera. But the mini elephant wound its trunk expectantly around Reber's thumb and he turned back to his charge.

What Reber had here wasn't just a scientific sensation; it was a walking fortune!

Pellegrini put his mobile away and got down from the bench. But rather than go to the door, he went the way he'd come, back to his car. He'd decided not to take any risks. He would show the video to Roux, who could make up his own mind whether or not to go to the police.

It was snowing so heavily that he could only see faint outlines of the footprints he'd made a few minutes ago.

15

Circus Pellegrini

6 June 2016

Roux could feel the blood rushing to his face.

He was sitting – Pellegrini had insisted that he sit – on the visitors' chair by the huge desk in the director's wagon. The director had turned the screen 180 degrees and stood beside the chair.

He realised at once that the sly bastard had screwed him like no one had ever screwed him before! That crook had diddled him out of the fruits of his many years of work!

Thoughts wildly assailed his mind. Victim! Deprivation! Debts! Silent partner! Failed experiments in Austria! Six months without driving licence! Miscarriage? Rubbish! Bright and cheery! The Burmese attendant! Dishonest swine!

'Again!' he commanded.

Roux put on his glasses and Pellegrini played the video through once more. It was perfect, his creature! Moving and behaving just like a young elephant! But it would fit onto a sheet of A4 paper! And it was pink! Perfect! He wouldn't be surprised if it glowed in the dark too! Sensational! His creature!

'Where is it?'

'Before I tell you that we need to agree on a few conditions – I'm sure you understand.'

'Conditions?' The blood surged to Roux's cheeks again.

'Well, the circumstances have changed. We're no longer dealing with a failed experiment. Now there are different financial arrangements. Quite different ones.'

Roux gave a dismissive wave of the hand. 'When I get hold of the result, money will no longer be an issue.'

'So let's discuss it briefly.'

'Briefly.'

'You owe me for Asha's care and upkeep according to the terms we negotiated for a successful procedure.'

'Agreed.'

'Plus the bonus we agreed if it was successful.'

Roux nodded.

'And a reward for finding the creature.'

This was too much for Roux. 'Your people nick the result of the research project and you want me to pay you a reward for finding it again? You know what? I'll find out myself where Reber's shacked up.'

'No you won't. You see, if you leave here without us having reached an agreement, I'll warn Reber. Then you can go hunting for your pink miracle.'

Roux thought about it. Finally he asked, 'What sort of reward did you have in mind?'

'When the time comes for you to present the animal to the public, Circus Pellegrini will have exclusive rights. For thirty performances my circus will be the only place on earth where the miraculous creature can be seen. I will determine the entrance prices and other conditions.'

Roux looked at him in disbelief. 'We're not talking about a circus act here. This is a highly important research project!'

Pellegrini laughed. 'In a few years' time there'll be dozens of research results like this. Patented and on the market at outrageous prices. What do you bet?'

They eventually agreed on fifteen performances, with Roux getting a small share of the takings.

16

The same day

Roux's feelings were still swinging between anger and euphoria, hatred and bliss. He'd done it! Although it hadn't gone smoothly, it had worked. Wow! He, Paul Roux, had made a scientific breakthrough; those other glowing animals were nothing next to this! And those had won their creators the Nobel Prize. Yes, he'd achieved a chance outcome, but wasn't St Chance the patron saint of researchers? Obviously he wouldn't be able to publish his findings until he'd found out how the dwarfism had come about, but he had the cell material. The clonable cell material! And he had the partner who possessed the technical knowhow and expertise to manufacture the product – in significant quantities – as well as the power to establish it on the market. He didn't need a Nobel Prize. The esteem and commercial success he would obtain would be more than sufficient to put Professor Gebstein deeply in the shade, where he belonged.

Roux knew that right now he mustn't let himself be steered by feelings of jealousy. There would be plenty of time for that later. Now he had to keep his cool; he needed a plan and he needed his silent partner.

17

Beijing

The same day

CGC was in an industrial area of Beijing, two hours from the centre in normal traffic. But those who worked there rarely travelled into the centre. Most lived in one of the large nearby housing complexes that all looked exactly the same.

Such sameness didn't bother them; they were used to it from their work. One of the most important interests of the Chinese Genetic Company was cloning.

An even more important mainstay of its activity was sequencing, the decryption of genetic codes. CGC carried out this work so rapidly and economically that for western laboratories it was often more efficient and cheaper to send their cells to China.

CGC wasn't the largest genetic factory in China, but it was one of the largest. It employed around 2,000 laboratory workers, technicians, chemists, doctors and other specialists.

Right now a few of them were sitting in one of the many conference rooms, watching for the umpteenth time the video being beamed onto the screen at the end of the table by a powerful, hi-res projector.

The men and women were all talking at once. Excitedly,

someone familiar with such company might say. They were debating whether the tiny pink elephant on the screen being fed by a slightly overweight man was mechanical or alive, real or a special effect. And they weren't in agreement. But those who believed the elephant was real were in the majority. It was nonetheless decided to send the material to the IT department and let the specialists check whether the creature had been morphed. The employees arranged to reconvene in an hour and the meeting broke up.

Exactly one hour later the specialist confirmed that the material hadn't been manipulated. At that point the circle of those present was reduced to the higher management. After a brief consultation, they decided to delegate the matter to the very top.

Following a lengthy discussion, the directors called in the head of security, who immediately briefed Tseng Tian and provided him with the necessary papers and equipment.

Just before seven o'clock the following morning, Tseng Tian was in economy class on board Air China CA5621 to Zürich.

18

Graufeld

The same day

Brudermatte Farm on that early morning was like a picture from an Advent calendar. The thick layer of new snow on the roof and garden stood out against a black-ish-blue sky where a thin sickle of moon and a few stars lingered. Two lit-up windows cast their light onto the glittering white. A bright column of smoke rose from the chimney into the daybreak.

Reber was kneeling in front of the stove to light it. Barisha stood beside him, swinging her trunk impatiently. On the cooker was a pan heating her bottle in warm water. On the other hotplate stood Reber's old aluminium coffee pot with its glazed lid. He loved the smell of hot coffee in a cold farmhouse kitchen.

The fire burned. Reber hauled himself to his feet. Seriously out of shape, he thought, especially for someone who had equalled the Swiss 400-metre medley record back in his student swimming days.

He filled a large cup of warmed-up coffee, added some sugar, took the baby bottle from the water bath, checked the temperature of the milk on the inside of his wrist, sat on the end of the corner bench beside the kitchen table with both coffee and milk, and started feeding Barisha.

For almost ten months Reber had been doing this five times a day – and occasionally at night too, if she demanded – but he'd never tired of it. On the contrary, he enjoyed it each time. His longest love story to date.

He fried two eggs and ate them with the farmhouse bread that Frau Huber brought him from the village bakery. This bread was partially responsible for his excess weight. He devoured it like cake. And between mouthfuls he gave Barisha bite-size pieces of apple and carrot.

After breakfast he took her outside. It wasn't Barisha's first experience of snow, but she still found it mysterious. She plodded around circumspectly and with stiff legs, stopping every few steps and lifting one foot, then another to warm them a little.

Reber watched Barisha for a while before taking pity on her and lifting her up.

As he was going back inside he noticed on his bench beneath the window something resembling old footprints. Faint, barely apparent dents in the new snow.

When he took a closer look Reber also saw some that led from the bench to the path, then became lost among his own, fresh footprints.

Just the hint of some tracks. Perhaps a fox seeking some warmth.

19

Zürich

7 June 2016

This time Roux arrived punctually at the airport. He was in the arrivals hall, holding a sign that read 'Mr Tseng'. He felt like a chauffeur.

The video hadn't failed to make an impact. He had barely sent the file link to his contact when his mobile rang. Roux had briefly outlined the circumstances and situation, and had been made to promise that he would do nothing until they called again.

It was almost three hours before the second call came. 'Play it safe' was the watchword. Act perfectly normally. Everything as usual. Do nothing that might offer any clue that something extraordinary had happened. Don't let anyone in on it who didn't know already. Did anyone else know? Yes? Then make sure they behaved in exactly the same way. 'Don't make a move. No police. Until our man comes. Play it safe.'

Tseng was taller than Roux had imagined; he towered above him. His shoulder-length hair was tied into a pony-tail and he must have been around thirty years of age.

He travelled with a small piece of hand luggage and a large suitcase. Both were on wheels but he carried them as if they weighed nothing. He'd spotted Roux's sign and now was coming towards him with large strides. Roux put on a smile, but Tseng didn't return it. He was on a serious mission.

Tseng greeted him with an iron handshake and a formal 'How do you do, Mr Roux?' that sounded like 'Ro-uggs'.

'Ru,' Roux corrected him.

On their way to the car park Roux plied his guest with small talk, asking about the flight and whether this was his first visit to Switzerland. Tseng's answers were monosyllabic.

Before they got into the car the Chinese man went on his hands and knees and checked the undercarriage with a small LED lamp. Then he searched the boot with rapid, professional hand movements. He opened the bonnet and gave that a thorough inspection, and finally he undertook a meticulous examination of the BMW's interior.

Only then did he take his place in the passenger seat.

Roux watched Tseng in silence, considering his security measures over the top. Now he sat behind the wheel.

'Play it safe,' the Chinese man said.

On the drive to the hotel Roux was given his instructions. He felt just like a chauffeur again.

20

Circus Pellegrini

11 June 2016

Strange, Reber thought when he hung up. Everything had been fine with Trisha on his last visit and the next one wasn't due for a fortnight.

Pellegrini had called and asked him to come by specially. He wasn't happy with Trisha.

'What's wrong with her?'

'I'd like to get your opinion on that. She's behaving funnily somehow.'

'What does Kaung think?'

Pellegrini sounded irritated. 'Can you come or should I ask Dr Hess?'

Reber promised to be there in a couple of hours.

Couldn't he come sooner? Pellegrini asked.

He was on his way to a patient, Reber lied. He could hardly tell Pellegrini that Barisha was due her next feed in an hour.

'You do house visits on Saturdays too?'

'I'm afraid animals don't stick to working hours,' came Reber's reply. As soon as he was off the phone he sent Kaung a text with their agreed message. 'Call,' it said.

It was twenty minutes before Kaung was able to phone

in private. Reber told him about Pellegrini's call and asked what was wrong with Trisha.

'Trisha okay,' Kaung replied.

'Pellegrini says he's worried. That she's behaving funnily.'

'Trisha okay. But director funny.'

Reber laughed. 'Isn't he always?'

'Now nervous too. Perhaps because of China man.'

'What sort of China man?'

'Is here.'

'An artiste?'

'Too tall for artiste.'

An hour later Reber fed Barisha, took her to the stable, left some twigs, locked the door and drove off.

It had turned a little warmer, but there were still patches of snow by the side of the road.

During the drive to Dondikon he mulled over what might be behind this. Not once since he'd started looking after the circus elephants had Pellegrini ever called himself. If there was something out of the ordinary Kaung would have taken the initiative. Kaung knew when an elephant needed a vet.

The more he thought about it, the stranger it seemed. It was as if Pellegrini were looking for an excuse to meet him. Did he suspect?

He briefly considered turning around, but then he put his concern down to the paranoia that had gripped him since Barisha's birth. Reber drove on.

Dondikon Common was a gloomy place even in the sunshine. Nearby were a few industrial buildings, pig sheds, farmhouses with enormous silos, a community hall, a petrol station and an exhibition space for agricultural equipment and vehicles. In the near distance was a wood, and where it met a narrow road stood a sign that read: 'Shooting Range'. There was a field with a few sad cows, and in front of it the common where Circus Pellegrini was set up.

Reber parked his SUV in the car park, took his case from the boot and went to the director's caravan.

Having seen him approach through the window, Pellegrini opened the door before Reber could ring the bell. 'Thanks for coming so quickly,' he said. 'Shall we go and see her straight away?'

On the way to the animal tent Pellegrini remarked, 'I may be mistaken, I mean I'm not exactly an elephant expert.' He followed this with a nervous laugh.

'Better to have rung the doctor one too many times,' Reber said, in direct contradiction to what he believed.

Trisha was in the pen beside Rupashi. Kaung was there, mucking out the stalls. He nodded to the two men and wheeled out the barrow full of dung.

Reber looked at the elephant cow. 'What struck you about her?'

'She's just different from usual. Unsettled. Nervous. Jumpy.'

Reber walked around Trisha, patted her trunk, looked into her eyes and lifted her tail.

'Any external indications? Discharge, diarrhoea, mucus?'

Pellegrini thought about this. 'No, I didn't notice anything concrete. It's more of a feeling. Quite possibly I'm mistaken. But I just don't want to lose another calf.'

'What does Kaung think?'

'He thinks she's okay. But Kaung's been wrong in the past too. That time with Sadaf, for example. He didn't anticipate that she'd be capable of killing her baby.'

Kaung returned with a bucketful of carrots and apples. If he'd heard Pellegrini's last comment he wasn't letting on.

'At any rate I'd be most grateful if you could take the time to give her a thorough examination. I'll be in the office if you need anything.'

Reber followed him to the exit.

'Where are you going?' Pellegrini asked, slightly shocked.

'I can't perform a thorough examination without an ultrasound scan. I need to fetch the kit from my car.'

The director looked as if he was going to demur, but all he said was, 'In that case we're heading in the same direction,' and went in front. Particularly slowly, Reber thought, as if he were carrying a heavy load.

At the door to the office he remarked again that he may have been wrong about Trisha, but he just wanted to make sure that he hadn't missed something. Only then did he enter his caravan.

Reber continued on his way to the car park. From a distance he saw a tall man with long hair, who looked briefly in his direction before getting into the passenger seat of a black car.

Reber couldn't be sure, but the man may well have had East Asian features.

* * *

Everything was fine with Trisha; Reber could tell this even without an hour-long examination. Now he drove a little faster than normal to make sure that he was back in time for Barisha's next feed.

Kaung was right: Pellegrini, not Trisha, was behaving strangely. Everything the director claimed to have observed about the elephant actually applied to himself: unsettled, nervous, jumpy.

Was Kaung also right in his suspicion that this might be connected to the Chinese man? And was this the person he'd seen in the car park? He was certainly tall, possibly Chinese too.

In any event, his fear that Pellegrini might have suspected the truth had proved unfounded. He'd surely have confronted Reber otherwise. Despite everything else you could say about Pellegrini, he was pretty straightforward.

But why had he made Reber come to the circus?

Whatever the truth, it couldn't hurt to be a little wary.

Once home he went straight to the stables. When he unlocked the door and was greeted by Barisha he felt relief. Even more than usual.

21

Berner Oberland

12 June 2016

'We'd have had enough time to drive to his house and just take it.'

'Better play it safe,' the man from Beijing replied as expected.

Roux had picked up Tseng early that morning from his hotel, a faceless new construction near Gentecsa. The Chinese man had insisted on this choice because of its location. Since his arrival he'd spent hours replacing the locks in the laboratories with hi-tech locking devices he'd brought with him, and installing all manner of surveillance and alarm gimmickry. The plan was to bring the dwarf elephant directly to the laboratory, take tissue samples and keep it there until Beijing reported success that could be built on. Only then would the sensation be introduced to the public.

Tseng's fussiness and nit-picking was royally getting on Roux's nerves. If it had been down to Roux, the man could have already been on the plane back home with the cell material.

But no. For Tseng everything had to be meticulously prepared and made failsafe twice, three times. No room for improvisation.

Roux had thought it a great idea for Pellegrini to summon Reber to the circus. Until he learned that Tseng was going to exploit the opportunity merely to attach a gizmo to Reber's car, allowing him to pinpoint his location at any time.

And then Reber had almost caught him red-handed! It had been Roux's turn to say, 'Play it safe,' but the Chinese man had dismissed his concerns, saying, 'No problem.' Another of his stock phrases.

Now they were sitting in an ordinary-looking Renault hire car with forged Chinese papers – as a precaution – beside a toolshed somewhere in the Oberland, staring at the display on Tseng's large smartphone. The flashing red dot near Graufeld, not ten minutes from where they were, hadn't moved for hours. Eventually even Tseng was satisfied that they would be ready to make their move as soon as Reber was far away enough from his house.

Roux was freezing, but Tseng wouldn't allow him to start the car to warm it up a little. 'Too conspicuous,' he said.

He found the Chinese man's taciturnity especially wearing. Roux was too on edge to keep quiet; it would be a welcome distraction if he could chat to someone. Like Pellegrini, who was also a bundle of nerves, but didn't express it in silence. Pellegrini and Roux had talked in a state of high excitement together and for the duration of their conversation had been able to forget how tense they were about the miraculous creature.

The dot moved. Roux's heart missed a beat.

22

Graufeld

The same day

Reber was at home alone with Barisha. He put on his baggy tracksuit – why on earth he possessed a *tracksuit* was a mystery to him – and carried Barisha downstairs into the kitchen. He lit the stove and realised that he was out of bread. A Sunday morning without bread was unimaginable.

Reber put the elephant in the sitting room and gave her a few pieces of apple as a first breakfast. Then he locked the door and drove to the village bakery.

At the entrance he bumped into Rita, the waitress at Löwen, carrying a bagful of rolls. 'Did the circus director find you?' she asked.

'Which circus director?'

'From Circus Pellegrini. How many circus directors do you get coming to visit you?'

'Oh, him. When was that?'

She thought about it. 'Thursday, I think. He didn't find you then. And I did him such a lovely map. Sepp says he's a friend of Dorothy.'

Reber didn't understand.

'Gay. Sepp says he's gay.'

'Could be.'

'Shame.'

Reber bought two rolls and drove back home.

Pellegrini had come looking for him? So why hadn't he found him?

The snow on the path to the front door had melted, all that remained was the trampled wet snow from the first flurry, which was now a layer of ice. Reber saw his own footprints coming and going.

Close to the front door a trail broke off from the path and led to his bench. Although he couldn't make out the pattern on the sole, it was a different shape. He followed the prints to the bench and saw that the person who'd left them had climbed up.

Reber got up himself. He only reached as far as the window sill and wasn't able to look inside. But it wouldn't have been a problem for a taller man.

Pellegrini was taller.

Reber leaped down from the bench and ran into the house.

23

The same day

If the pulsating red dot passed Graufeld they would get moving too. Roux started his motor when the dot reached the centre of the village. But it stopped. Roux turned off the engine.

A few minutes later the dot started moving again quickly in the opposite direction, then stopped at Reber's house.

'Shit!' Roux exclaimed.

Tseng showed no emotion; he just sat there and waited.

He didn't need to wait long. The digital clock on the display showed eight minutes before the red dot got moving once more.

This time it drove past Graufeld. And fast.

Roux started the engine and was about to pull away. But Tseng laid a hand on his forearm. 'Wait,' he said. 'Two more minutes.'

These two minutes seemed to Roux like an eternity.

When the Chinese man finally said, 'Go!' he put his foot down so hard that he left two black tyre marks outside the shed.

'Too conspicuous,' Tseng muttered, before falling silent until they reached Brudermatte Farm. 'Wait here!' he ordered.

This was too much for Roux. Pointing to his chest, he said, 'My elephant!' and followed Tseng.

They rang the bell like bona fide visitors, hoping that nobody would answer.

After a while they rang again, and then Tseng took a bunch of skeleton keys from his bag and opened the door as if he were holding the genuine key.

The front door led straight into the warm kitchen. In the sink was a small pot full of milky water. The door to a sitting room stood ajar. The heat from a green tiled stove filled the room.

On the floor Roux discovered a slice of apple and a colourful rubber ring. And something else: tiny balls, perhaps a little larger than goat poo. He lifted one up; it was crumbly like elephant dung.

'Tseng!' he called out.

No reply.

He went into the kitchen. The third door, which had been shut when they came in, was now open to the barn. There Tseng stood by another door, picking its lock.

They entered an empty stall, which was set up like a miniature elephant pen. There were small logs, stones and hollows, some filled with water, and bare branches fixed vertically into the ground like small trees, with balls hanging from them.

And everywhere the tiny droppings, one of which Roux was still holding and now tossed to the ground with the others.

No pink mini elephant anywhere to be seen.

Roux was certain that Reber had smelled a rat and done a runner with the animal. But Tseng searched the entire house before he gave in to Roux's urging and followed him to the car.

On the screen the red dot was already near the city.

'Shit!' Roux shouted again.

24

Zürich

The same day

Reber didn't have a plan. He'd often worried that something might go wrong and he'd have his cover blown, and each time he'd concluded that he'd have to flee with Barisha and hide somewhere. But where? It was a question he'd never been able to answer.

To begin with he'd thought that the only ethical way out of the situation was to put the result of the experiment to sleep and ensure that not a single cell remained. But that was a theoretical scenario, a scientific one, so to speak. At the time he hadn't been quite so fond of Barisha as he was now.

He realised that by running away he was putting everything on the line – his existence and his future. But Reber didn't care. Some things were more important.

There was hardly any traffic on that dismal Sunday morning and he made good progress. Or at least as good progress as you could make if you had no destination in mind. But he didn't need a destination. Instinctively he drove towards the city. Where else? He knew his way around Zürich better than anywhere else. And if you had to hide, you'd be best off doing it somewhere familiar.

Zürich was where he'd been born, gone to school, studied, fallen in love and got divorced. The city was so full of memories that once upon a time he'd had to escape it. Now he was on the run again, however, he couldn't think of anywhere else to go.

He drove through the woods of the recreation area. In the car parks on the fringe of the woods stood vehicles belonging to a few indefatigable joggers and hikers. Soon he was passing the first properties on the Villenhügel; in better visibility he would have had a view of the city and the lake from here.

Barisha was standing in an open shoulder bag in the footwell of the passenger seat. She'd stood the entire way, as if frozen. She froze each time something unusual happened. When she heard unfamiliar voices. Or when he left her alone in an unfamiliar place. The first time she'd had to wait for him in the sitting room, he found her three hours later in the same position as when he'd left. Judging by the heaps of dung behind her she hadn't moved from the spot.

Now, too, she only moved to maintain her balance, when Reber braked or took a bend. This was the second car journey of her life, the first having been the taxi ride with Kaung on the day she was born.

Kaung! He'd forgotten Kaung!

He stopped so abruptly by the side of the road that he was only just able to prevent Barisha from falling over. Reber took his mobile from the pocket of his tracksuit bottoms and typed, 'Call!' Reber waited for a while, but there was no response.

He kept driving through the 30 kph zone, where the

214

properties now became smaller and the villas were more densely built.

At the junction where the road led down steeply into the city centre, he paused briefly, then turned right to the north, heading for the suburbs and the river.

It started to rain.

25

The same day

'Big mistake!' Roux said again furiously.

Tseng didn't respond. The first time he'd pointed out that if he hadn't taken the precaution of attaching the tracker to Reber's car they wouldn't now have a clue where Reber and the tiny elephant were. After that he ignored Roux.

Roux knew that Tseng was right. He just needed someone to blame. And he was too nervous to say nothing.

Reber was heading straight for the city. They were roughly twenty minutes behind him and, as Reber seemed to be observing the speed limit, Roux could make up some ground. Not as much as he would have liked, because Tseng kept slowing him down with his 'too conspicuous'.

It was asking a little much of Roux to stay patient, so close to their goal. But of course Tseng was right. It was crucial they kept their nerve and avoided doing anything rash. And now it had started raining too. Shit!

For a while it looked as if Reber was going to drive right into the city centre. Or perhaps straight through and then onto the motorway heading south. Italy!

'I hope he's not aiming for Italy!' Roux couldn't help but say it out loud. 'If we have to follow a pink elephant through Italy then it's game over!' He burst into hysterical laughter. Tseng looked at him in astonishment and pointed at the display.

The red dot had turned off and was now heading north. Was he making for Basel? France? Germany?

Tseng gave him another tap on the forearm; in his fervour Roux had been driving too quickly again. He took his foot slightly off the accelerator.

They were approaching the industrial district by the river when Tseng pointed to the display. 'Slow,' he ordered.

Reber had turned off the main road and was driving slowly through the district by the river.

Now he stopped.

Tseng switched the map to satellite view.

On the screen was an aerial shot of the area where Reber had stopped.

Tseng zoomed in on the spot. 'Recognise?'

Of course Roux recognised it. Those were the allotments beside the river path. Did Reber have an allotment? Was he planning on hiding there?

Ten minutes later they found Reber's SUV in a parking space for the allotments at the end of a cul-de-sac. 'Stop!' Tseng ordered.

Roux stopped at the side of the narrow street. Another car wouldn't be able to pass coming the other way.

Tseng took out his small binoculars from the bag and gazed at the vehicle for what seemed like an eternity.

'Well?' Roux asked for the third time, when the Chinese man put down his binoculars and stated, 'Car empty.'

'Shit!'

'Go!' Tseng ordered, pointing at Reber's car.

Roux drove the Renault up to the SUV and stopped three parking spaces away. Apart from them there were two estate cars. A sign said, 'Plot-holders only!!' Beneath that was a clumsy drawing of a tow truck.

They got out and strolled up to the SUV. In the boot they could see the pilot bag that Roux could remember Reber using for his veterinary equipment, and the black cloth bags he transported his ultrasound gear in.

On the back seat lay a wheelie suitcase.

While Roux was still peering through the windows, Tseng had already opened the driver's door and unlocked the rear doors. He opened the suitcase, which consisted of hastily packed clothes, washing, some fruit and vegetables, a Thermos flask and an empty baby bottle.

Tseng closed the car door and pointed to the narrow footpath that led between the allotments to the river.

26

The same day

The allotments had been an inspiration.

As a student Reber had had a girlfriend whose parents were allotmenteers. Allotmenteers, that's what they'd called themselves. They'd leased a plot here by the river and grown their vegetables. Record-breaking specimens, not biodynamic or organic, but cultivated with highly potent artificial fertilisers they secretly mixed into their home-made compost, and with fungicides and pesticides that they stirred discreetly into the infusions of nettle and horsetail.

Nora had hated them for this. Not because it was dishonest, but because they used the only smidgen of deviousness in their bones for something as petty as screwing other petty individuals in a competition for the largest pumpkin or the most abundant head of lettuce.

But the allotment had its good side too. Outside the growing season the garden hut was an ideal love nest for a student couple who still lived with prudish parents and didn't have the money for a hotel room.

This hut was a perfect hideaway for a few days. Although they were in the middle of the growing season there wasn't much gardening to be done in this washout June.

Reber felt confident he'd find the plot again even after all these years. He certainly hadn't forgotten the name of the hut: Blue Bayou. Nora hadn't stopped apologising for this either.

All of a sudden there he was, outside it. It was now called дома, rather than Blue Bayou, and the Macedonian flag flew from the roof, whipped in the wind that was building up to a storm. The vegetable beds were a little smaller than he remembered, but now there was a built-in barbecue, its chimney inset with painted ceramic plates.

The plot-holders must have changed, so Reber didn't even bother to check whether the key was still in its old place, resting on the diagonal beam that supported the right-hand side of the gable over the door.

He glanced in the shoulder bag. Barisha had lain down, but she wasn't asleep. Her eyes peered up anxiously at him.

Reber turned around and walked along the narrow path back to the car.

In the distance he saw two figures coming his way. He crouched beneath a blooming lilac tree bending heavy and wet over a fence, and spied through the leaves. A tall man and a shorter one. The taller one had East Asian features. The other was Dr Roux.

He crouched down and hurried from his hiding place.

He didn't know whether they'd seen him and were now following.

Reber's excess weight was a hindrance, while the bag with Barisha further impeded his progress. If they were after him, he'd have no chance of shaking them off. His only hope was to remain undetected.

He reached the river path. Reber knew his way around, because he'd often come swimming here as a youngster. He crossed the path and climbed down the overgrown embankment. Stumbling and slipping, he headed towards the river, using each bush and willow as cover.

Behind a group of shrubs he got his breath back and noticed that here the earth beneath the river path had been eroded, creating a cave. He climbed in and tried to stifle his panting.

Footsteps approached quickly then went away again. Soon afterwards came more laboured footsteps and a man's voice, out of breath, exclaimed, 'Shit!' His pursuers had passed him.

But they'd soon realise that he couldn't be so far ahead of them and they'd come back to search the embankment. It wouldn't be long before they discovered him. Before Barisha fell into their hands.

He opened the bag, took out the tiny elephant and whispered, 'Wait here. I'll be back soon.'

Reber slid on his knees deep into the cave and put Barisha down where the roof and floor met.

He crept back to the entrance and peered out. Far ahead he saw the Chinese man. He'd stopped and was waiting for Roux, who'd stopped running and was now sauntering to his companion, hands on hips and head bowed.

Reber put the empty bag on his shoulder, crept out of the cave and, as soon as he was certain that the two men weren't looking in his direction, slid down the embankment.

Upstream stood willows, their low-hanging boughs tugged by the brown mass of water. Reber hid behind their trunks and spied on his pursuers.

Roux had now caught up with the Chinese man and they were in conversation. The Chinese man pointed in the direction they'd been running in, while he himself started heading in the other direction. Loose-limbed, he sped towards Reber.

Reber crouched as low as he could behind his cover and waited till the man had gone past.

The two had divided up their hunting ground. Reber couldn't stay where he was; he was too close to where Barisha was hiding. Faced with the choice between the bloodhounds, he chose the slower one and headed in the direction Roux was going.

As far as the weir the vegetation on the embankment was so dense that he could move undetected. But after that it grew more sparse. Reber could see Roux just before the railway bridge and waited until he'd entered the pedestrian underpass by the bridge pier. Then he made a run for it.

Before he could reach his next cover, however, Roux came back out of the narrow tunnel entrance and spotted him.

Reber froze.

Grinning, Roux took his mobile out of his pocket and calmly dialled a number. While he spoke a few words into the phone he moved towards Reber. He put the mobile away and kept walking until he was standing directly above him.

Reber began heading down to the river again.

Roux didn't follow him. 'Go ahead!' he called out. 'My friend will be here any minute! He was with the Chinese Snow Leopards, the best commando unit in the world!'

Reber stopped again. He'd seen the Chinese man run. He didn't stand a chance. He started clambering up the embankment; Barisha was safe for the time being.

When he saw the Chinese man trotting towards him in the distance he stopped. It wouldn't take him five minutes to get whatever information he wanted out of Reber.

At that very moment his mobile rang and, after a brief hesitation, he took it out of his pocket.

The screen said 'Kaung'. He answered and said softly, 'In a cave by the river where the allotments are,' switched off the phone and put it back.

Now he carefully lifted the shoulder bag, as if it contained something valuable, opened the zip and pretended to whisper a few words into it. Then he went down to the riverbank, took off his trainers, tied them together, held them by the laces and entered the water. It wouldn't be the first time he'd crossed this river, even with the water like this.

'Hey! Are you off your head?' Roux called out.

The water was freezing. Reber held the bag by the shoulder strap and let it swim on the surface as he used to do with his clothes when he was going for a long swim in the river.

'Hey!' Roux shouted. 'Heeeey!'

Reber looked back. The Chinese man was running along the river path downstream. Roux followed at a considerable distance.

The river was taking him quickly. He put the shoulder strap around his neck to free up both his arms for swimming.

He had to reach the other side before the weir.

27

The same day

He ought to have slid down the embankment and appre-hended Reber before Tseng arrived. Now all he could do was watch him swim away. With the mini elephant and all his hopes and dreams.

That fucking Chinaman and his over-cautiousness!

Exhausted, Roux ran along the river in the pouring rain. Far ahead was Tseng, the only hope of salvaging the fruit of his research.

Half a kilometre below the weir was a pedestrian bridge. Roux crossed it and took the path upstream.

A soaked cyclist came towards him.

'Did you pass a tall Chinese man?'

The cyclist shrugged.

Roux hurried on, but he couldn't run any more.

The path led into a small wood, where all of a sudden he heard someone calling his name: 'Ru!'

He stopped and looked around. Again: 'Ru! Here!'

The voice was coming from the embankment. 'Come!' it called.

Spying Tseng between the trees, Roux climbed down to him.

For more than an hour they searched the riverbank as

far as the hydraulic power station, where they stood for a while, staring at the flotsam in the grille. Neither Reber nor Roux's dwarf elephant were there.

They gave up and went back upstream to the allotments.

The rental car and Reber's SUV were the only vehicles in the car park. Notes were tucked behind the windscreen wipers of both cars, which read: 'Next time you'll be towed away!!!'

The only option left now was to drive off and keep monitoring the SUV via the tracker.

28

The same day

They were about a kilometre away from Reber's car, watching for movement on the screen. Tseng thought that Reber would wait until the coast was clear and then return to his vehicle. Roux doubted this. Unlike the man from Beijing he didn't believe that Reber would worry about abandoning his car with all the equipment. For what were a few ultrasound devices when you had a mini elephant?

Tseng also thought it possible that Reber had drowned. But Roux didn't believe this either; the man was a strong swimmer. Pellegrini had told him that in his youth Reber had been a member of the national squad. You don't forget how to swim.

But that didn't mean the mini elephant had survived.

If it hadn't, it was vital they recovered the corpse as quickly as possible so that the cells were still usable, i.e. clonable.

Nothing was moving on the screen.

From time to time Roux got out to smoke a cigarette. At one point he went to a nearby petrol station and bought sandwiches and mineral water.

It was getting dark. Perhaps Reber was waiting for nightfall to return to his car unobserved.

But when night came the dot on the screen was still motionless.

Around one o'clock Roux suggested they took turns to keep watch. Tseng went first and was going to wake him in two hours. But when he shook Roux awake it was daylight and commuter traffic was on the road. It was seven o'clock.

Tseng pointed at the screen. The dot was moving!

They waited until they were at a safe distance before setting off.

The dot moved slowly out of the city. Past the former industrial district to the current one, where it crossed the railway tracks and came to a stop on the other side.

Roux stopped too.

They waited five, ten, fifteen minutes before driving to the car's location.

It was full of parked cars and the entrance was blocked by a gate, above which a sign read: 'Toptow Towing Service'.

The allotmenteers had made good on their threat.

29

13 June 2016

When he was at his second highest level of frustration, Roux was talkative. At his highest, he was silent. He drove the car grimly and without a word through the early morning traffic back to the river, and left it in a car park from which it wouldn't be towed away.

Grey rain fell from the overcast sky. They shared the yellow umbrella with the car rental firm's logo and walked past the allotments to the riverbank. The two men wandered slowly along the path, scouring the embankment with their eyes.

An old man in a poncho was standing by his mini greenhouse, pinching out the side shoots of a tomato plant. 'Lost something?' he called out to the two men.

Before Tseng could stop him, Roux said, 'Yesterday a friend of ours went swimming in the river and hasn't been seen since.'

'Have you informed the police?'

'He's an excellent swimmer.'

'Upstream or downstream?' the elderly man asked.

Roux pointed upstream. 'Up there,' he said. 'By the bridge.'

'Upstream from the whirlpool of death, then,' the allotmenteer said.

Roux and Tseng didn't understand.

The man came out of the gate. 'Come on, I'll show you.'

He walked slightly ahead until they reached a point not far from his allotment, where bushes and willows blocked the view of the river. The man walked on until through the vegetation they could see a small platform and a long rescue pole. A sign carried the warning: 'Only to be used in an emergency!'

'If he didn't manage to get ashore before this point then he's fish food, I don't care how good a swimmer he is. When the river rises to this level an eddy forms here that refuses to let anything or anyone go. Many a poor soul has drowned in the past. They spin around and around until they're propelled here. And then this is where you fish them out.'

Roux and Tseng stared at the brown spume from which a piece of driftwood, a car tyre and a mangled shopping trolley kept bobbing up then disappearing again.

'If I were you, I'd notify the police,' the old man advised them, before returning to his tomatoes.

The two men kept staring at the eddy. 'Shit!' Roux cursed.

Tseng took the rescue pole from the hooks and plunged it into the whirlpool.

The car tyre almost knocked the pole from his hand, then vanished again.

Tseng kept prodding about. The hook at the end of the pole got caught in the shopping trolley. He almost lost his balance and Roux hurried to his assistance. Combining forces they managed to haul their catch ashore.

A knot of twigs and rubbish had got caught round the shaft. Tseng freed it and unravelled it on the platform. The tangle had formed around a pair of worn-out trainers tied together by the laces.

Roux cursed again. 'His shoes. He took them off before getting into the water.' He lifted the pole, submerged it as deeply as he could in the eddy and pulled it back up.

'Hey! Hello!' a voice called out. 'Has someone fallen in?'

Roux turned around. On the river path stood a bearded man wearing a yellow raincoat like a roadworker.

'My dog!' Roux cried.

The man raised his shoulders and shook his head. 'Whirlpool of death,' he shouted. 'Nothing gets out of there alive. It's swallowed plenty already. Forget the dog and concentrate on not falling in yourselves!'

Roux ignored the tramp and turned back to the river fall. 'Thanks!' he heard Tseng call out in English.

Always polite, this loser.

30

The same day

The more he thought about it, the stranger the whole thing seemed. A friend tried to swim across the river yesterday? In this weather? With the water this high? And hasn't been seen since? And they're not telling the police, but searching the riverbank themselves?

Albert Hadorn stood up with a groan. Your back's going to put you in a wheelchair, his wife had always said. She'd been dead for more than ten years now, while he was still picking snails out of the beds on rainy days.

He carried the brown earthenware dish in which he usually let his potato salad marinate – he was famous for his potato salad – into the hut, filled the kettle and switched it on. The kettle immediately started singing.

Maybe those men had something to do with the two unfamiliar cars in the car park yesterday. One of them bore the logo of a rental company – that would fit the Chinese man. He'd given them a chance, warned them in writing! The rental car had availed itself of this chance and vanished before the tow truck came. The light-grey Land Cruiser, on the other hand, had been nabbed.

Albert counted eighteen snails, a few of which were trying to escape. No doubt word had got around the snail community of the fate awaiting them. He pushed them back with his finger. As ever he'd forgotten to put on his gardening gloves for this task. It was almost impossible to get the slime off your fingers afterwards.

Maybe he ought to call the police.

The kettle beeped. He took it from its base and poured the boiling water over the snails in the bowl. Not especially nice, but better than the methods employed by a few others on the allotments: cutting them with clippers or using salt, sugar or pellets.

He took the bowl outside and tipped the dead snails into the compost. Then he called the police and noted the time.

It took twenty-eight minutes for a patrol car to arrive, its lights flashing and sirens howling! He showed the two officers to the weir, but if the men hadn't already left before then the sirens would have sent them packing. Unless they had nothing to hide, an assumption he found more unlikely the longer he thought about it.

On the platform by the whirlpool of death lay a broken shopping trolley beside a pair of trainers, tied together by the laces.

He gave the policemen the two car registration numbers, having noted them yesterday for the tow-away service.

One of the officers moved away and spoke into his radio. Albert Hadorn looked at his watch.

It was almost two hours before a river police recovery boat was put out onto the water.

And almost three before they hauled aboard the heavy body of a man in a tracksuit.

A shoulder bag hung around his neck.

Part Three

1

Zürich

12 June 2016

Despite the strange phone call, Kaung had milked Rupashi, but he'd suspected that something bad had happened. The suspicion became a certainty later that evening, when Hans told him at their secret rendezvous that he hadn't found Reber when he went to pick up the empty Thermos.

Half crazy with worry about Barisha, Kaung spontaneously changed his plans and jumped into Hans's car.

Brudermatte Farm was in darkness. They'd fetched Hans's mother, who had a key.

The house looked as if Reber had left in a great hurry. The stable door, which was always locked, stood open. For the first time Frau Huber and her son saw the miniature elephant pen and tiny balls of dung, and wondered what kind of an animal the vet was keeping here.

Kaung retired to the guest room. He was going to wait for Reber to get back.

He spent the night in meditation and prayer, his hopes fading in the fragrance of his incense sticks.

The following morning he drove back to the circus with Hans and decided to milk Rupashi nonetheless.

When he handed Hans the Thermos he made him promise to call if there was any news.

But it was Frau Huber who called, in tears. Two policemen had turned up at the door and told her that Dr Reber had drowned in the Limmat. She was being asked to go to Zürich and identify the body.

That afternoon came the confirmation that it really was Reber. An empty shoulder bag had been found hanging around his neck, which had got caught in the river fall and strangled him. Even though he'd once been a champion swimmer.

Kaung went to Pellegrini's secretary to ask her what the word 'allotment' meant.

'Why do you want to know?' she asked.

'Learn better German.'

He embarked on his hunt for Barisha. In between training and the show he took the train into town and walked from the station to the river.

On the river path he met a homeless man wearing a raincoat like a roadworker and carrying a holdall. He was unsteady on his feet.

'Please, where is cave?' Kaung asked.

He had to ask twice before the man understood.

'No caves here,' he replied.

Kaung wasn't satisfied with this answer. 'You sure?'

'Piss off,' the homeless man growled at him.

The following day he had more luck, asking an old man who was working on the allotments. He laughed and said, 'Caves? They're all occupied.'

So there were caves.

And he found it the next day, hidden beneath the river path. There were clothes stuffed inside, while dried twigs, grass and leaves lay on the floor. And it smelled of elephant! On the ground he saw dried dung. And tiny elephant prints in the sand! Barisha had been here!

He stayed in the cave until he had to leave to get back to the circus in time.

When he returned the following day the clothes were gone.

And a day after that the cave had been cleaned.

On this occasion Pellegrini was waiting for him and he asked Kaung what he'd been looking for down by the Limmat.

After the show Kaung packed a bag and said goodbye to each of his elephants. 'Little sacred elephant alive,' he told them. 'Must find her.'

2

Circus Pellegrini

18 June 2016

Kaung's disappearance was a problem for a number of reasons.

It was a problem for the circus because the elephant act had to be improvised. Pellegrini came into the ring in his tailcoat and stood there in the spotlight, arms outstretched, until Ben and two other circus workers managed to coax the elephants in.

They put their legs up on a podium only with reluctance and if Willi, the long-serving circus clown, hadn't been inspired to make a comic routine out of the director and his disobedient elephants, they'd probably have been booed off. But at least this way they got some applause and a few laughs when the elephants ignored Pellegrini's commands, while little Willi fruitlessly scolded the huge animals and grovelled his apologies to the director for their insubordination.

The circus orchestra improvised too, accompanying the act with crashing and spinning sounds, and Laurel and Hardy music.

For Roux and Tseng the problem was that Kaung's disappearance had severed their last connection to the mini elephant. They'd hoped that Reber might have given it to someone or hidden it somewhere before he'd gone into the river. And that the oozie could lead them to it.

A pretty unlikely scenario, maybe, but Reber had taken a phone call before embarking on his mad swim. From Kaung, perhaps?

To check this, during a performance Tseng had stolen Kaung's mobile from his caravan and scrolled through the caller list and text messages. Or that had been his intention, but Kaung had deleted all his calls and messages.

The move had not been entirely in vain, however. He'd installed a geolocation app on Kaung's phone, which allowed them to discover where he went in his few hours out of the circus. He'd gone to the banks of the river, where Reber had drowned.

But Roux and Tseng had failed to tell Pellegrini this, which was a silly mistake. Because he'd received the same information as them, albeit from a different source, when his secretary told him that Kaung had asked what 'allotment' meant.

And that oaf Pellegrini only went and asked Kaung what he was looking for in the allotments by the river!

A few hours later Kaung had vanished. He'd left his mobile behind.

3

Zürich

The same day

Valerie Sommer had dealt with alcoholics too often to be bothered by a relapse.

The moment she entered the kitchen she could see what was wrong. Dirty dishes in the sink, Sabu's droppings on the floor, empty wine bottles on the table in the staff area where they tended to eat.

Schoch wasn't obsessive about order, but nor was she. Still, for a homeless alcoholic on the wagon he'd been surprisingly neat and tidy up to now.

Valerie put the shopping down on one of the sideboards and took the lift.

When the lift door opened she could hear him singing: 'The moon has risen high, stars glitter in the sky, the night is clear and bright.' His voice was remarkably tuneful.

As she entered the room, a comic scene greeted her: Schoch beside the bed on all fours, singing to Sabu, who was presumably curled up beneath it.

When he saw Valerie he got up uncertainly and slurred, 'I'm singing my lap elephant a lullaby. What do you think of "lap elephant"? I'm going to trademark the term and sell it to those who breed Sabus. Lap elephants.'

Valerie didn't reply.

Schoch started singing again and Valerie started tidying up.

It had been a mistake to believe that he'd manage it without help. The most dogged alcoholics were those who claimed they weren't. Not for nothing did you have to start off at Alcoholics Anonymous by announcing your name and saying, 'I am an alcoholic.'

What hope did she have of protecting Sabu from the genetic engineering industry if she left her in the care of a homeless alcoholic?

While deliberating what to do she stumbled across the dark-blue suede bag that her mother had bought for Sally, her chihuahua. Sally used to bark incessantly, lived to almost sixteen years old and lost all her hair by the end. Inside the bag was some of Sabu's dung and her mother's black Persian stole.

She knew at once what that meant. And now she *was* going to make an issue of Schoch's relapse.

'Have you already gone for a stroll or is that still to come?' she yelled at him, holding the bag and stole under his nose.

'Both,' was his laconic answer.

'Did anyone see you?'

'Yes. Me and my dwarf poodle.'

Sabu, who by now had crept out from under the bed, looked faintly terrified. Valerie had never been this loud.

'Where were you?'

Schoch's answer sounded defiant: 'At home.'

'Why, for heaven's sake?'

'I was homesick.'

Valerie shook her head, sighed and slumped into an armchair.

'Plus I wanted to check if my things were still there. But they weren't.'

Valerie paused to compose herself, then asked, 'Do you plan on making any other excursions?'

'It was spontaneous. I don't plan spontaneous things.'

'You just do them when you're pissed enough.' She was getting annoyed and now she sounded like an alcoholic's wife.

'I drink spontaneously too.'

'I'm afraid you're going to have to modify that in future. I don't give a shit how much you drink and when. But you can't do it spontaneously any more. You have to coordinate it with me first. Someone has to look after Sabu. Is that clear?'

She got up from the armchair and left the room, hopping mad. With him, but also with herself.

4

Zürich

19 June 2016

It took Schoch quite a while to realise where he was. From the dry mouth, sticky eyes and thumping heart it felt as if he were at home in the River Bed. But the air was muggy and it smelled of dust and stables.

He was in a dark room. The only light came from a tiny pink elephant.

Now fragments of his memory returned and assembled themselves to give the whole picture. The most irksome detail was that yesterday he'd been completely smashed.

He lay fully dressed on the carpet with Sabu standing beside him, swinging her trunk. He checked the time. Almost nine. Her breakfast was overdue.

Schoch pulled himself together and as he got to his feet the door opened and the light went on. Valerie was holding a tray with a full baby bottle, two cups of coffee, a bottle of water, a basket of croissants and another with pieces of carrot.

'Good morning, you two,' she said with slightly strained cheerfulness. She put the tray on the chest of drawers, filled a large glass with water and handed it to Schoch.

Now he recalled that she'd been angry yesterday. He also remembered why.

'Morning,' he replied, downing the glass in one.

She picked up the bottle and gave Sabu some to drink. 'You can't go downstairs, there are people there,' she said.

'What sort of people?'

'My father's wine dealers.'

'Why are you buying wine?'

'I'm not buying it, I'm selling it. There's quite a tidy sum to be made getting rid of his old vintages. Especially the clarets.'

'I see.' Schoch picked up the cup of coffee, hoping he wasn't coming across as too remorseful.

Maybe he would have managed it if he hadn't asked, 'Do I need to apologise?'

'Nonsense. If anyone does it's me.' After a pause for thought, she added, 'But we do need a plan.'

Both of them fell silent as if searching for one.

Schoch poured himself another glass of water and drank it. 'Got it. I simply won't drink any more.'

Valerie smiled. 'I mean a *good* plan.'

Having finished the bottle Sabu went over to Schoch and lifted her trunk. He took a few pieces of carrot from the basket and began feeding her.

After a while he looked up. Valerie was smiling at him. Only now did he realise that she must have been smiling the whole time he'd been feeding Sabu.

'If you think you can't cope, please let me know before-hand, would you? No more spontaneity.' Valerie drank up her coffee and went downstairs to see how the wine men were getting on.

5

The same day

It was a day like they hadn't had in a long time: blue sky, 23 degrees and a light summer breeze rustling the plane trees of Freiland Park. Mothers were chatting away at the sandpit, a jogger with headphones was doing his laps, lost to the world, and two uniformed workers from SIP – Security, Intervention, Prevention – ensured that the harmonious scene wasn't disrupted by the alcoholics, junkies and homeless people celebrating this long-awaited summer's day.

Among them was one-eyed Bolle, drawn to anywhere he could hope to meet others of his ilk.

He had two six-packs of litre beer cans that he generously offered for general consumption. Yesterday was the day he'd collected his weekly benefits from the Stadtkasse.

They'd mobbed two park benches and Bolle had to keep talking louder to drown the others out. Which wasn't particularly hard since on the way to Freiland Park he'd had a few pit stops – as he liked to call them – to refuel. Lilly had already knocked back the first beer and was now begging him for a second. She sat on Bolle's lap and started groping him.

'If you like I could come and visit you in your new cave,' she whispered, sticking her tongue into his ear.

'I'm not living in Schoch's cave, he's come back,' Bolle replied, rubbing his ear dry with his sleeve.

'Rubbish, Giorgio says Schoch hasn't been seen again. Can I have the other half?'

Bolle loosened a can from the six-pack and passed it to her. 'I saw him with my own eyes.'

'Where?'

'In the cave.'

'Did he say where he'd been?'

'Didn't ask.'

'Why not?'

'Bugger off and drink your beer.'

Lilly trudged off in a sulk.

By the late afternoon their spontaneous summer gathering had grown into a party. Word had got round all the usual hangouts that there was a bash in Freiland Park and so they arrived with their beer, wine and hooch. Even the dog lovers turned up; they usually stuck faithfully to their own patch.

Bolle's beer supplies were running low and now he had to rely on the generosity of others. That of the dog lovers, for example, who'd set up camp on the edge of the park and were cheering on their frolicking dogs.

'I brought twelve big ones. All necked,' Bolle said to Giorgio.

'Not by me,' Giorgio protested.

'You should've come earlier.'

Giorgio handed him a can. 'Right then, you saw Schoch in his cave, did you?'

Bolle opened the can and nodded.

'When was that?'

'Yesterday.'

'Are you sure?'

'Don't you believe me?'

'Why should I, given the crap you spout?'

'I'm not forcing anyone to believe me.'

'Funny. I live a hundred metres away and I've never seen him. Always empty.'

'I'm only saying what *I* saw.'

'Why didn't you ask him where he'd been, then?'

'Didn't want to intrude.'

'Because he would have realised you were after his sleeping place.'

Bolle got up. 'Thanks for the beer.'

Giorgio waved him away. 'I'm regretting it already.'

No longer completely sure on his legs, Bolle rejoined the other drinkers.

Nobody had noticed that a black bank of clouds had gathered in the west. Only when there was a rumble of thunder and the first gusts shook the plane trees did the raucous company look up at the sky and seek shelter under the canopy of Café Freiland.

Soon afterwards the raindrops fell heavily and noisily.

Bolle's voice could clearly be heard above the general racket: 'I've got to stop anyway or I'll start seeing little pink elephants again!'

6

The same day

On the way from his cave to the dog lovers' hangout, Giorgio had once counted 463 puddles, which is why he was keen to have the leptospirosis boosters done a few months earlier than planned. Although his dogs had learned not to drink out of puddles, thirst was sometimes stronger than reason. Nobody knew that better than Giorgio.

Access to the street clinic's waiting room was via Just a Second, Cynthia's second-hand clothes shop. This was the only drawback of the clinic, for Cynthia didn't let anyone pass without a 'natter', as she called it. Cynthia was American and had cultivated her accent since her arrival in Switzerland almost thirty years earlier. After embarking on a further education course at the art college, she was hooked. On a painter and performance artist.

It felt as if the main purpose of the shop was to satisfy Cynthia's own desire for clothes. She helped herself without restraint to the stock and wore the most outrageous combinations and garish items in her collection. Those things she'd worn and discarded after a while were sold in a corner of the shop marked 'Third Hand'.

It was said that Cynthia had a small annuity that an aunt had left her in her will. She never confirmed the rumour herself, but it was obvious that she couldn't make a living from Just a Second alone.

Cynthia, her hard-to-tame hair currently bright blonde with a slight hint of raspberry, was arranging the hangers on a clothes rack. She greeted Giorgio with the question, 'Has Schoch turned up again?'

'Not that I know of,' he replied.

'Strange. He was here just a few days ago.'

'Everyone's somewhere before they disappear,' Giorgio said, trying to get past her.

'Valerie had already closed up for the day, but she still saw him. And treated his dog.'

'Schoch doesn't have a dog.'

'Well, it may have been a cat. I didn't see the animal; he was carrying it in a bag. But …' She held her nose and rolled her eyes.

'What did Valerie say it was?'

'Vet confidentiality.'

Giorgio and his dog managed to get past Cynthia into the small waiting room. Ahead of them in the queue were three other dogs and a rat.

7

20 June 2016

Not drinking was going pretty well. The tremors improved and with enough distractions he sometimes forgot for a whole quarter of an hour that he was desperate for a drink.

Sabu was an excellent distraction. Schoch took short videos of her on the mobile and played with her when she demanded it. Or he simply watched her carry out her peculiar rituals: the one where she stood there motionless; when she mechanically took a step forward and then a step back; when she fanned her ears; when she put her ears forward, raised her trunk and launched mock attacks on the furnishings; when she withdrew under furniture as if seeking the darkness to glow more beautifully.

Occasionally Sabu just lay there without sleeping. Her eyes would be open but her gaze didn't follow him.

'She looks melancholy to me sometimes,' he once remarked to Valerie.

'Maybe she's missing someone. Elephants are very affectionate.'

'Maybe she was happy where she was. I've never thought about that.'

'I have. It can't have been easy to rear her from birth.'

'But why did they abandon her?'

Valerie shook her head. 'I expect that will remain a mystery for ever.'

Increasingly, it was Sabu who determined Schoch's daily routine. Which wasn't always easy for him, because without any booze he got tired much more rapidly and needed the occasional lie-down. Sometimes she let him sleep, but mostly she woke him up. If he was sleeping on the floor for old times' sake she'd use her trunk. When he lay on the bed out of her reach she'd trumpet. Although her noises were more like whistles and beeps, it was enough to wake him.

When Valerie wasn't on call she came twice a day. In the morning she'd have coffee with Schoch and give Sabu her first bottle, while in the evening she'd make something for them to eat. Schoch, whose appetite had returned now the ethanol had been discontinued – as Valerie put it – remarked, 'If you go on cooking like this I'll soon fit into your father's suits,' and pointed to his stomach.

'I can't talk,' Valerie said, indicating her own tummy.

'Nothing to see,' Schoch replied gallantly.

'It all goes straight to my arse and thighs.'

'More comfortable for sitting.'

Valerie laughed. 'I've never looked at it that way.'

'I have. I used to sit very comfortably. Back in the day your father's things would almost have been a little too tight for me.'

'He was a bit of a yo-yo. In his wardrobe you'll find clothes in at least three sizes.'

It took Schoch a while to realise that Valerie didn't cook any meat. He watched her make lasagne. She spread

253

two spoons of béchamel on a baking dish, covered this with sheets of cooked pasta and then a thick layer of ragout that she'd prepared at home. 'Don't get too excited – I've left out the wine.'

'But not the mince this time.'

'That's not mince, it's soya granules.'

'Are you a vegetarian?'

'Yes.'

'Why?'

'For the same reason I'm a vet.' As far as she was concerned the subject was closed.

One evening during the second week of his stay at Valerie's parents' house she arrived earlier than usual, looking edgy and flustered.

'Has something happened?' he asked.

'Bolle saw you.'

Ever since his reckless excursion Schoch had been afraid of something like this. He was just surprised it had taken so long for word to get around. 'How do you know?'

'Everyone knows. I mean, you know Bolle,' she said indignantly.

'It was silly, but it's not a disaster.'

'I wouldn't be so sure. He didn't see you wandering down the street with your bag, but in your cave!'

Now Schoch was horrified.

'Did you let Sabu out of the bag?'

He didn't need to answer.

'You imbecile!'

'She needed some fresh air.' He paused for a moment, then jutted his chin at Sabu and asked, 'Did he see her?'

'Those who've spoken to me about it didn't mention a pink elephant. But maybe only because that would have made the story sound unbelievable. "I saw Schoch with a little pink elephant." Maybe Bolle kept this quiet too, for the same reason.'

'I hope so.'

'At some point he's bound to start chit-chatting.'

'And nobody will believe him.'

'Apart from those who know that the pink elephant actually exists.'

'I've already apologised. Do you want me to do it again?'

'It wouldn't hurt.'

'Sorry.'

'Forget it.'

But he couldn't. The idea that Bolle – Bolle of all people! – had seen Sabu worried him. The feeling of security he'd had in this strange house had dissipated. He started cocking an ear to the sounds outside: voices, lawnmowers, car doors. He peered through the Venetian blinds for no reason. He kept checking whether the doors were locked and the curtains drawn. And he made preparations for a speedy exit.

It was true that Valerie's father had clothes in three different sizes. The smallest were still a little too baggy for him, but not so baggy that he looked like a clown. More like someone who couldn't afford a better tailor.

The suits were all bespoke, as he could tell by the workmanship, the buttonholes, the buttons on the sleeves that could be unfastened. And by the label on the inside pocket with the customer's name and the date it was finished. Schoch had an eye for this sort of stuff as there was a time when he'd worn tailor-made suits too.

They were all three-piece suits and the trousers had buttons for braces, of which there was an entire collection in one of the drawers.

The shirts were a problem, but it was solvable. Although the collars were all a couple of sizes too large, he wasn't intending on wearing a tie. If he left the top button undone it didn't show.

There was a solution for the double cuffs too. Even though he couldn't find any cufflinks he just rolled up the sleeves and it didn't look odd.

The only thing he couldn't find were appropriate shoes, as they were three sizes too small. If necessary he'd have to make do with his tatty trainers.

Schoch presented himself to Sabu dressed like this. 'Do you still recognise me?'

She came up to him and stuck out her trunk. Schoch bent down and tickled her behind her pink ears.

In front of the mirror in the dressing room he had to admit that he didn't look right. With his shaggy beard and matted hair he looked like a homeless person in disguise. From previous attempts he knew that the problem couldn't be solved with brush and comb, so he reached for the scissors. He trimmed his beard, a little at first, then a bit more, then some more again. But no matter how much Schoch trimmed, it remained a shaggy beard, just shorter.

The same was true of his hair. In front of the mirror he still looked like a down-and-out in a suit.

Schoch could have saved himself a lot of time if he'd started off by doing what he decided to do now. On Valerie's father's side of the parents' bedroom he found a razor and a dispenser with fresh blades. He lathered his beard and head and shaved himself smooth. A little blood was drawn, but once he was finished, there stood before him a slightly gaunt, middle-aged man, who looked just like the ones who got out of the tram in the morning or drank alcohol-free beer outside Sausalito.

When he returned to the bedroom he sensed that Sabu was staring at him in some astonishment.

8

21 June 2016

No trace of Kaung.

Roux and Tseng had done their research at the allotments, which wasn't an easy task as they had to avoid the old man who'd showed them the whirlpool. Another woman on the allotments did recognise Kaung, however, from the photo that Pellegrini had given them. She remembered that he'd been looking for a cave.

'Well? Is there a cave around here?' Roux asked.

'More than one, so long as the city keeps neglecting the river path,' the woman replied reproachfully.

'What could he have been looking for in a cave?' Roux pressed her.

'A place to sleep maybe. He wouldn't be the first.'

'Really? People sleep here?'

'Drunks, junkies, lowlifes.'

'Where are these caves?'

The woman pointed towards the river. 'Underneath the path. But watch out, one of them's got dogs.'

Tseng and Roux found both the caves, and both were empty. But when they returned the following morning a man with one eye was snoring in one of them. They woke him.

He hadn't seen anybody who looked like the man on the photo with the elephant. 'Maybe Giorgio has – he's in the other cave,' he suggested.

'There's nobody there.'

'He's normally with the other dog lovers around this time.' He told them where the place was and described Giorgio's twirly moustache.

Although finding Giorgio wasn't hard, getting anything out of him definitely was. Who was saying that he slept in a cave by the river? he asked.

'Your one-eyed neighbour,' Roux replied.

'Bolle?' Giorgio laughed. 'He's seeing pink elephants again.'

9

The same day

To begin with Kaung spent the night in the homeless shelter. In the evenings you had to get there between nine and half past midnight, while in the mornings you had to be out by ten.

He'd spend the day in places where the people who lived on the streets hung out. In the Morning Sun, Presto, Sixty-Eight, Meeting Point, AlcOven, the street kitchen and the Salvation Army hostel.

He'd stopped shaving and a patchy little beard had grown on his face. He acquired a new wardrobe at the Clothing Store, where each month the destitute could take five items for free.

Kaung's expertise with animals soon earned him the respect of the dog lovers, though this was slightly tarnished by the fact that he didn't drink.

Over the course of his many years in Switzerland, Kaung had built up some savings – a tidy 43,000 francs – because his board, lodging and work clothes were provided by the circus. He was planning to use the money to realise his dream of one day returning to Myanmar and setting up an elephant sanctuary for tourists. The severe government restrictions on forestry meant that there were now thousands of unemployed worker elephants.

He'd withdrawn this money from his account the day he went underground and now kept it in a military rucksack he'd picked up from the flea market. The money meant he didn't have to register for welfare benefits and so was able to vanish like someone without any documents.

He only dipped into his savings when it was absolutely unavoidable. But he'd sacrifice it all for Barisha if necessary.

Kaung was a spy working for himself. He said little and listened a lot. This is how he first heard about Schoch, the man who'd lived in the cave and then disappeared.

Now Kaung was sitting with the dog lovers in the tram shelter. The wind blew fine mizzle beneath the umbrellas of passers-by and overnight the temperature had fallen to below 15 degrees.

The weather dampened the dog lovers' spirits. They weren't as noisy as normal at this time.

'Do you know who I think about sometimes?' asked someone sitting next to Giorgio on a bench.

'Who?'

'Schoch.'

'I can't help thinking about him either. I wonder what he's up to?'

'Maybe he's not on the streets any more.'

'Where else would he be?'

'Back in the rat race.'

'After nine years?' Giorgio shook his head.

'Maybe he's met a woman.'

'Women land you on the streets, not the other way round.'

'I knew someone once who fell in love, dried out and became a hard worker.'

'Who do you imagine Schoch would fall in love with?' Giorgio asked. 'And, more importantly, who would fall in love with him?'

Both of them laughed.

'Who is Schoch?' Kaung asked.

'Was,' Giorgio corrected him. 'A neighbour. He disappeared.'

'Long time ago?' Kaung said.

'Not particularly,' the man beside Giorgio said.

'Fourteenth of June,' Giorgio asserted.

The man who sometimes thought about Schoch looked at him with raised eyebrows.

'By chance I happen to know the precise date,' Giorgio explained. 'Five days before I had Valerie give the dogs their jabs. Schoch was seen with her that evening. Fourteenth of June.'

10

The same day

He waited until Tseng's large frame had reached the counter and the passport formalities were concluded. Then Roux trudged back to the car park, got into his car and drove off in a huff.

A few days ago his partners in Beijing had started giving him deadlines for Tseng's return. They no longer believed that the result of his experiment could be found and were saying he'd be better off investing his time in trying to repeat it.

Roux had tried to secure an extension after Giorgio's comment, 'He's seeing pink elephants again.' But the one-eyed man dismissed the expression as nothing more than the English version of 'seeing white mice', and the Chinese experts were of the same opinion. Tseng was ordered back to Beijing immediately. All Roux got in recompense was that Tseng left him one of his tiny magnetic trackers, the locating software and his hi-tech mini binoculars, as well as an assurance to return if there were any promising developments.

But there hadn't been anything even vaguely promising, so once more Roux focused on finding a suitable surrogate mother for his final cryoconserved blastocyst.

11

The same day

Valerie got a fright when she saw the shaven-headed man crouching beside Sabu in the kitchen staff area.

Then she laughed and said, 'I thought you were someone else.'

'That's how I feel too.'

Once he'd helped her with the shopping bags she scrutinised him. 'Once the wounds have healed it'll look just about passable.'

'Wounds' was a slight exaggeration. But two cuts from a double blade were visible on his skull: one above the right ear and the other right on the little bump on the back of his head. The razor had left its mark on Schoch's face and neck too: a cut beside his Adam's apple and one beneath his ear lobe.

But the change was staggering. Now Schoch had a distinct profile and a shapely head. He must have been a handsome man in his younger years and even today he could be described as nice-looking, if you ignored the burst blood vessels in his cheeks and his slightly stooped gait.

'And despite the suit you bear no resemblance to my father,' she stated.

'Unfortunately his feet were too small.'

'What size are you?'

'Forty-three, forty-four.'

'Where would you buy shoes?'

'I haven't bought a pair for going on ten years. The ones I wear are freebies from the Clothing Store.'

'I can't risk popping into the Clothing Store to look for a pair of men's shoes.'

Schoch saw her point.

'Where did you buy them in the past?' she asked.

'They cost a fortune there.'

She looked at him thoughtfully. 'Some time you'll have to tell me about your past.'

'Some time.'

Schoch started mixing Sabu's milk and cutting up the pieces of apple and carrot. He gave her a few beech twigs to keep her occupied till feeding time.

Valerie put a pot of water onto the hob and started grating some Parmesan.

It was strange how the change in Schoch's external appearance had turned him into a different person for her. She thought that she'd shed all her prejudices, that after so many years of working with those on the margins of society, appearances no longer had any effect on how she judged people. Now she had to admit, however, that just some washing, shaving and different clothes had taken their relationship to another level. Valerie didn't feel ashamed that she now viewed Schoch as her equal, but that she quite clearly hadn't done so beforehand.

Did she secretly look down on people she did social work for?

Valerie washed the salad and made a simple dressing with three parts olive oil and one part balsamic vinegar, which she'd throw on the leaves just before serving.

Schoch crouched next to Sabu and gave her the bottle. 'It's not every day you bottle-feed a mini elephant that glows pink,' he remarked. 'In fact, I find it harder and harder to believe.'

Valerie nodded. 'Somebody wanted to design a luxury toy and the result was a sentient creature.'

The water was boiling. It fizzed briefly when she added the salt and she turned down the heat. She felt a new sense of intimacy with her two guests. 'We're crazy! The day you arrived with Sabu we ought to have taken her straight to the police. We've got mixed up in something that's way out of our league.'

The bottle was empty, so Schoch started feeding Sabu the chopped pieces of fruit and vegetables. 'We still could.'

'I know,' Valerie replied. She turned the hob up again and opened a packet of fresh ravioli filled with spinach and ricotta.

'Why don't we then?' Schoch asked.

'I can't speak for you, but for me it's quite simple: I'm repulsed by genetic engineering. I'd do all I can to damage the industry.'

Valerie quickly placed ten of the flour-dusted ravioli on a slotted spoon and lowered them carefully into the water.

'There could well be dozens of these mini elephants around, in which case the genetic engineering industry could easily cope with the loss of one of them.'

Sabu's appetite had waned and now she started to play with a piece of carrot.

Valerie tossed the salad. 'If that's the case then we're merely making a small contribution to protecting humanity from genetic modification. Just like not eating meat is a tiny contribution to protecting humanity from the destruction of the ozone layer.'

When the pasta parcels rose to the surface Valerie fished them out, let them drain, arranged them on two plates, seasoned them with pepper from the mill, sprinkled them with Parmesan and drizzled olive oil on top.

When they were eating, Schoch asked, 'Wouldn't it be easier for you to sleep here?'

Valerie gave him an amused look. 'I don't think so.'

12

The same day

The large drawing room was done out with 1960s period furniture: oval coffee tables, bulbous chests of drawers with inlays and velour and machine-tapestry upholstery. Heavy damask curtains hung in front of the French windows that led to the terrace and garden. Valerie had pushed two of these to the side and opened the windows to refresh the stale, dusty air with some oxygen. The shutters remained closed. On the walls hung landscapes and engravings from unknown contemporary artists. Among these Schoch could again see light, shield-shaped patches where trophies had been removed.

'Was that you?' he asked. 'Did you get rid of all those hunting trophies?'

Valerie poured them both some tea. 'Yes.'

'Because of your love of animals?'

'Because of my love of animals, but also because they reminded me of my father.'

'You didn't like him.'

'You wouldn't have liked him either.'

'I don't suppose he would have liked me much.'

'You might be right there. He didn't like anyone. Apart from himself, but he adored himself.'

'And your mother?'

'He didn't like her either. But she didn't like him. She was also someone who didn't like anybody.'

'Only herself.'

'No. Not even herself. My mother only liked Sally, her chihuahua. Not liked, *worshipped*. They even died together.'

'How?'

'In a Learjet.'

'Plane crash?'

'Over the French Alps on the way to the Côte d'Azur. Father, mother, chihuahua, pilot and co-pilot. Human, rather than mechanical failure.' She couldn't help laughing. 'Human failure! The leitmotif of my father's life!'

'Judging by this house he was pretty successful.'

'*Human* failure, not *commercial*. He was a good businessman and a good hunter, but a bad husband, a bad father and a bad person.'

Schoch took a sip of tea. 'What sort of business was your father in?'

'He ran a subsidiary in Johannesburg. Until 1994, the end of apartheid. You understand what I'm saying?'

'Totally.'

'He was often down there afterwards too. He said "down there". Hunting.'

'What did you do with the trophies?'

Valerie took her time and drank some tea. Eventually she said, 'I buried them.'

'You buried those trophies? Where?'

On a piece of land I bought for that very purpose.' She

put her teacup back onto the tray. 'You think I'm mad, don't you?'

'Not mad, perhaps just a bit eccentric. Why did you do it?'

She didn't need to think long about her reply. 'Out of respect.'

'For the animals?'

'For life.'

Sabu, who'd been lying beneath a chess table, stood up and walked sedately across the Persian carpet. Valerie and Schoch watched her.

'Out of respect for life, however it may have come about,' Valerie added.

'Creation or evolution, you mean?'

'Sometimes I think they're one and the same. The only difference is the time span. Seven days or a few million years – time is relative. Everything's a question of perspective. How long does a mayfly think its life is?'

Valerie paused and Schoch sensed that there was something to follow.

'But there's a volition, a plan behind it. I don't believe in chance.' Another pause. 'How about you?'

Schoch laughed. 'Talking philosophy with a tramp.'

'Diogenes was homeless too.'

Sabu was standing by the open window, feeling with her trunk the gaps between the slats.

'Yes,' Schoch said, 'I do believe in chance, coincidence, whatever. For example, it was pure chance that we met.'

'That's a minor coincidence. I'm talking about major ones. This bunch of flowers, for example,' she said, pointing to the rather crude still life of some Michaelmas daisies in a clay vase, which hung in a gilded plaster frame and bore a huge signature. 'Just assume that those were real flowers in a real vase. Can you imagine the vase appearing of its own accord by chance?'

Schoch shook his head.

'But its contents, five Michaelmas daisies, highly complex creations – they're supposed to be a product of chance?'

Schoch poured them both some more tea. 'So that's why we're fighting against genetic modification. Because it's interfering in creation.'

'And/or in evolution.'

'Even if you can use it to cure or prevent disease?'

Valerie shrugged.

'When you look at it like that, your job is interfering too.'

'I don't agree. Treating and curing is just restoring the natural state, which is to be healthy.'

Sabu turned away from the slats, spread her ears and plodded over to them.

'If you believe in creation,' Schoch said warily, 'you believe in God too.'

Valerie sighed. 'I don't know.'

'Up till now those who believe in him still haven't given us any proof of his existence,' Schoch pointed out.

'Nor has the other side come up with any proof that he doesn't exist.'

Sabu was now standing beside them, raising her tiny trunk.

'Maybe she's the proof.'

'That he exists or that he doesn't exist?' Valerie asked.

Schoch thought about this for a moment, then said, 'Perhaps both.'

13

22 June 2016

Valerie was there for a long time the following evening as well. And once again they chose the grand drawing room over the kitchen staff area. They'd eaten *Gschwellti* – potatoes in their skins with cheese – and although dinner was long finished, they hadn't yet tidied away the plates and were still picking at the cheese.

'Fritz as in Friedrich?' Valerie asked.

'No, just Fritz. My parents christened me Fritz because you couldn't shorten it.'

Valerie tried the name out. 'Fritz Schoch, Fritz Schoch. Two monosyllables. Like a Chinese name.' Then she said it again, this time very slowly: 'Fritz Schoch.'

'How long is it since you lived here?' Schoch asked, to change the subject.

'Twenty-two years.'

'Has the house been standing empty that long?'

'It's been empty for nineteen. But I moved out twenty-two years ago. On the day I turned eighteen.'

'When your parents died you could have renovated the house and moved in yourself.'

'There are certain memories you can't just paper over. Nor certain other things either. I can still smell the stench

273

of the venison, partridge and pheasant, which used to hang downstairs in the cold store until they were putrid enough for my father.' She shuddered.

'Have you got brothers or sisters?'

'No, I'm an only child.'

'Why did you keep the house?'

'Legal stipulation. The house couldn't be sold for twenty years and there was an executor to make sure of that.'

'You could have let it.'

'No.'

'Why not?'

'Legal stipulation.'

'I'm gradually realising why you don't like your father.'

'That's not the reason.'

'Why then?'

'I don't feel I know you well enough to say.'

There was silence for a while until Schoch said, 'What about the money? I mean, you're not exactly living the high life, are you?'

'There wasn't much left; he lost most of it in the Asian currency crisis.'

'Ah yes, 1997.'

Valerie looked at Schoch in surprise.

'And the money that was left?' Schoch asked before she could get her question in.

'Went into the Sommer Foundation.'

'Another legal stipulation?'

'No, it's something I set up.'

'For what?'

'Animal protection.'

'Of course.'

'It funds the street clinic, for example.'

'And pays your salary.'

'I don't draw a salary, which is why I work 60 per cent of the time in the animal hospital.'

'When can you sell the house?'

'In a month.'

'What will you do with the money?'

'Put it into the Sommer Foundation.'

'Are you an idealist?'

'No. I just don't want any of my father's filthy money.'

'Money has no smell.'

'I'm not so sure about that.'

Schoch said nothing for a while. Then he muttered, 'Nor am I.' He scraped some of the overripe Camembert from the plate and spread it onto a piece of black bread.

'How did you end up on the streets?'

'I'll tell you another time.'

'You know so much about me and I know nothing about you.'

Silence.

'Come on, talk.'

'It's not something I like to talk about with a woman.'

'Why not?'

'Because it concerns a woman.'

'Interesting. Tell me.'

Schoch paused, then said, 'I used to be married.'

'What was her name?'

'Why's that important?'

'It'll help me get a better picture of her.'

'Paula.'

'Fritz and Paula Schoch. Sounds terribly middle class.'

'It was.'

'Was she pretty?'

'An absolute stunner.'

'So what went wrong?'

'What always goes wrong?'

'You or her?'

'Three guesses.'

'Children?'

'One. From the other guy.'

'Why didn't the two of you have any?'

'She didn't want them.'

'Ouch. And then you chucked the whole thing in?'

'I no longer saw any reason to earn so much and work so hard. I let her have everything I had.'

'And made sure that no more came in,' Valerie said with a knowing smile.

'I'd have had to give her most of it anyway.'

'With another man's child?'

'She said it was mine.'

'You can do paternity tests these days.'

'I didn't want a huge row about it,' Schoch said.

'Better just to chuck it all in. I understand.'

'Really?'

'I chucked all of this in, didn't I?' she said, pointing at the room they were in.

'That's true.'

Valerie cut off the last bit of a rind. 'Did you never feel the urge to get back in the game again?'

'Not till now.'

Their eyes met then immediately looked away again.

'It was the big catastrophe of my life.'

'What about now? After … how many years?'

'Almost ten.'

'After almost ten years, are you over it now?'

'I was long ago. But I thought it was too late.'

'But you don't think that any more?'

Schoch didn't reply.

Through a chink in the curtains they could see the horizontal strips of the twilight in the blinds that weren't quite closed.

'What was your job?'

'You don't want to know.'

'That bad?'

'I worked in a bank.'

Valerie laughed. 'A banker!'

'A bank employee.'

'A big beast?'

'Pretty much.'

'That's why you're so comfortable in my father's suits. Which bank?'

'I've forgotten.'

14

23 June 2016

A morning like in the tropics: still fresh from the night, but already heavy from the humidity that would soon fall as rain. Roux had a cool bag over his shoulder and was struggling up the embankment to the bushes that concealed the entrance to the cave.

The one-eyed man was awake, but probably only just. He was rolling up his sleeping bag and cursing quietly to himself.

The cave reeked of alcohol, stale smoke and urine.

'May I come in?' Roux said.

The man got a start. It took him a moment to recognise Roux. 'Oh, it's you. I'm not geared up for visitors.'

Roux crept into the cave.

'What do you want?' the one-eyed man said.

'To see you.'

'Are you from social services or the police?'

'Neither. I'm a researcher.'

'Ha! A researcher. What are you researching?'

Roux took his mobile from his pocket, fiddled about a bit, then stuck it under the man's nose. 'That's a skinny pig. A naked guinea pig.'

The tramp stared at the photo. 'It's pink,' he declared.

'That's what I'm researching.'

The man laughed, then his laugh turned into a coughing fit and it took a while before he could talk again.

In the meantime Roux had opened the cool bag, taken out two glasses and one of the two bottles and was uncorking it.

'Prosecco?' the one-eyed man gasped.

'Champagne,' Roux corrected him. 'Veuve Clicquot.'

'I can't remember the last time I drank champagne. Maybe never.'

Roux carefully allowed the gas to escape from the bottle, then poured two very unequal glasses. Raising the less full one, he said, 'Paul.'

The other man raised his, said, 'Bolle, everyone calls me Bolle,' toasted Roux and drank it with relish. 'Mmm,' he said, smacking his lips. 'Does it get you pissed, too?'

'Happy,' Roux corrected him.

'Great.' Bolle grinned. 'I can't remember when I was last happy – certainly longer ago than since I was last pissed.' He finished the glass. 'But small glasses.'

Roux filled it again. 'Large glasses take too long to drink and the champagne gets warm.'

'Not if it's my glass,' Bolle said, triggering another laughing and coughing fit that prevented him from drinking.

'So you're researching pink guinea pigs?' he finally said.

'Among other things.'

'What else?'

'Small pink elephants.'

This shut Bolle up. He downed his glass and held it out to Roux, who refilled it and asked, 'Ever seen one?'

Bolle took a large gulp. 'You're having me on, Paul.'

'I've heard you sometimes do see them.'

'White mice too. This is what's responsible.' He lifted his glass and necked it. 'Not from having too much of it, but too little.'

Roux refilled. 'Were you already in this cave when a man drowned down here?'

'No, just heard about it.'

'Are you sure?'

'Totally.' He finished his glass. 'I could get used to this stuff. Anything left in the bottle?'

Roux poured the last of it.

'What about you?' Bolle said, pointing to Roux's glass that still contained most of the dribble he'd allowed himself.

'I've still got some, thanks.'

Bolle grinned. 'Still got some research to do, eh?'

'How long have you been sleeping here?'

Bolle finished his glass. 'Good stuff, isn't it?'

Roux nodded.

'How long have you been sleeping here?'

'Wanna know why everyone calls me Bolle?'

'I can imagine.'

Bolle started singing, '*Bolle left for Pankow, at Whitsuntide one June …*'

With a sigh, Roux took the second bottle from the cool bag and uncorked it.

Bolle stopped singing. 'That's what I call a gentleman. Always with a second bottle on him. I mean one of them could have been corked.'

Roux poured him some.

'... *His left one looked like slime.* With me it's the right eye, but it looks like slime all the same.'

'How long have you been sleeping here, Bolle?'

'Since Schoch.'

'Who's Schoch?'

'The guy who slept here before me.'

'Why doesn't he sleep here any more?'

Bolle shrugged and held out his glass.

'He vanished all of a sudden.'

'When was that?' asked Roux, holding back the bottle.

'Fourteenth of June.'

Roux filled Bolle's glass. 'How can you be so precise?'

'Giorgio says so.'

'How come he knows?'

'He says it was five days before his dogs were vaccinated. Schoch just disappeared, but then he turned up at the street clinic and was never seen again.'

Roux's heart was pounding. So the former inhabitant of this cave disappeared two days after Reber drowned.

'Or almost never,' Bolle held out his glass again.

15

The same day

On the pavement outside Just a Second was a single parking space. A sign said 'Private' and showed a registration number. Parked there was a Peugeot estate, dull red in colour.

Kaung had come to take a look earlier, but the street clinic was in the back rooms of the second-hand shop and it was closed. He'd made a note of the opening times and returned at the next opportunity.

Twenty metres in front of him a man Kaung thought he recognised was walking along. He slackened his pace and ducked behind the cars parked by the kerb.

A sensible precaution, for the man suddenly turned around.

Dr Roux.

His destination seemed to be the same as Kaung's. Outside the entrance to Just a Second, behind the parked car, he turned around again. Then he bent down as if to tie his shoelace, but for a moment it looked as if he'd done something to the car. He stood back up and went into the shop.

Kaung had to wait until Roux left before paying his own visit.

16

The same day

Valerie put down her shopping. 'Someone's looking for you.'

'What kind of person?'

'Someone from social services. Kellerberger, Kellerman – Keller something. He said it was a routine matter. When someone who's registered and regularly receives payments suddenly stops collecting them, they run a search for that person.'

'Did you ask for ID?'

'I've never asked anyone for ID in my life.' She gave him the bag from a shoe shop. 'Try these. Those that don't fit you I'll have to take back tomorrow.'

'You asked for a selection of men's shoes?'

'Why not?'

'How did you explain that the customer wasn't there himself?'

'He's not good on his feet.'

'Why does he need shoes then?'

Both of them laughed.

Sabu announced herself with a high-pitched noise that sounded like a piccolo.

They dutifully started preparing her meal. Valerie

chopped up the fruit, Schoch mixed the formula milk.

'How did he find you?'

'On the streets they know that you came to see me before you disappeared.'

'Then you'd better glance over your shoulder before you drive here.'

'In case I'm being tailed by social services you mean?'

'Assuming the guy *was* from social services.'

'He looked like he was.'

'What did he look like?'

'Thickset, almost completely shaved head, red-haired.'

'But you could still see the hair colour?'

'From the hair on the back of his hands. Women look at men's hands.'

Schoch gave Sabu the bottle. 'Let's assume the guy isn't from social services, but he's one of the people looking for Sabu.'

'So why is he looking for *you*?'

'Why has he linked me to her?'

'Because Bolle talked.'

Schoch grimaced. 'Of course.'

'I'm quitting at the animal hospital.'

'Why?' Schoch said, surprised.

'To give me more time for this,' she said, pointing at Sabu, him and everything around them.

'I can manage.'

'It's practically a round-the-clock job. And I'll keep going at the street clinic.'

'I thought that was voluntary.'

Having finished her bottle, Sabu now lay beside Valerie, who started stroking her neck.

284

'The foundation is paying me a small salary now.'
'And you can live off that?'
'The foundation has just increased it slightly.'
'I thought you were the foundation?'
'I am,' Valerie said with a smile.

17

The same day

'What about *your* love life?' Schoch asked.

Again they were sitting on one of the sofas in the drawing room, having eaten in the kitchen staff area. Valerie had made a stir-fry in the wok with diced tofu that she'd deep-frozen, let thaw, then marinated in soy sauce to give it a meatier taste and texture. 'Just let me know when you can't do without meat any more in the evenings,' she'd said.

'It's nothing compared to booze,' he replied.

After dinner they'd made tea and repaired to the drawing room. Sàbu had stayed in the kitchen, but they'd left the doors open in case she wanted to join them. Some days she was more attached to them than others.

'My love life?' She feigned a yawn and held a hand in front of her mouth. 'I'd rather you told me about your life as a banker. Have you remembered now which bank you were with?'

'GCBS, I think it was called.'

Valerie laughed. 'You forgot that? It's on every second corner.'

'If you spend ten years trying to forget something, it works occasionally.'

'What did you do there?'

Schoch hesitated. 'I was an investment banker,' he said finally.

'Those are the ones with the bonuses, aren't they?'

'And the sixty-hour weeks.'

No light was coming in from outside any more. Reaching behind her, Valerie pulled a brass chain beneath the shade of a standard lamp, and the sofa they were sitting on was instantly bathed in a yellow glow.

'What does an investment banker do?'

'Makes people like your father even richer.'

'Or poor.'

'Can happen too.'

They heard the wind in the treetops outside.

'Did you plan to go on living like this? Without a home?' Valerie asked out of the blue.

'Homeless people don't make plans.'

'I understand.'

Sabu had been on her own for long enough; now she came to the door with her ears spread wide and trunk in the air, and stood there expectantly. Valerie put out her hand and the little elephant wrapped its trunk around her finger.

'There was a strange man in the street clinic today.'

'The guy from social services?'

'No, a different one, he was Burmese. He arrived after the other man. I thought he was one of the dog lovers at first because he came into the consultation room with one of them who had an Alsatian mix with a bite wound. The dog refused to be touched, it snapped at me and even its owner. I was just about to sedate it when the Burmese man laid his hand on its neck and spoke to it, in Burmese I assume. And do you know what? The dog calmed down and let me administer the local anaesthetic and stitch the wound.'

'A dog-whisperer maybe?'

'He asked me if he could help out sometimes. I said I couldn't afford an assistant, so he suggested I give him a probation period: 986 francs per month.'

'That's the basic welfare payment. He'd get that even without having to work.'

'He said he wasn't working for money. And I believe him.'

'Did you say yes?'

'I said I'd think about it.'

'And? Will you?'

'It would be a great help to have someone like that.'

All of a sudden a dog barked fiercely outside and another joined in.

'I didn't know there were dogs around here.'

'They're old and you rarely hear them.'

'So why now?'

'One's barking because the other one is.'

'How about the other one?'

'Because it's heard something.'

'Did you hear anything? I didn't.'

'Dogs have better hearing.'

'Even old ones?'

Sabu had let go of Valerie's finger and turned her head to the window. 'Just dogs, Sabu,' Valerie whispered.

But Sabu kept facing the window, even when the dogs had quietened down.

Valerie, who'd been waiting for Sabu's trunk to grab her finger again, pulled her hand away and took hold of Schoch's.

18

The same day

To begin with Roux had difficulty working Tseng's software, but he soon got the hang of it. Now the vet's Peugeot was a flashing dot moving across the map on his smartphone.

He followed the object at a safe distance. Once it entered the car park of a shopping centre. Roux had to drive around a few times until the dot started moving again.

Then it stopped outside a pharmacy. This time Roux had more luck, as he found a parking space three cars behind. Just a few minutes later he saw the vet come out again with a shopping bag.

The next stop was a shoe shop, where she spent almost ten minutes. Then he followed the dot for quite a while around the periphery of the city. It stopped at a building project near the motorway exit.

When Roux arrived there he couldn't see the Peugeot. It must have disappeared into the garage that said: 'Tenants only'.

Her private address wasn't in the telephone book, but now he knew where she lived.

To be on the safe side he waited for five minutes, then drove away.

The apartment block was still in sight when the dot moved again, crossed the river and climbed through the university quarter up to the villas, gardens and parks.

Then the dot came to a stop in a little side street.

Roux stopped too.

The dot moved a tiny bit more before stopping again.

Roux waited a quarter of an hour before driving on. The car with the tracker was parked behind a wrought-iron gate and an overgrown hedge.

He could only guess what a house that boasted such fancy surroundings must be like up close.

Roux drove slowly along the road. On either side were silent houses and old gardens, screened by massive hedges. Nowhere he could stop and wait inconspicuously. At least not while it was still light.

After an aimless drive through the woods above the city he came back. In some of the houses he could see light shimmering through the dense vegetation, and just as he arrived the streetlamps went on. He went on a few streets and parked in a restricted zone.

Was the apartment block where she'd stopped briefly her real home? And the house where she was now her hideaway? Or where Schoch and his stolen mini elephant were hiding?

For wherever Schoch was, the mini elephant must be too. This, at least, he'd found out from the one-eyed tramp. Bolle had seen Schoch once after his disappearance. And next to Schoch he thought he'd seen something like a glowing pink, electric toy elephant that looked almost real.

Roux had notified his Chinese partners at once, but the

statement by a homeless alcoholic wasn't good enough for them. Once he could 'positively confirm' that he'd seen the animal, they'd send Tseng again, not a moment before.

The occasional car drove past and the odd person taking their dog for its evening walk peered warily into his BMW. Roux noticed that his hands were trembling with anxiety.

The red dot on the screen of his smartphone hadn't moved again and night had shrouded the villas and gardens in its darkness.

Roux got out and walked the short distance to the hidden villa.

The gate to the driveway was made of the same wrought ironwork as the fence, but a metal sheet was welded behind it. The ornate decorations on the fence provided support for both hands and feet.

Roux wasn't particularly dextrous or sporty, but that night he was assisted by fortune and the power of desperation.

He climbed rapidly and silently over the gate.

A forecourt, a double garage, a front door, barred windows on the ground floor, closed shutters on the first floor.

Roux walked quietly around the house and came to a tree-lined lawn that vanished into the darkness after about forty metres.

A few steps led up to a terrace that ran along the entire length of the back of the house. All the shutters were closed, but light peeped through the slats of one of them, which were at a slight angle.

Roux climbed the steps to the terrace, sneaked over to the shutters and spied through the slats.

The vet was sitting on a sofa beside a gaunt man in a suit. He couldn't understand what they were saying.

All of a sudden they interrupted their conversation and looked in the same direction.

What now emerged into his field of view made his heart thump wildly: the little pink elephant! The perfect toy for children who had everything. It plodded up to the two people, fanning its ears and trunk in the air, and stood beside the woman. She held out her hand and the tiny elephant wrapped its trunk around her finger. The two of them continued talking.

Suddenly a dog barked, immediately followed by another. Roux froze. The people inside turned their heads to the window Roux was spying through.

The pink elephant had turned its head too.

Roux held his breath.

Finally the dogs stopped barking.

The little elephant was still looking in his direction, but now the vet and the man were kissing.

She stood, pulled him up from the sofa and turned off the standard lamp.

In the darkness of the room he could barely make out the couple any more.

But the glowing pink elephant following them was easier to see.

19

24 June 2016

The following morning Kaung was waiting for Valerie outside Just a Second at half past seven.

'Think about?'

Valerie laughed. 'Yes, let's give it a try. One month, then we'll see.'

He offered her his hand. 'Kaung.'

'Valerie.'

'Frau Doctor better.'

'Nobody calls me Frau Doctor here.'

'Mistake. Frau Doctor make better healthy than Valerie.'

She unlocked the door and led him through the still empty shop, the waiting room and into her surgery.

'The practice opens at half past eight. Before then I do a bit of admin and tidy up. So you should really start work at half past eight.'

'Frau Doctor do admin, Kaung tidy up.'

The bins were full of the previous day's rubbish: blood-spattered tissues, used bandages and cotton wool, inside-out disposable gloves. The container for disposable syringes was full too, as was the waste-paper basket. The floor was dirty from the dog lovers' shoes and a yellow puddle had dried by a table leg. The mobile instrument table was utter chaos and Kaung also had to tidy the cabinets with the medicines and bandaging.

For the most part he didn't need Valerie's help and could let her work undisturbed but sometimes he had to ask her where things went.

Just before Kaung called the first patient in at half past eight and the Frau Doctor got up from her computer to take a look around, she said, 'My surgery hasn't been as tidy as this in ages.'

This wasn't the only compliment she paid Kaung that morning. She praised his way with animals, his calming effect on the often neurotic street dogs, as well as their owners, some of whom were no less anxious.

Soon after one o'clock the waiting room was empty and Kaung began to clear up. He saw the Frau Doctor open the medicine cabinet, take out a variety of preparations and put them on the desk. Some of these he knew: colostrum, lactobacillus, calcium, vitamins E and B and a bottle of coconut oil – while tidying earlier he'd noted there was a small supply of this in the cabinet.

She packed everything into a crumpled shopping bag and locked the surgery behind her.

The music of Ravi Shankar was playing in the shop and the biting smoke of a beedi hung in the air. Cynthia was sitting behind her painted counter, meditating. The Frau Doctor quietly piloted Kaung past her and out into the street.

'See you tomorrow,' she said, getting into her Peugeot.

Kaung watched the car drive off.

He'd have loved to know where she was going with her supplements and coconut oil. As well as the other ingredients that went into formula milk for young elephants.

20

26 June 2016

Tseng had rented a car at the airport and they'd arranged to meet in the lobby of the same hotel as last time.

First of all they had to know who they were dealing with and, more importantly, how many.

Roux was certain that it was Schoch, the man from the cave. But Tseng had asked whether Kaung might not be involved as well, seeing as he'd been Dr Reber's accomplice, was spotted hanging around the cave and had also disappeared. He knew something about elephants too. It was possible that Kaung had taken Schoch's place or was a reinforcement. In the first scenario Schoch would probably have emerged again; in the second he'd stay in hiding.

Tseng insisted they did their research first.

They drove to the tram stop at the station with the intention of interrogating Giorgio, the man with three dogs who'd given the tip-off that Bolle had seen pink elephants.

Giorgio wasn't there, but the other dog lovers were already in a talkative mood and the two six-packs of beer that Roux had brought along loosened their tongues further.

'Schoch?' one said. 'If he turns up again, we'll be the first to know.'

'He won't turn up again,' another said. 'He wouldn't be the first river sleeper to drown.'

'I've heard,' a third man roared, forming a heart with his grubby thumbs and forefingers, 'that he's smitten.'

'In love?' a fourth bellowed. 'He'll soon be back here then.'

They all laughed.

Roux indicated that it was pointless, but Tseng took his wallet from his jacket and slipped out a photo – the same one they'd passed around when they were first looking for Kaung. Pellegrini with the elephant routine, Kaung in the background.

The picture did the rounds.

'What about him?' Roux said, acting as interpreter. 'Has he turned up?'

'That's the guy who helps out in the street clinic, isn't it?' one said. 'The dog-whisperer.'

So Kaung had reappeared. And he was working for the vet. The advantage of this was that they had him in their sights. He'd be in the clinic when they struck.

Tseng's plan was to wait till it was night, then make a recce of the villa. He needed to examine the lock on the garden gate and the one on the front door too. They'd carry out the actual raid during the daytime when only Schoch was in the house.

For this Tseng and Roux would have to enter the villa through the front door. Like a Chinese prospective buyer with his estate agent who had the key to the property. They would have to be quick – they'd take Schoch by

surprise and force him to give them the food for the creature, as well as the recipe for the formula milk, as it was
unlikely that Kaung would have another source of real
elephant milk.

What happened afterwards would have to be meticulously planned too. They would take the animal to the
Gentecsa laboratory, where Roux would examine, measure, document and film it. And, most importantly of all,
take the necessary cell material.

They'd leave the prototype in the care of Roux's two
assistants, Vera and Ivana, who were both reliable and
discreet, and Vera also had a good way with laboratory
animals. This was important; Roux knew how tricky
young elephants could be. Robbed of their attachment
figure, they could fall into depression and sometimes even
die.

Which wouldn't be a tragedy in this case, because he'd
have the cell material.

Now they were sitting in Tseng's hotel room, staring at
the red dot on the smartphone.

It hadn't moved since 4 p.m.

Roux put a capsule into the coffee machine and made
another insipid lungo. The situation and the waiting
were making him fidgety, not helped by the mixture
of fussiness and composure that Tseng was again
exhibiting. What difference would a little bit more
caffeine make?

Roux moved to the window and watched the strange
dusk. Blue and mother-of-pearl grey, like the polar night
he'd been so tormented by during a year-long academic
exchange a long time ago in northern Norway.

Tseng rummaged in his hand luggage and took out a set of skeleton keys, some binoculars, two small LED torches and a few cable ties.

It was now dark, but Tseng wanted to wait till midnight when fewer people were about.

21

The same day

Her boss in the animal hospital was not a good loser. He couldn't stand people handing in their notice. He was the one who sacked people. And he took Valerie's resignation particularly badly, because he thought the world of her and he felt offended. When she then asked for the earliest possible leaving date, that was the last straw.

'If you're in such a hurry,' he griped, 'you can pack up now.'

She took him up on his offer without hesitation.

And so Valerie was already back at the house by four o'clock that afternoon. She was moved by the scene that greeted her: Schoch in one of her father's slate-grey suits and the Oxford shoes she'd bought for him – the larger shoes were the ones that fitted him – playing ball with Sabu. He must have taken bundles of wool from her mother's knitting basket and rolled it all together to make one large, solid ball, which he nudged to her. Sabu would stop the ball and push it back nimbly with her trunk and legs.

When she saw Valerie, Sabu hurried over to greet her.

Schoch came over too and embraced Valerie. She caught herself checking whether he smelled of alcohol.

Valerie took his hand and led him to the lift and up to the bedroom. Sabu followed.

In the middle of the night Valerie and Schoch awoke at the same time, without knowing why. Sabu's pink reflection on the ceiling seemed to be moving.

Valerie sat on the edge of the bed. She nudged Schoch, who came and sat next to her.

Her trunk pointing straight up at the ceiling and ears spread wide, Sabu kept running at the dark and heavy curtain hanging in front of the shutter, which was open to let some fresh air in through the slats.

Sabu would stop just before the curtain, turn around, go back to the starting point, rock her head from side to side and swing her trunk. Then she'd resume the attack position and charge again.

Valerie held Schoch's hand and they watched this performance, captivated.

Sabu launched about ten mock attacks then stood facing her superior enemy and stiffened like an elephant statue in the victory position.

She seemed to glow more intensely than ever before.

As he had during their first encounter, Schoch put his palms together in front of his face and bowed, like a Thai greeting. Valerie copied him.

22

27 June 2016

It was a busy morning in the street clinic. Two new, neglected dogs without chips – nobody knew where they were from or if they'd been vaccinated – needed to be examined, while a drunken couple brought in a shaggy mongrel with a wound on its neck that required urgent stitching. Neither of its owners knew where the wound came from.

The next stage of Kaung's plan was to tell the Frau Doctor that he was an oozie by profession and had been working with elephants since he was six. Depending on how the conversation went, he was also considering talking to her about the ingredients for elephant formula milk. But given the activity in the surgery there was no question of broaching the subject for the time being.

He fetched the next patient from the waiting room.

'Hey, you, dog-whisperer,' a voice said. It came from one of the dog lovers who'd brought his collie mix to be vaccinated. 'Did the Chinese guy find you?'

'Which Chinese guy?' Kaung asked.

'Tall Chinese chap with long hair. And a shorter Swiss guy with him.'

'Red hair?'

'Yeah, but not much of it.' The man laughed. 'He showed us a photo of you and a few elephants in the circus.'

Kaung was horrified. Roux and the tall Chinese man!

He went back into the surgery without bringing a patient. The Frau Doctor raised her eyebrows.

'On day when I come, before come man with short red hair.'

She nodded. 'What about him?'

'What man want?'

'He was from social services, looking for someone.'

'Looking for Schoch?'

'Yes.'

'You tell him where is Schoch?'

The doctor didn't reply immediately.

Kaung pressed her. 'Not say where Schoch is. Man not from social services. Bad man. Look for small pink elephant. Schoch have it? You know where?' Kaung was speaking more rapidly and urgently.

'I don't know what you're talking about,' the Frau Doctor said. But Kaung didn't believe her. In her eyes he could see that she knew exactly what he was talking about.

'Then Barisha die. Perhaps Schoch too.'

The Frau Doctor went to the door and locked it. She pushed the visitors' chair over to him and said, 'Sit down.'

Kaung obeyed and she sat opposite him.

'Talk.'

Kaung hastily told her about Roux's experiment with the elephant cow in Circus Pellegrini, the embryo's growth disorder, his conspiracy with Dr Reber and the time when Barisha lived with Dr Reber and he, Kaung, milked Rupashi and sent the milk to the doctor. Then he explained how the Chinese man had appeared and Reber had obviously left the house in a hurry with Barisha. And how Reber drowned in the river.

'I wonder how they found him?' The Frau Doctor's question was aimed more at herself than Kaung.

He put his palms facing upwards and shook his head.

'Maybe they followed the car that brought the milk.'

'Difficult. Hans always drive very fast,' Kaung explained.

'Maybe they put a trace on his phone.'

'Maybe.'

'Or the car.'

'Is possible?'

'You see it in every crime show. They put small magnetic trackers under the car and these let you track them.'

Kaung got up and went to the door. 'Back soon.'

He went through the room full of impatient people waiting with their pets, through the second-hand shop and out to the Frau Doctor's car.

At the place where Roux had tied his shoelaces, he felt the undercarriage and discovered a tiny box. It offered some resistance when he tugged at it, but then came off in his hand. It was dirty from water splashes and weighed less than 100 grams.

Kaung went back through the shop, past Cynthia who wanted to engage him in conversation, past the restless patients and into the surgery. He held out the tiny, dirty trophy in the palm of his hand. 'Man put this on car. Not from social services.'

She grabbed her mobile and speed-dialled a number. 'Answer, answer,' she implored in a whisper.

No answer.

'Come!' she ordered, opening the door.

'Emergency!' she called out to the expectant faces and locked the door. 'The surgery is closed and will reopen in the morning.'

They pushed their way past the protesting mass of people and got into the car.

23

The same day

Just as Tseng was about to give the signal to go in, the alarm went off. The red dot had moved.

They'd already driven down the narrow street three times to make sure that no neighbours, delivery drivers, gardeners or any other unwanted witnesses were in sight. On one occasion a yellow postal van stopped outside a neighbouring house, on another a florist's van stopped outside the villa opposite and then the refuse collection emptied the bins on the street.

And now, on the fourth time, when the air was clear, the dot had started moving.

The surgery had only opened a couple of hours ago. Was it closed again already?

They drove back into the side street and watched the huge screen on Tseng's phone.

The dot was stationary again.

24

The same day

Sabu was drinking the bottle with her head raised and trunk curled up. Schoch watched her and thought of Valerie.

He'd never imagined that there would ever be another woman in his life he'd think about as often as he thought of her. As often and as affectionately.

He'd thought of Paula often too. With sheer hatred at first, then sadness, bitterness and disdain. But more recently he'd almost felt a little sympathy for her.

Because things were going well for him. Because he felt something – if only slightly – that he'd never expected to feel again in his life: happiness.

Another thing he hadn't expected was that he was making plans. And Valerie and Sabu were part of these.

These plans weren't very concrete; they were perhaps more dreams than plans. The three of them far away somewhere, undisturbed and content.

Sabu had finished the bottle and now wanted her apples and carrots. Schoch got up and took his coffee to the work surface in the kitchen where the chopping board and knife were lying ready.

He found his mobile there too, which showed two missed calls, both from Valerie. The second soon after the first. He'd switched it to silent.

Schoch dialled her number and Valerie answered straight away. She sounded agitated.

'We're on our way to pick both of you up. They know where you are. Pack the essentials and get Sally's bag. We'll be there in five minutes.'

'Who's we?'

'Me and Kaung, my Burmese assistant.'

Schoch picked up Sabu and ran upstairs to the first floor. He packed a few things into a small case, placed Sabu in Sally's bag, chucked in the Persian stole in case he had to disguise her as a dwarf poodle, hurried back into the kitchen, packed a bag with Sabu's food, dashed into the trophy room, smashed the glass of the weapons cabinet and grabbed a rifle. He couldn't find any bullets but at least the gun might be good enough to scare someone. Then he returned to Sabu.

25

The same day

Tseng had declared that they'd wait ten minutes. If the dot hadn't moved again they would drive past the villa to check out the scene. If everything looked all right, they would go round again, then park on the pavement by the garden gate where the yellow postal van had stopped.

Roux would position himself so that any potential witnesses wouldn't realise that it was his Chinese client rather than himself opening the gate, and they'd undertake the same procedure at the front door. The locks were easy to pick, as Tseng had established last night.

Although the coast was clear on their first run, Tseng made Roux drive straight past. Roux groaned.

Three minutes later, on their second run, an old Peugeot stood by the drive. Roux recognised it at once. 'Shit!'

'Go on! Go on!' Tseng ordered.

When they drove past they saw the gate sliding to the side. Two people were in the car. On the passenger seat beside the vet sat a short, slim man.

Tseng looked at his mobile. The red dot was still in the same place at the street clinic.

This time it was the Chinese man who hissed, 'Shit!'

'Let's go get them!' Tseng said after a brief pause for thought.

Roux turned and drove back.

At the end of the narrow street they just glimpsed the back of the Peugeot disappearing around the bend.

Roux parked the rental car by the garden gate and they got out. Roux was carrying an empty briefcase and, with expansive gestures, gave a fake sales pitch to his fake client.

The garden gate was open in a jiffy and the front door wasn't a problem for Tseng either.

Quietly they entered the large, dismal hall.

They could hear nothing save for the plinking of a dripping tap. Tseng signalled to Roux to wait while he slunk towards where the sound was coming from.

He entered a large kitchen with stainless-steel work surfaces, like in a restaurant. Vegetable peelings, pieces of apple turned brown and salad leaves lay around, while strewn across the floor were small twigs and nut-sized balls.

Tseng picked one up and gave it a sniff.

'Elephant shit,' whispered Roux, who couldn't wait any longer and had followed Tseng.

On the cooker was a pot filled with water, inside it a smaller one with traces of a milky liquid. Beside it lay a whisk with the same residue.

An open door led into a room where a light was on. They went inside.

Here the floor was likewise messy: leaves, twigs, droppings and a ball of wool.

In the centre of the room stood a table with six chairs. On it were a few used plates and a half-full coffee cup.

'They've done a runner!' Roux snorted.

They started searching the house.

Half an hour later they left it empty-handed.

A parking ticket was clamped behind the windscreen wiper.

26

The same day

There wasn't much of a lake view any more from Hotel du Lac. Two office blocks further down the valley had obstructed it since the 1980s. The hotel had held on to its four stars by the skin of its teeth and kept its head above water through expats who stayed there while waiting to find an apartment. But it was a well-run establishment, its bar was famous for its single malts and its Thai restaurant had been an insider's tip for more than twenty years.

Even though the Hotel du Lac had seen better times, it wasn't used to welcoming guests such as the ones now pulling up outside.

The guests arrived in a rickety old Peugeot estate with local number plates, and their luggage consisted of a dated Louis Vuitton suitcase, a cheap wheelie case, several supermarket carrier bags and an old military rucksack.

The woman was in her early forties, not made up and dressed practically rather than elegantly. She carried a tattered dog bag, its dark-blue suede decorated with golden rivets.

One of the men was short, Asian and middle-aged. He wore jeans that hadn't seen the washing machine in a while, trainers, a green stained parka and a grey felt hat.

The other man was more elegant, wearing a slightly old-fashioned yet classy suit. He was gaunt and had a shaved head.

He asked for Herr Gautschi, the porter of many years, who to the great relief of his designated successor had finally retired four years ago, but still worked on a temporary basis and by chance happened to be on duty that day.

Herr Gautschi was fetched from the office, where he was having a coffee break. He greeted the new arrival formally, took the tattered ID card, compared its photo with the man before him, smiled and gave him a warm handshake.

The man waved his companions over, then all three of them went into the little office at the back. The Asian man insisted on bringing the rucksack.

They stayed in the office for some time while Herr Gautschi came out on three occasions. The first time to talk to the duty manager, the second to organise the room allocation and status of the guests, and the third time to hand the new arrivals over to the receptionist.

Now Herr Schoch and his companions were staying in apartment 312 which had a connecting door to room 314. Herr Gautschi had made sure that they didn't appear anywhere in the hotel computer system.

27

The same day

Up in the room Valerie asked, 'Can I see your passport picture again?'

Schoch took the passport from his chest pocket and gave it to her.

A chubby man in pinstripes, his shirt collar looking slightly tight, gazed back at her seriously. She looked back and forth between him and the photo. There was no similarity between the two men.

'I don't think you'd be let into any country with this.'

'I'm amazed they ever did.'

'No wonder Herr Gautschi didn't recognise you.'

'Actually I was a bit thinner when I was last here too. Lovesickness is the best diet.'

'How long did you stay here?'

'The few weeks it took to get my divorce sorted out.'

There was a knock at the connecting door. It was Kaung, carrying the little elephant. 'Sabu ill.'

He put her on the floor. She stood with droopy ears on the carpet. Kaung offered her a carrot, which Sabu ignored and lay down.

This was nothing like the happy creature who had

performed a greeting dance when Kaung arrived at the villa.

'She's never not eaten, apart from right at the beginning.' Schoch tried to get Sabu to take the carrot too. 'Maybe all the excitement.'

Kaung shook his head. 'No, ill.'

Valerie bent down to Sabu, stroked her and stood her up.

Kaung knelt a short distance away and called her over in Burmese.

She took a couple of steps.

'What's wrong with her leg?' Schoch asked.

'Not leg,' Kaung said. 'Brain.'

Schoch looked at Valerie. She wanted to rock her head from side to side but it came out as a nod.

'Must go to *sararwaan* for elephants,' Kaung said with determination.

'What's that?' Schoch asked.

'Elephant doctor. But in my country.'

28

28 June 2016

Frau Iten recognised the voice immediately, but she thought she hadn't heard correctly.

'Yes, yes, it's me, Frau Iten.'

Frau Iten was secretary to the successor of Schoch's successor. It would be her last stint as she was on the verge of retirement.

Herr Schoch had been her favourite boss. She'd got to know him when he was a young investment adviser; he was sixteen years her junior. Up till then she'd worked in various positions in the back office of the bank, always on the lookout for a better job. Then his offer came. He'd just reached a stage in his career that entitled him to a secretary of his own, so he asked her. To this day she'd never found out why.

Frau Iten didn't spend long thinking about it and she followed Schoch up every new step of the ladder. Until the day his wife ... She could have told him from the start that the woman was a slut. First he'd turned up to work unshaven and with red eyes, then with boozy breath, then drunk, then not at all.

And now he was calling her to ask for a meeting. Lunch in the Thai Restaurant at the Hotel du Lac, where he'd lived before he fell off the radar. Lunch today. He needed her help – it was urgent.

This was the first time Herr Schoch had asked for her help. Of course for tiny things he'd done that on a daily basis, but this time it sounded serious and urgent. That's why she agreed even though she'd have preferred to come the following day, fresh from the hairdresser's.

He was waiting for her at an alcove table in the almost empty restaurant. She wouldn't have recognised him if he hadn't got up and come over to her. His handshake was still firm, but the hand was slender and bony. He was shaven-headed and slim. No, gaunt. The suit was a little too baggy and she cursed herself for sounding all maternal when she asked – barely had they sat down – 'Are you ill, Herr Schoch?'

'I've just lost a bit of weight.'

They opted for the set menu and he ordered a glass of champagne for her, just like old times, and a mineral water for himself, unlike old times.

He was asking a lot of her. If she were found out it would cost Frau Iten her job, just before retirement.

But she had his word that he would pay back the money within the current accounting period and she knew how to make such transactions invisible in the books.

Eventually she said, 'I'll do it. Do you know why, Herr Schoch? Because I'm a silly, sentimental old woman.'

That afternoon she booked the Gulfstream G550, but not through the bank's internal travel agent.

29

The same day

Outside Just a Second stood a cluster of alcoholics, dog owners, hippies and junkies, patiently waiting for the street clinic to open.

Roux and Tseng had parked Roux's BMW in sight of the shop and they were also waiting, albeit not quite so patiently. The previous evening they'd driven straight to the vet's apartment and lain in wait for her for hours, without success. After that they'd driven aimlessly around the villa district, about three times down the narrow street where they'd last seen the Peugeot, and eventually they'd returned to Tseng's hotel.

Roux's anger and hatred had faded away; now he was resigned. Or as good as. For sometimes he was struck by how unbelievable it was that they'd failed a second time so close to their goal, and for a moment he'd feel sure that everything *had* to take a turn for the better.

In the night they'd broken into the vet's apartment. Nothing suggested that she'd left in a hurry, but there was considerable evidence that she wasn't an especially tidy individual.

They found no clues as to where the people they were after might be. Only a folder on the back of which it said

'Hainbuchstrasse', which implied that the villa where Schoch had been hiding belonged to her.

When they'd arrived at the street clinic early that morning, a good hour before it opened, Roux's heart was pounding. But the longer they waited and the larger the group of people waiting grew, the more listless he became.

Now it was nine o'clock, half an hour after the official opening time.

'Go and ask,' ordered Tseng, who'd hardly said a word since they'd arrived.

Roux got out and joined the group. He vaguely recognised one them, probably one of the dog lovers from Giorgio's lot.

'Do you know why it's not open?' Roux asked.

'She had an emergency yesterday and said we should come back today. But when today, I've no idea.'

While they were still puzzling over what might have happened, the vet's Peugeot drove up. A young man got out, pushed his way through the throng of people, climbed the handful of steps to the door and said to the crowd, 'Good morning. Please excuse the delay. My name is Dr Peter Grimm and I'm standing in for Frau Dr Sommer while she's on holiday.'

He unlocked the door and entered the second-hand shop, which today smelled of patchouli.

30

Singapore

2 July 2016

Sabu's condition hadn't got worse, but she was still refusing solids. Kaung, who called her Barisha, kept trying to feed her the bottle and sometimes she drank a little. He also got her to move and she'd take a few steps, but the right hind leg always dragged behind.

The flight had been gruelling for all of them. Although the Gulfstream G550 was a spacious business jet, it was a small aircraft that didn't have much to counter the turbulence above the Indian Ocean. It could accommodate twelve passengers and usually a flight attendant was included in the price. They'd dispensed with one to avoid Sabu being seen.

They'd also requested 'absolute privacy', which meant that the door to the crew rest area, with its lavatory, bed and galley kitchen, had to remain closed throughout the entire flight.

In the short periods without any turbulence, Valerie and Schoch had tried to get some sleep. Neither had enjoyed much during their short stay at the Hotel du Lac; at night their worry about Sabu had kept them awake, while during the day there was much to sort out: Schoch's emergency passport, Valerie's stand-in, meetings with her trustee who needed instructions and power of attorney, and the issue of a pet passport with the necessary vaccinations for Sabu the dwarf poodle.

And all this in the constant fear of being recognised by someone.

They were mightily relieved when they'd concluded the border formalities and the aircraft finally took off, leaving the overcast sky beneath them.

After their dawn landing at Singapore's Changi Airport, they were met at the plane steps by the bank's VIP agents and driven to the VIP terminal in a limousine. A bleary-eyed immigration officer stamped the passports without any questions, even Kaung's Burmese one, which time and again he'd renewed and extended in preparation for the day when his dream would come true and he'd return to his home country.

Now Valerie and Schoch were sitting at a table laid for breakfast in the Palm Court of the Raffles Hotel, looking over the veranda railings and between the lady palms at the lawn, where an elderly gardener in a broad-brimmed straw hat was repositioning the sprinklers.

Kaung was in his room, watching over Sabu. She'd drunk a little milk and eaten a slice of the apple that the waiter had brought up with breakfast.

'Barisha feeling better,' Kaung had said. 'Can travel soon.'

Valerie put her hand on Schoch's.

'Kaung believes that Sabu is sacred,' Schoch said.

'I know.'

'How about you?'

'Why do you ask?'

'Because you believe in creation.'

'Not exactly. I don't believe in the distinction between evolution and creation.'

'Okay. But in something sacred?'

'Sabu is very, very special. Maybe there's no difference between very, very special and sacred.'

'So you believe in miracles too?'

'Sabu is one.'

'I thought she was the result of genetic engineering.'

'Do you think they'd go to all this fuss finding her if she were so simple to manufacture?'

31

Zürich

Autumn and winter 2016

The villa in Hainbuchstrasse was sold for 15.4 million francs to an anonymous buyer, who was said to be Russian. The renovation work began a few weeks after the contract was signed by the buyer's and seller's proxies.

Right after the sale the Sommer Foundation received a transfer of 212,000 francs in recompense for a payment it had made for the same amount to a certain Frau Iten. She in turn transferred the sum to a travel expenses account of GCBS bank and deleted a booking for the same amount made to JetFlug, a private charter company.

Dr Peter Grimm was taken on full time as the street clinic's vet.

Circus Pellegrini enjoyed unexpected success with its new comic elephant act.

Dr Horàk was commissioned by Dr Roux to implant the last of the modified blastocysts in Asha. With success.

In Beijing the Chinese Genetic Company instructed their security department to undertake an international hunt for the pink dwarf elephant, without Dr Roux's involvement. The team entrusted with this mission was headed by Tseng Tian, who was already familiar with the matter.

32

Beijing

29 August 2017

Without any success to show for itself, 'Project Pink' sank ever lower in the list of the Chinese Genetic Company's priorities over the months that followed. Tseng and his team were assigned other tasks and Roux, the partner still resident in Switzerland, was given ever shorter shrift. The plan was to shelve 'Project Pink' completely after eighteen months.

But then one day, one of Tseng's internet researchers stumbled upon an obscure Buddhist blog mentioning a shrine to a sacred pink dwarf elephant by the name of Sabu Barisha.

This discovery created a stir at the team meeting and Tseng instructed two other researchers to search the internet and the dark net for Sabu Barisha.

Results came quickly. The search item kept taking them to a relatively new elephant sanctuary in Myanmar to the north of Rangoon, between the Irrawaddy and Sittaung rivers.

The sanctuary was called Sabu Barisha after a small temple there, where a tiny, glowing pink elephant of the same name was worshipped.

There were several photos of the temple complex and

of statues of the miniature elephant god. They also discovered three videos with eyewitness statements of pilgrims – two elderly women and a young man – who had seen Sabu Barisha and gave credible descriptions of her. There were no video clips or photos of Sabu Barisha herself.

Tseng presented the material to his superior, who informed the CGC management. They approved a three-man expedition to Myanmar under Tseng's command with the goal of capturing the creature, but at the very least they were to obtain usable cell material.

Three days later the group landed in Rangoon, each equipped with a diplomatic bag and diplomatic passport. At the airport they picked up their reserved Land Cruiser and set off.

After a long drive on poor roads, sections of which had been washed away by the monsoon rains, they reached the huge entrance gate. SABU BARISHA ELEPHANT SANCTUARY stood in colourful letters above the entrance.

They drove in and followed the signs to the reception, a large bungalow in the shade of an old teak tree, where they were greeted with ice-cold ginger tea by a young woman in traditional dress.

The camp had more than ten guest bungalows, staff houses and stalls. Some of the buildings dated from the time when the camp still belonged to the British colonial power or the national logging corporation; the rest had been built by the new owners.

Tseng and his companions moved into their bungalows.

33

Myanmar

1 September 2017

The large bungalow now housing the reception was where the camp manager and his family had lived in the colonial era. The building was mainly constructed from the teak that grew locally. The polished parquet floors, the doors and windows, the roof and most of the furniture were made from it.

The former living room was now a dining room with space for twelve tables.

Six others were occupied besides the one where Tseng and his companions now sat, all by Indian, Chinese and Burmese groups in traditional dress.

The CGC men silently ate their curry, washed down with a bottle of Myanmar Beer.

After pudding – coconut milk with sago – a European woman in Burmese dress entered the dining room and went from table to table. Although Tseng had only glimpsed the vet fleetingly from the car outside the villa, he knew it had to be her.

She came to their table, welcomed them on behalf of the management, wished them a pleasant stay and gave them a flyer with information about the sanctuary.

It lay on the edge of a huge area of wild and cultivated

teak forests from the colonial era, and bordered an extensive forest conservation area. The government had now imposed a logging ban on the commercial plantations too, as each year the country's forest land was declining by more than 100,000 hectares, representing 2 per cent of the total forest land annually.

The new owners had adopted the thirty-two elephants who'd worked in the now protected forest, taken in another fourteen former worker elephants since and had raised the total population to fifty-five with nine elephant orphans.

The aim of the project was to find a species-appropriate way to care for both their own animals and those in the neighbouring eighty square kilometres of conservation area, and to gradually reintroduce the healthy elephants into the wild. The weak and sick elephants would be looked after until the end of their lives.

The sanctuary offered an insight into the lives of elephants. The visitors could observe the herds on the huge expanse of land from off-road vehicles. They could watch them bathe, and visit the baby area where elephant orphans were hand-raised.

What you couldn't do was ride, feed, wash or have direct contact with the animals. But it was possible to sponsor elephants and help out with the reforestation.

The flyer made no mention of Sabu Barisha or her temple.

34

The same day

Fritz Schoch was slim, but no longer scrawny. He wore a checked *longyi* and a white shirt with stand-up collar. His face and head were still smoothly shaven and he no longer had the shakes.

Schoch was sitting at his desk typing on the computer. He'd refreshed his IT skills, marvelling at the quantum leaps made in this area over the past ten years. Now he looked after the administration of the camp and the Sommer Foundation. Not a full-time job, but enough for someone who hadn't lifted a finger in ten years.

Valerie entered the small office they shared. She was wearing a *longyi* too and a traditional Burmese blouse. She'd greeted the guests in the dining room, as she did every evening, and now sat down in front of her computer.

Valerie had been back to school as well. She'd been instructed in Burmese elephant medicine by the *sararwaan*, the vet who Kaung had called on because of Sabu Barisha, and also learned about conventional medicine for *Elephas maximus* on the internet. Now she was looking after the health of her growing elephant population, helped always by Kaung and the *sararwaan*.

Valerie and Schoch went about their business quietly. It was palpable that both of them felt comfortable in each other's presence.

Valerie interrupted the silence. 'Have you seen the three newcomers? Chinese.'

'No.'

'Strange. Not our typical guests.'

'How do you mean?'

'Just not the sort of people to visit an alternative elephant sanctuary. More like men on a mission.'

'You mean …?'

'It's just a feeling.'

Since their successful and adventurous escape to Myanmar they'd never stopped keeping a watchful eye out. But this wasn't the first time they'd had a strange feeling about some visitors, so they weren't overly worried by Valerie's inkling.

She went behind Schoch, placed a hand on his neck and said, 'Shall we? It's time.'

He turned off the computer and got up. At that moment the rain started pounding on the roof.

35

The same day

The temple lay in a small clearing a kilometre from the main bungalow. A six-sided pagoda, pistachio green, white and golden, as if crafted by a confectioner, and with a glistening wet golden roof, its spire rising about five metres into the night sky.

The entrances were guarded by ferocious lion statues.

Inside, right in the centre, stood a golden cube, each of its sides a metre wide. On top, in the middle of orchid flowers and incense sticks, stood the statuette of a tiny, glowing, pink elephant.

Kaung, his eyes closed, knelt in front of it and moved his lips. He heard the rain fall silent as suddenly as it had begun, then lost himself again in meditation.

All of a sudden he sensed somebody entering the temple. He opened his eyes and saw three men, one of whom he knew. It was the tall Chinese man who'd been looking for Sabu Barisha.

Kaung closed his eyes again.

'Kaung,' the man said.

Kaung didn't react.

'Where is Sabu Barisha?' the Chinese man asked in English.

Kaung pretended not to understand.

'Where is the little elephant?' It sounded louder and more menacing.

Kaung stood and tried to escape past the men outside. When the tall man gave a signal, his companions flanked Kaung and held him by the arms.

'Come,' Kaung said.

The Chinese man nodded to the other two and they led him out of the small temple.

36

The same day

Valerie and Schoch went to the temple, as they did every Friday, to bring their offerings. Followed by those oozies who could spare an hour that evening, and their wives. There must have been around thirty people, many of them carrying candles or petrol lamps.

The clouds had broken and an almost full moon shone on the gold of the pagoda's roof.

A group of men stepped out of the main entrance, dimly lit by a pink light. They took a few steps forward then stopped. One of them was Kaung.

Valerie and Schoch walked up to them. Now they could see that the other men were the Chinese newcomers. Two of them were holding on to Kaung.

'Everything okay, Kaung?' Schoch asked.

The tall Chinese man gave the other two a sign; they let go of Kaung and he leaped over to Schoch and Valerie.

'What do the men want?' Valerie asked.

'Sabu Barisha,' Kaung said.

'The experimental animal doesn't belong to you,' the tall Chinese man said. 'We are here on behalf of Dr Roux, the legal owner. We demand you hand the animal over to us.'

The oozies and their wives had caught up with Valerie and Schoch and formed a circle around the group.

Now Kaung spoke. 'Sabu Barisha not belong Dr Roux. Sabu Barisha belong nobody. Sabu Barisha sacred being.' He turned to the temple, put his palms together in front of his face and bowed. Those standing around him did likewise.

Valerie whispered something to Schoch. He thought about it for a moment, then nodded.

'Come,' he told the Chinese men.

They went first along a narrow path through a section of forest. The rainwater dripped from the leaves. They reached another, smaller clearing, with a bungalow that looked as if it also dated from the pre-independence era. It was built on stakes and surrounded by a wooden veranda with five steps leading up to it. The oozies and their wives sat on the veranda; Valerie, Schoch, Kaung and the three men went in.

They entered a living area with a mixture of traditional Burmese and old colonial furniture. Schoch flicked a switch and a few fans started rotating on the ceiling.

Kaung sat on the floor.

Valerie invited the men to take a seat, fetched a laptop and booted it up.

She attached a memory stick and started the video.

37

The same day

The words SABU BARISHA appeared in pink on the screen like a film title, while a variety of drums, cymbals and harps played traditional Burmese music.

The title remained for a few seconds then faded into a still image of the tiny elephant with her trunk in the air. Her mouth was open and it looked as if she were laughing. The three Chinese men whispered to each other.

The image started moving. Sabu Barisha walked across the Persian carpet of a gloomy room. Occasionally her glow overexposed the picture, bathing the entire screen in her pink.

A different scene now emerged: the small elephant sucking powerfully on a baby bottle being held by a hairy hand.

A cross-fade showed the same hand rolling a ball of wool towards the mini-elephant. Sabu Barisha trapped it with her trunk and pushed it back skilfully with her foot.

In the next scene her playfulness was gone and she stood like a glowing statue beneath a piece of furniture – a chest of drawers or a bed.

The image changed again and now the little elephant was lying on her side next to a blue dog basket. Her pink torso rose and sank. Sabu Barisha was asleep.

The Chinese visitors had stopped commenting on the clips. It was silent in the room, save for the soundtrack of Burmese music.

But then the three men suddenly started whispering again. Sabu Barisha appeared to be injured. Kaung was standing facing the elephant, beckoning her. She moved with difficulty, dragging a leg behind, made two or three steps then gave up and lay down.

'Is she sick?' the tall Chinese man said, but didn't receive an answer.

From now on the little elephant was mostly seen on Valerie's lap. Or on Kaung's lap or in his arms, surrounded by oozies bringing her flowers, incense sticks and sweet things. In one shot the pagoda was visible, still under construction. Only in one scene did the elephant try to walk, but the drag of her hind leg had got so bad that she gave up.

Sabu Barisha's little head now looked shrunken. The bones in her body too were protruding beneath her pink skin. She was always garlanded and surrounded by people in traditional dress, kneeling before her. The camera panned in and her trunk could be seen moving among the flowers.

The music fell silent and the picture cross-faded to a stony-faced Kaung. He lifted up the lifeless body and carried it out of the darkened room. Its glow was extinguished.

Heavy raindrops started hammering onto the corrugated iron of the bungalow, releasing the viewers from the oppressive silence.

On the screen was a large gathering of festively dressed

people, kneeling around a pile of logs, decorated with flowers, on top of which Sabu Barisha lay. Two monks and Kaung lit the wood.

The burning of the pyre in long cross-fades was again accompanied by music, but this was drowned out by the rain.

The final scenes showed Kaung and two monks recovering the still-smoking ashes, depositing them into a small, brass urn and bricking this up in the cube in the centre of the pagoda.

The video ended. All that could be heard was the rain.

'Barisha,' Kaung said. 'Rain.'

Valerie wiped the tears from her eyes, pulled the memory stick from the laptop and offered it to Tseng.

He took it without saying anything and left the bungalow, followed by his team.

38

8 March 2018

A small, rusty tugboat, its structure leaning aggressively forward, was pulling a plump container barge with a square, turquoise cabin. A wreath of old tyres protected it from damage when mooring.

'Just think of all the places these tyres went when they were still attached to wheels,' Valerie said dreamily.

They were sitting in deckchairs on the small balcony of their cabin, gazing down at the river. The Irrawaddy was greenish brown, the riverbank green, the sky above it grey, blue and pink, like a Zürich pigeon.

They were on their first holiday since they'd set up Sabu Barisha Elephant Sanctuary: one week on a steamer on the Irrawaddy. The visit from the three Chinese men, the detection they'd long feared, had freed them. It was Valerie's idea to book the trip on the steamer. 'Let's do something normal people would do,' she'd suggested.

'Are we normal people, then?' Schoch had asked, raising a smile on both their faces.

Their cabin was in the prow. The only noises were the gurgling of the water beneath the ship's hull and the drone of the motor far at the back.

Valerie put her hand on Schoch's, which lay on the armrest of his deckchair. Colourful Buddhist fortune bracelets were tied around both wrists. The river drifted past.

Nests of water hyacinths. A fishing boat. A buoy with the yellow–green–red flag and the white star, marking the presence of a net.

Only rarely would they hear the metallic engine sound of a fishing boat, chugging away from a freshly laid net.

There was no gentler means of transport on air, land or water.

39

Circus Pellegrini
9 April 2018

Dr Roux, Dr Hess and Ben, the elephant keeper, were in Asha's pen. She was sixteen months pregnant and Dr Hess, on the insistence of Roux, was undertaking yet another – he couldn't remember the precise number – unnecessary ultrasound scan.

When he'd finished he said cheerfully, 'As ever, the embryo is perfectly healthy and developing normally.'

'Normally!' Roux yelled. 'Fuck you!'

Asha, whose four legs had been chained up by Ben, as they always were for vet visits, got a fright. She lashed out with her trunk, caught Roux and sent him smashing against the partition wall. Behind it the other elephants trumpeted.

It was the second fatal accident caused by an animal in almost ninety years of Circus Pellegrini.

40

16 December 2018

Six months later Asha gave birth to a healthy baby. It weighed 110 kilos and was 95 centimetres at the shoulder.

The only remarkable thing about this baby bull elephant were the pigment disorders on his forehead, at the root of his trunk and on his ears.

Such a phenomenon occurred from time to time, but in this instance the pink of the depigmentations was more intense.

And in the dark it gave a faint glow.

Acknowledgements

First of all I'd like to thank Prof. Dr Mathias Jucker, director of the Hertie Institute for Clinical Brain Research at the University of Tübingen, because he was the person who told me ten years ago at the international conference on '100 Years of Alzheimer's' that it would be possible to produce a tiny pink elephant using genetic engineering. This idea has stuck with me ever since.

It was also Prof. Jucker who put me on to Prof. Dr med. Anita Rauch, director and professor of Medical Genetics at the University of Zürich. She told me about her specialist field, primordial dwarfism, and filled me in on the opportunities and dangers of genetics. Many thanks to her.

I'm also most grateful to Dr Robert Zingg, elephant expert and senior curator at Zoo Zürich. He made great efforts to introduce me to the nature and behaviour of elephants, and referred me to another expert, to whom I owe a great deal.

This is Prof. Dr Thomas Hildebrandt, the international expert in the artificial insemination of elephants at the Leibniz Institute for Zoo and Wildlife Research in Berlin. He sacrificed much of his time and exhausted his patience explaining reproductive and genetic engineering techniques. He, Prof. Rauch and Dr Zingg checked and corrected the relevant parts of my manuscript. Any remaining mistakes are all mine.

My warmest thanks also to Captain Helene Niedhart, president and CEO of CAT Aviation, who helped me with the description of the flight in the private jet to Singapore and corrected the text.

Thanks, too, to Ewald Furrer and Hans Peter Meier, both of whom earn their living selling the remarkable street magazine *Surprise*. They gave me an insight into the world of the marginalised and homeless, and a sense of what their lives feel like.

As ever I'm very grateful to my editor, Ursula Baumhauer, for her important creative contributions and her survey of the sometimes rather messy chronology. And thanks to my publisher, Philipp Keel, for his friendly and constructive intervention.

My wife, Margrith Nay Suter, gets a big hug for once again undertaking the difficult task, as first reader, of letting me know what she thought was good and what needed improving.

And to my daughter, Ana: I'm sorry that I'll never give you a tiny, living, pink elephant, but I hope you'll understand.